THANK YOUR LUCKY STARS!

In the 2008 Astrological Guide, you'll find:

- All 12 signs individually represented—for a person-alized look at *each month* in the year to come
- The days that will be most memorable for you
- Answers to many questions
- Essays by leading astrologers
- And much more!

"Astrology told me about my life even before I wrote it as an autobiography."   —Bette Davis

"Whether or not I would have succeeded without as-trology, I don't know."   —Sylvester Stallone

SYDNEY OMARR'S®

ASTROLOGICAL GUIDE FOR YOU IN

2008

by Trish MacGregor

A SIGNET BOOK

SIGNET
Published by New American Library, a division of
Penguin Group (USA) Inc., 375 Hudson Street,
New York, New York 10014, USA
Penguin Group (Canada), 90 Eglinton Avenue East, Suite 700, Toronto,
Ontario M4P 2Y3, Canada (a division of Pearson Penguin Canada Inc.)
Penguin Books Ltd., 80 Strand, London WC2R 0RL, England
Penguin Ireland, 25 St. Stephen's Green, Dublin 2,
Ireland (a division of Penguin Books Ltd.)
Penguin Group (Australia), 250 Camberwell Road, Camberwell, Victoria 3124,
Australia (a division of Pearson Australia Group Pty. Ltd.)
Penguin Books India Pvt. Ltd., 11 Community Centre, Panchsheel Park,
New Delhi - 110 017, India
Penguin Group (NZ), 67 Apollo Drive, Rosedale, North Shore 0745,
Auckland, New Zealand (a division of Pearson New Zealand Ltd.)
Penguin Books (South Africa) (Pty.) Ltd., 24 Sturdee Avenue,
Rosebank, Johannesburg 2196, South Africa

Penguin Books Ltd., Registered Offices:
80 Strand, London WC2R 0RL, England

First published by Signet, an imprint of New American Library,
a division of Penguin Group (USA) Inc.

First Printing, July 2007
10 9 8 7 6 5 4 3 2 1

CONTENTS

PART TWO: What Other Astrologers Are Saying

Introduction

2008 is a pivotal year. Pluto, the outermost planet in our solar system, symbolic of permanent and profound change, leaves fiery Sagittarius, where it has propagated religious wars, divisive politics, and exposed the dark underbelly of the American dream—the stark differences between the haves and the have-nots. Pluto now enters earth sign Capricorn and remains there until 2024, a mighty long time by anyone's standards.

If we look back at Pluto's last transit through Capricorn in the 1700s, before the planet had even been discovered, we were in the midst of a revolution, fighting for our independence from Great Britain. This time around, the fight is to free ourselves from what we have become—a divisive nation that adheres to a paradigm that no longer works. Pluto exposes the shadow side of existing power structures—the aftermath of Hurricane Katrina, the war in Iraq, and the depletion of the earth's resources are just three examples—and challenges us to change those structures. If we don't do it willingly, then profound change is thrust upon us through loss and deprivation.

The result of the 2008 elections will prove critical to how we experience Pluto's transit through Capricorn. Instead of politicians spouting the same old rhetoric, we need elected officials with global vision, who embrace a new paradigm. Alternative power, a severance of our dependence on oil, human rights, affordable health care, a narrowing of the gap between haves and have-nots, a foreign policy that promotes goodwill instead of vilifying us in the eyes of the world . . . well, you get the idea.

When Pluto enters Capricorn, it doesn't matter if you vote red or blue, purple or yellow or pink. It doesn't matter if you're a lifelong Republican, a die-hard Democrat, or a proud Independent. It doesn't matter whether you're a Methodist or a Catholic, a Jew or a Muslim. What matters is the collective spirit of what we are as human beings, sharing the same space, on that third rock from the sun. Earth is our world. It has sustained us, embraced us, put up with our travesties, our greed, our cruelties.

Once Pluto enters Capricorn, the planet begins to defend itself in earnest. It will eliminate and purify. Whether it's a pandemic or a hurricane that's off the charts or a pole shift, upheaval becomes business as usual. We are seized, humbled, shocked. We are shaken to our collective core. And, hopefully, we wake up. Hopefully, we elect representatives who seek to embrace profound and permanent change. Hopefully, we find within ourselves the ability to build new and better structures in our government, our politics and policies, our individual lives. Because if we don't change, we're history.

So what can you do as an individual?

Astrology is and always will be about you as a person. *You.* Your soul, mind, spirit, energy. Whatever it is that makes you unique. Each of us chooses to be born to a particular family, under a particular set of circumstances, in a particular era, with particular challenges, talents, and lessons to be learned. So in the course of reading about your sign's potential and predictions for the year, consider these questions:

- How can I bring about positive change in my own life?
- What can I, as an individual, do to promote

greater harmony in my family, community, or my corner of the world?

- Who am I in the larger scheme of things?
- Why did my soul choose to be born in this particular time and place?
- What abilities do I possess intuitively, intellectually, emotionally, and spiritually that support the strength of the collective?
- Do I walk the talk?

At the end of each sign's annual summary is a brainstorming activity. Have fun with it. Be creative, bold, imaginative, honest. Express who you really are.

PART ONE

Sun Sign Predictions

Star Stuff

How much do you know about the day you were born? What was the weather like that day? If you were born at night, had the moon already risen? Was it full or the shape of a Cheshire cat's grin? Was the delivery ward quiet or bustling with activity? Unless your mom or dad has a very good memory, you'll probably never know the full details. But there's one thing you can know for sure: on the day you were born, the sun was located in a particular zone of the zodiac, an imaginary 360-degree belt that circles the earth. The belt is divided into twelve equal 30-degree portions called signs.

If you were born between March 21 and April 19, then the sun was passing through the sign of Aries, so we say that your sun sign is Aries. Each of the twelve signs has distinct attributes and characteristics. Aries individuals, for example, are independent pioneers, fearless and passionate. Virgos, born between August 23 and September 22, are perfectionists with discriminating intellects and a genius for details.

The twelve signs are categorized according to element and quality, or modality. The first category reads like a basic science lesson—fire, earth, air, and water—and describes the general physical characteristics of the signs.

Fire signs—Aries, Leo, Sagittarius—are warm, dynamic individuals who are always passionate about what they do.

Earth signs—Taurus, Virgo, Capricorn—are the builders of the zodiac, practical and efficient, grounded in everything they do.

Air signs—Gemini, Libra, Aquarius—are people who live mostly in the world of ideas. They are terrific communicators.

Water signs—Cancer, Scorpio, Pisces—live through their emotions, imaginations, and intuitions.

The second category describes how each sign operates in the physical world, how adaptable it is to circumstances.

Cardinal signs—Aries, Cancer, Libra, Capricorn—are initiators. These people are active, impatient, and restless. They're great at starting things, but unless a project or a relationship holds their attention, they lose interest and may not finish what they start.

Fixed signs—Taurus, Leo, Scorpio, Aquarius—are deliberate, controlled. These individuals tend to move more slowly than cardinal signs, are often stubborn, and resist change. They seek roots, stability.

Mutable signs—Gemini, Virgo, Sagittarius, Pisces—are adaptable. These people are flexible, changeable, and communicative. They don't get locked into rigid patterns or belief systems.

Table 1: Sun Signs

Sign	Date	Element	Quality
Aries ♈	March 21–April 19	Fire	Cardinal
Taurus ♉	April 20–May 20	Earth	Fixed
Gemini ♊	May 21–June 21	Air	Mutable
Cancer ♋	June 22–July 22	Water	Cardinal
Leo ♌	July 23–August 22	Fire	Fixed
Virgo ♍	August 23–September 22	Earth	Mutable
Libra ♎	September 23–October 22	Air	Cardinal
Scorpio ♏	October 23–November 21	Water	Fixed
Sagittarius ♐	November 22–December 21	Fire	Mutable
Capricorn ♑	December 22–January 19	Earth	Cardinal
Aquarius ♒	January 20–February 18	Air	Fixed
Pisces ♓	February 19–March 20	Water	Mutable

The Planets

The planets in astrology are the players who make things happen. They're the characters in the story of your life. And this story always begins with the sun, the giver of life.

Your sun sign describes your self-expression, your primal energy, the essence of who you are. It's the archetypal pattern of your Self, the Apollo in your corner of the world. When you know another person's sun sign, you already have a great deal of information about that person. Let's say you're a Taurus who has just started dating a Gemini. How compatible are you? On the surface, it wouldn't seem that you have much in common. Taurus is a fixed earth sign; Gemini is a mutable sign. Taurus is persistent, stubborn, practical, a cultivator as opposed to an initiator. Gemini is a chameleon, a communicator, social, with a mind like lightning. Taurus is ruled by Venus, which governs the arts, money, beauty, love, and romance, and Gemini is ruled by Mercury, which governs communication and travel. There doesn't seem to be much common ground.

Yet suppose the Taurus has Mercury in Gemini and suppose the Gemini has Venus in Taurus. This would mean that the Taurus and Gemini each have their rulers in the other person's sign. They probably communicate well and probably enjoy travel (Mercury) and would see eye to eye on romance, art, and music (Venus). They might get along so well, in fact, that they collaborate on creative projects.

Each of us is also influenced by the other nine planets (the sun and moon are treated like planets in astrology) and the signs they were transiting when you were born. Suppose our Taurus and Gemini have the same moon sign. The moon rules our inner needs, emotions, and intuition, and all that makes us feel secure within ourselves. Quite often, compatible moon signs can overcome even the most glaring difference

9

in sun signs because the two people share similar emotions.

In the sections on monthly predictions, your sun sign always takes center stage and every prediction is based on the movement of the transiting planets in relation to your sun sign. Let's say you're an Aquarius. On February 17 of this year, Venus enters your sign and stays there until March 12. What's this mean for you? Well, since Venus rules romance—among other things—you can expect your love life to pick up significantly during these three weeks.

Table 2 provides an overview of the planets and the signs they rule. Keep in mind that the moon is the swiftest-moving planet, changing signs about every two and a half days, and that Pluto is the snail of the zodiac, taking as long as thirty years to transit a single sign. Although the faster-moving planets—the moon, Mercury, Venus, and Mars—have an impact on our lives, it's the slowpokes—Uranus, Neptune, and Pluto—that bring about the most profound influence and change. Jupiter and Saturn fall between the others in terms of speed.

In the section on predictions, the most frequent references are to the transits of Mercury, Venus, and Mars. In the daily predictions for each sign, the predictions are based primarily on the transiting moon.

Now glance through table 2. When a sign is in parentheses, it means the planet corules that sign. This assignation dates back to when we thought there were only seven planets in the solar system. But since there were still twelve signs, some of the planets had to do double duty!

Table 2: The Planets

Planet	Rules	Attributes of Planet
Sun ☉	Leo	Self-expression, primal energy, creative ability, ego, individuality
Moon ☽	Cancer	Emotions, intuition, mother or wife, security

Mercury ☿	Gemini, Virgo	Intellect, mental acuity, communication, logic, reasoning, travel, contracts
Venus ♀	Taurus, Libra	Love, romance, beauty, artistic instincts, the arts, music, material and financial resources
Mars ♂	Aries (Scorpio)	Physical and sexual energy, aggression, drive
Jupiter ♃	Sagittarius (Pisces)	Luck, expansion, success, prosperity, growth, creativity, spiritual interests, higher education, law
Saturn ♄	Capricorn (Aquarius)	Laws of physical universe, discipline, responsibility, structure, karma, authority
Uranus ♅	Aquarius	Individuality, genius, eccentricity, originality, science, revolution
Neptune ♆	Pisces	Visionary self, illusions, what's hidden, psychic ability, dissolution of ego boundaries, spiritual insights, dreams
Pluto ♀	Scorpio	The darker side, death, sex, regeneration, rebirth, profound and permanent change, transformation

Houses and Rising Signs

In the instant you drew your first breath, one of the signs of the zodiac was just passing over the eastern horizon. Astrologers refer to this as the rising sign or ascendant. It's what makes your horoscope unique. Think of your ascendant as the front door of your horoscope, the place where you enter into this life and begin your journey.

Your ascendant is based on the exact moment of your birth and the other signs follow counterclockwise. If you have Taurus rising, for example, that is the cusp of your first house. The cusp of the second would be Gemini, of the third Cancer, and so on around the horoscope circle in a counterclockwise direction. Each house governs a particular area of life, which is outlined below.

The best way to find out your rising sign is to have your horoscope drawn up by an astrologer. For those of you with access to the Internet, though, there are a couple of sites that provide free birth horoscopes: www.thecosmicpath.com, http://astro-software.com, and http://0800-horoscope.com/birthchart.html.

In a horoscope, the ascendant (cusp of the first house), IC (cusp of the fourth house), descendant (cusp of the seventh house), and MC (cusp of the tenth house) are considered to be the most critical angles. Any planets that fall close to these angles are extremely important in the overall astrological picture of who you are. By the same token, planets that fall in the first, fourth, seventh, and tenth houses are also considered to be important.

Now here's a rundown of what the houses mean.

ASCENDANT OR RISING: THE FIRST OF FOUR IMPORTANT CRITICAL ANGLES IN A HORO-SCOPE
- How other people see you
- How you present yourself to the world
- Your physical appearance

FIRST HOUSE, PERSONALITY
- Early childhood
- Your ego
- Your body type and how you feel about your body
- General physical health
- Defense mechanisms
- Your creative thrust

SECOND HOUSE, PERSONAL VALUES
- How you earn and spend your money
- Your personal values
- Your material resources and assets
- Your attitudes toward money

- Your possessions and your attitude toward those possessions
- Your self-worth
- Your attitudes toward creativity

THIRD HOUSE, COMMUNICATION AND LEARNING
- Personal expression
- Intellect and mental attitudes and perceptions
- Siblings, neighbors, and relatives
- How you learn
- School until college
- Reading, writing, teaching
- Short trips (the grocery store versus Europe in seven days)
- Earth-bound transportation
- Creativity as a communication device

IC OR FOURTH HOUSE CUSP: THE SECOND CRITICAL ANGLE IN A HOROSCOPE
- Sign on IC describes the qualities and traits of your home during early childhood
- Describes roots of your creative abilities and talents

FOURTH HOUSE, YOUR ROOTS
- Personal environment
- Your home
- Your attitudes toward family
- Early childhood conditioning
- Real estate
- Your nurturing parent

Some astrologers say this house belongs to Mom or her equivalent in your life, others say it belongs to Dad or his equivalent. It makes sense to me that it's Mom because the fourth house is ruled by the moon, which rules mothers. But in this day and age, when parental roles are in flux, the only hard-and-fast rule is that the fourth belongs to the parent who nurtures you most of the time.

- The conditions at the end of your life
- Early childhood support of your creativity

FIFTH HOUSE, CHILDREN AND CREATIVITY
- Kids, your firstborn in particular
- Love affairs
- What you enjoy
- Gambling and speculation
- Pets

Traditionally, pets belong in the sixth house. But that definition stems from the days when "pets" were chattel. These days, we don't even refer to them as pets. They are animal companions who bring us pleasure.
- Creative ability

SIXTH HOUSE, WORK AND RESPONSIBILITY
- Day-to-day working conditions and environment
- Competence and skills
- Your experience of employees and employers
- Duty—to work, to employees
- Health
- Daily work approach to creativity

DESCENDANT/SEVENTH HOUSE CUSP: THE THIRD CRITICAL ANGLE IN A HOROSCOPE
- The sign on the house cusp describes the qualities sought in intimate or business relationships
- Describes qualities of creative partnerships

SEVENTH HOUSE, PARTNERSHIPS AND MARRIAGE
- Marriage
- Marriage partner
- Significant others
- Business partnerships
- Close friends
- Open enemies
- Contracts

EIGHTH HOUSE, TRANSFORMATION
- Sexuality as transformation
- Secrets
- Death, taxes, inheritances
- Resources shared with others
- Your partner's finances
- The occult (read astrology, reincarnation, UFOs, everything weird and strange)
- Your hidden talents
- Psychology
- Life-threatening illnesses
- Your creative depths

NINTH HOUSE, WORLDVIEW
- Philosophy and religion
- The law, courts, judicial system
- Publishing
- Foreign travels and cultures
- College, graduate school
- Spiritual beliefs

MC OR CUSP OF TENTH HOUSE: THE FOURTH CRITICAL ANGLE IN A HOROSCOPE
- Sign on cusp of MC describes qualities you seek in a profession
- Your public image
- Your creative and professional achievements

TENTH HOUSE, PROFESSION AND CAREER
- Public image as opposed to a job that merely pays the bills (sixth house)
- Your status and position in the world
- The authoritarian parent and authority in general
- People who hold power over you
- Your public life
- Your career/profession

ELEVENTH HOUSE, IDEALS AND DREAMS
- Peer groups
- Social circles (your writers' group, your mother's bridge club)
- Your dreams and aspirations
- How you can realize your creative dreams

TWELFTH HOUSE, PERSONAL UNCONSCIOUS
- Power you have disowned that must be claimed again
- Institutions—hospitals, prisons, nursing homes, what is hidden
- What you must confront this time around, your karma, issues brought in from other lives
- Psychic gifts and abilities
- Healing talents
- What you give unconditionally

In the section on predictions, you'll find references to transiting planets moving into certain houses. These houses are actually solar houses that are created by putting your sun sign on the ascendant. This technique is how most predictions are made for the general public rather than for specific individuals.

Lunations

Every year, there are twelve new moons and twelve full moons, with some years having thirteen full moons. The extra full moon is called the Blue Moon, and in 2008 it falls in May. New moons are typically when we should begin new projects, set new goals, seek new opportunities. They're times for beginnings.

Two weeks after each new moon, there's a full moon. This is the time of harvest, fruition, when we reap what we've sown.

Whenever a new moon falls in your sign, take time to brainstorm what you would like to achieve during the weeks and months until the full moon falls in your sign. These goals can be in any area of your life. Or, you can simply take the time on each new moon to set up goals and strategies for what you would like to achieve or manifest during the next two weeks—until the full moon—or until the next new moon.

Here's a list of all the new moons and full moons during 2008.

New Moons
January 8—Capricorn
*February 6—Aquarius
March 7—Pisces
April 5—Aries
May 5—Taurus
June 3—Gemini
*August 1—Leo
August 30—Virgo
September 29—Libra
October 28—Scorpio
November 27—Sagittarius
December 27—Capricorn

Full Moons
January 22—Leo
*February 20—Virgo
March 21—Libra
April 20—Scorpio
May 19—Scorpio
June 18—Sagittarius
*August 16—Aquarius
September 15—Pisces
October 14—Aries
November 13—Taurus
December 12—Gemini

The asterisk next to two of the new moon entries indicates a solar eclipse; next to two of the full moon entries, the asterisk indicates a lunar eclipse. Every year there are two lunar and two solar eclipses, separated from each other by about two weeks. Lunar eclipses tend to deal with emotional issues, our internal world, and often bring an emotional issue to the surface related to the sign and house in which the eclipse falls. Solar eclipses deal with events and often enable us to see something that has eluded us. They also symbolize beginnings and endings.

Look to the entries for that month for more information.

Mercury Retrograde

Every year, Mercury—the planet that symbolizes communication and travel—turns retrograde three times.

During these periods, our travel plans often go awry, communication breaks down, computers go berserk, cars or appliances develop problems. You get the idea. Things in our daily lives don't work as smoothly as we would like.

In the overview for each sign, check out the dates for this year's Mercury retrogrades and how these retrogrades are likely to impact you.

Using This Book

This book can be used alone, to get a sense of the patterns that may be coming up for you in a particular month, or it can be used along with the book for your sun sign that contains daily predictions. Whether you use one or both, the information is intended to inform you ahead of time about possible issues, challenges, situations, and relationships that may be surfacing in your life. To be informed is to be empowered.

The Big Picture for Aries
in 2008

Welcome to 2008, Aries! It's your year for cooperation, partnerships, patience, arbitration, and relationships. Given your independence and need for action,
there could be some inherent challenges in what's
called for this year. But no challenge is big enough to
daunt your pioneering spirit.

You have major, positive changes coming up this
year in your career. Whether you're just starting out
on a career path, are in the middle of it, or nearing
retirement, Jupiter and Pluto in your tenth house of
careers both expand and radically change what you're
doing. New opportunities come your way that are
more in line with your spiritual and personal beliefs,
individuals enter your life who may act as guides or
mentors, or you may fulfill that role for someone else.
You'll do well in business partnerships this year as
long as you don't get into power plays with other
people.

Other areas to watch for this year concern Saturn,
the planet that represents rules, restrictions, and
karma. For the last two and a half years, Saturn has
been in your fifth house of romance. You may have
experienced delays or restrictions related to romance
or your joy may have been squashed for some reason.
Even if other areas of your life have flourished, you
may have been disappointed in the love department.

That ended once Saturn moved into Virgo on September 2 of last year. Until the fall of 2009, you may

experience restrictions related to your daily work routine. You could be saddled with more responsibility. Just do the work, Aries. The payoff comes in several years. Since the sixth house also represents your daily health, it's important to keep yourself in good shape once Saturn moves into Virgo. Pay closer attention to your nutrition and exercise routines.

Uranus, the planet that symbolizes sudden, unexpected change, is still in your twelfth house this year. It's been there for quite a while, so you should be well acquainted with its energies. You may experience events or relationships that touch upon deeply buried issues and allow you to confront these issues and resolve them once and for all. Since the twelfth house symbolizes what we can't see, what is hidden, you could have some associations with people in hospitals, nursing homes, or other institutions. Your dreams could be particularly vivid this year and can bring you intuitive information, insight into your own unconscious, and answers to questions.

BEST TIME FOR ROMANCE

Mark the dates between April 6 and 29, when Venus is in your sign. Your romantic quota soars. You're also more artistic then and others see you in a whole new light. You feel more confident and your sex appeal soars. Great backup dates for romance fall between July 12 and August 4, when Venus is transiting your fifth house of love and forming a beautiful angle to your sun.

BEST TIME FOR CAREER DECISIONS

Make career decisions between the first of the year and May 8 or between September 8 and the end of the year, when Jupiter is moving direct through your tenth house. During the four-month period between early May and early September, Jupiter is moving retrograde—it's essentially dormant.

There are some especially lucky days this year for career decisions. They fall between May 11 and 13 and September 3 and 5, when the sun and Jupiter see eye to eye and there's a nice flow of energy between them.

MERCURY RETROGRADES

Every year, there are three periods when Mercury, the planet of communication and travel, turns retrograde. During these periods, it's wisest not to negotiate or sign contracts, to travel, to submit manuscripts, or to make major decisions. Granted, we can't live our lives entirely by Mercury retrogrades! If you have to travel during the periods listed below, however, expect changes in your plans. If you have to sign a contract, expect to revise it.

It's also a good idea to back up computer files before Mercury turns retrograde. Quite often, computers and other communication devices act up. Be sure your virus software is up to date, too. Pay special attention to the house in which Mercury retrograde falls. It will tell you the area of your life most likely to be impacted. The periods to watch for in 2008 are:

January 28–February 18: retrograde in Aquarius, your eleventh house of friends.

May 26–June 19: retrograde in Gemini, your third house of communication and travel.

September 24–October 15: retrograde in Libra, your seventh house of partnerships.

ECLIPSES

Every year, there are four eclipses, two solar and two lunar. Solar eclipses trigger external events that allow us to see something that eluded us before. When an eclipse hits one of your natal planets, it's especially important. Take note of the sign and house placement. Lunar eclipses bring up emotional issues related to the sign and house into which they fall.

Here are the dates to watch for:

February 6: Solar eclipse at seventeen degrees Aquarius, your eleventh house of friends, wishes, and dreams. Those of you born between April 4 and 8 are likely to feel the greatest impact, in a positive way. But check your natal chart to find out if you have any planets at seventeen degrees.

February 20: lunar eclipse at ten degrees Virgo, in your sixth house of daily work and health.

August 1: solar eclipse, nine degrees Leo, in your fifth house of romance. If you were born between March 27 and 31, this eclipse will impact you strongly, in a positive way.

August 16: lunar eclipse at twenty-four degrees Aquarius, your eleventh house of friends, wishes, and dreams.

LUCKIEST DAYS IN 2008

Every year, Jupiter forms a beneficial angle with the sun, usually a conjunction, when both planets are in the same sign. In 2008, the angle is a lovely trine and it occurs during two time periods: May 11–13 and September 3–5. If you're going to buy a lotto ticket, do it during these periods!

Now let's take a look at what 2008 has in store for you month by month.

Twelve Months of Predictions
for Aries
January–December 2008

Aries—January 2008

The year gets off to a running start with a new moon in Capricorn on January 8 that promises fresh opportunities and strategies related to your career. If you decide that the professional path you've been following isn't in line with your passions and interests, then you make plans to gain the skills or knowledge you need to do what you love.

On January 8, expansive Jupiter is close enough to the new moon to bring about serendipitous happenings. You're in the right place at the right time, meet exactly the right people who open doors, and know exactly what to say and when to say it. Jupiter is the Midas touch. Use that energy wisely. Jupiter will be transiting your tenth house of careers for the rest of the year, so you can expect more expansion and successes in publishing, higher education, and foreign travel and business dealings.

You enjoy the Mercury transit this month (except when it turns retrograde). It's in Aquarius and your eleventh house, attracting friends of all types and belief systems. Your nature accommodates just about anything! Between January 28 and February 18, when Mercury is moving retrograde, there could be some strains in friendships—misunderstandings, mostly, or revisiting old territory.

On January 24, Venus joins Jupiter in your tenth house. Talk about smooth sailing! Things may be so smooth that you could be tempted to take off for a couple of weeks. Don't do it unless you absolutely have to. You have opportunities now to advance your agenda, goals, and vision. Venus may be a distraction in career matters because you get involved with someone you meet through work. Or with a boss. Or a professional peer. Be careful, Aries. A little restraint goes a long way in mitigating your passions.

With Mars retrograde in Cancer and your fourth house until January 30, you may have some home expenses you didn't count on. These expenses coming on top of holiday bills could put you in a blue funk for all of about five minutes. You're rarely down for long. Your natural enthusiasm and vigor for life and new experiences urge you to leap out of bed and embrace whatever awaits you.

The full moon in Leo on January 22 holds incredible surprises as it lights up your fifth house. Think romance, creative adrenaline, emphasis on children. This full moon could put a strain on a friendship, but it forms a beautiful angle to your sun. You feel very good about the direction of your life and about your love life in particular. If you're not involved at the full moon, your search will astonish you.

Dates to watch for: January 8, with several days on either side; January 19–20, when Saturn and Jupiter join hands to bring rewards in daily work and career; and the beautiful full moon on January 22. Reread the material on Mercury retrogrades and follow those guidelines between January 28 and February 18. On January 25, Pluto joins Jupiter in your tenth house, adding an element of power plays in your professional picture.

Best date: January 24, when Venus and Jupiter link up in your career house.

Aries—February 2008

The two eclipses this month pack a wallop. On February 6, the solar eclipse (new moon) in Aquarius, your eleventh house, brings insights about friendships, any groups to which you belong, and your own wishes and dreams. Mercury is very close to the moon and sun in this eclipse, suggesting lots of discussion and conversation concerning friends and friendship issues. Neptune—illusions and higher inspiration—is also close to the sun and moon, indicating that you may be called upon to walk your talk, Aries.

The lunar eclipse on February 20, in Virgo and your third house, may bring up emotional issues related to your daily work and health routine. You absolutely have to talk to a trusted friend about events that occur several days before or after this eclipse.

What happens in between these two dates? Plenty. Mark February 17 on your calendar. Venus enters Aquarius, your eleventh house. Hmm, Aries. Fire and air in romance. Are you ready for that? Ready to speak your mind as easily as you reveal your heart? Chemistry with someone you consider a friend is a real possibility. Or, you meet someone special through friends.

On February 18, Mercury turns direct in Gemini. That means you go from *ouch* to jubilation! Now you can sign contracts, make your travel plans, and write from the heart. But to write from the heart you have to know what you want, what you're trying to say, and do you know that yet, Aries?

With both Jupiter and Pluto now in Capricorn, your tenth house, you're in the driver's seat when it comes to your career. There are power plays going on, but you're on top of it. The odd thing is that you may decide you don't want to play. You're so innately blunt and honest that you just can't be bothered with playing games. And that's fine. Never deny any facet of who you are and never, never change to suit someone else.

With Uranus still continuing its transit through Pisces and your twelfth house, you should check the Omarr daily guides to your sign for insights into what this means and how to use this energy to your benefit. Hint: a secret affair is in the stars.

Dates to watch for: February 6, 18, 20.

Best date: February 29. The sun and Uranus make a wide conjunction to each other, indicating an unexpected surprise or insight concerning that secret romance. It's also a good time to recall your dreams. Meditation would be a plus, even if it's just five minutes on the run, while you're listening to the Rolling Stones or Santana on your iPod and are tuned in to Air America for the latest straight talk on politics.

Aries—March 2008

The new moon in Pisces on March 7 makes you introspective for most of the month. But not to worry. You don't have to meditate on your navel, Aries. Much of your inner work unfolds in dreams. Simply keep a notepad, light, and pen next to your bed at night, and before you sleep give yourself a suggestion to remember your dreams. As you become proficient at dream recall, you can ask for dreams that illuminate concerns and issues. By the end of the month, you'll be as comfortable in your dreams as you are in waking life.

Another nice facet of this new moon is that it draws unusual people into your life. These individuals definitely don't fit into any box and their particular genius shakes up your status quo, perhaps changing what you believe is possible, perhaps even proving that the universe is still a very magical place.

On March 12, Venus enters Pisces, and on March 14 Mercury joins Venus in your twelfth house. This combination urges you to continue your exploration of your dream world, but also could trigger a secret

26

romance. Enjoy the secrecy while it lasts. After Venus moves into your sign on April 6, the secret will be out.

On March 4, Mars enters Cancer and your fourth house. Mars symbolizes your physical and sexual energy and will be forming a challenging angle to your sun between now and May 9. You may encounter conflict at home with your partner, kids, even one of your parents. Mars in Cancer is deeply intuitive, however, and you'll know how to handle things.

Mark March 21, too. The full moon in Libra brightens up a romance or triggers the beginning of a romance. Even though this full moon is opposite your sun, which can cause some tension, it's a romantic evening. A relationship may be taken to newer and greater heights.

With Neptune still in Aquarius, your friendships right now are unusual, perhaps even spiritual. They involve a common idealism and a certain intuitive awareness of how you and your friends fit into the larger picture.

Dates to watch for: March 7, plus or minus several days on either side; March 12, 14, 21.

Best dates: March 1–2, when Mercury and Venus in Aquarius bring in social invitations and a possible romance with someone you considered a friend.

Aries—April 2008

This could be one of your best months all year and it starts on April 5, with the new moon in your sign. This moon should usher in a whole new chapter in your personal life. There could be a new relationship, career, job, trip, virtually anything on which you place your attention. Mercury is close enough to the moon to sharpen your communication skills. This new moon happens only once a year, so take advantage of it.

On April 6, Venus enters your sign, signaling the beginning of a twenty-four-day period that should be one of the most romantic times this year. If you're not involved in a committed relationship right now, you probably will be before this transit ends on April 30. If you're involved, then the relationship enters a pleasant and upbeat period, in which you and your partner should see eye to eye on just about everything.

On April 17, Mercury enters Taurus and the money sector of your chart. Until May 2, your conscious mind and daily life are focused primarily on financial issues—what you earn, spend, and how your balance sheet adds up. You may be looking for safe investments. Stay away from the stock market unless you really know what you're doing. If you feel you need to buy stocks, then buy in companies whose products you use.

April 20 brings a full moon in Scorpio, not exactly your favorite sign unless you have planets in water signs. Joint resources are spotlighted. Your partner or anyone else with whom you pool money and resources may have a change in income. Or, if you're in the midst of a divorce, this full moon brings everything out into the open.

When Venus joins Mercury in Taurus on April 30, your mind and your heart are in synch where money is concerned. But more than that, you're able to use emotional security issues as fodder for a creative project. So any angst you've been feeling now has a positive outlet. With Jupiter also in an earth sign (Capricorn) and Saturn in earth sign Virgo, the focus should be on what's practical, efficient, and useful to others.

Dates to watch for: During the first ten days or so this month, Jupiter and Uranus travel at a harmonious angle to each other, bringing excitement and surprise to your career and also to your inner life.

Best dates: April 1–2, when Mercury and Venus in Pisces bring insights and psychic experiences related to a romantic relationship, creativity, and your inner life.

Mark May 2. Mercury enters Gemini, an air sign compatible with Aries, and doesn't leave until July 10. Except for the three weeks or so when Mercury is retrograde, this transit stimulates all your writing and communication projects, your travel, and your relationships with brothers and sisters. You're in a gregarious and celebratory mood, upbeat, and most appealing to family and friends.

Then, from May 26 to June 10, things get confusing. Mercury retrograde messes up your travel plans, causes your computer to act as though it has a mind of its own, and plays havoc with your communications. The best way to negotiate this period is to rethink, rewrite, revise. If you have to travel, expect changes in your plans and schedules.

The new moon in Taurus on May 5 should bring about new financial opportunities. If you don't like what you do to earn your living or feel that financial opportunities aren't coming your way quickly enough, this new moon brings some nice, positive changes. Think serendipity. You're in the right place at the right time.

Jupiter turns retrograde in your tenth house on May 9. This movement indicates that there could be some delays in terms of job changes or promotions during the next several months. You may be scrutinizing your career path and trying to figure out if it's in line with your worldview and spiritual beliefs.

On May 19, the full moon in Scorpio brings to light an insurance issue or highlights a concern you have about resources you share with others. If you're in the midst of a divorce, for example, this full moon illuminates the full scope of what's on the table.

Venus enters Gemini and your third house on May 24. This transit is terrific for writers or anyone in the communication and travel businesses. It portends a generally smooth atmosphere and stimulates your creativity as well. During much of this transit, however, Mercury is retrograde, mitigating some of the benefits of the Venus transit.

Dates to watch for: May 3–25. During this period, Mercury is moving direct through Gemini, a sign compatible with Aries, and stimulates all kinds of activity related to travel, communication, and your relationships with brothers, sisters, neighbors, and your community in general. Also on May 3, Saturn turns direct in Virgo, your sixth house of health and work. While you may still feel burdened by responsibilities at work, things will ease up considerably after that date.

Best dates: May 23–30. Mercury and Jupiter are forming harmonious angles to each other in your second and tenth houses. Even though Jupiter is retrograde, you still experience financial and career expansion in some way.

Aries—June 2008

The new moon in Gemini on June 3 should be immensely pleasant for you. Despite the Mercury retrograde, you can expect new opportunities related to travel, writing and communication, your community, and education. Give the timing four days on either side of June 3.

The full moon two weeks later, on June 18, falls in Sagittarius, your ninth house, and falls very close to Pluto, the great transformer. This combination indicates that the full moon will be especially powerful for you. If you're a writer in search of an agent or publisher, then this full moon could bring a major break. Since the ninth house also represents overseas travel, you may have an opportunity to travel overseas. Make sure your passport is current!

Also on June 18, Venus enters Cancer, your fourth house, where it will remain until July 12. This transit should promote a more harmonious atmosphere at home and augurs well for romance. Since Venus represents the arts, it's possible that the energy of this transit shows up in your creative life. Perhaps you should consider setting up a home office for your creative projects, whatever they might be.

Mercury turns direct again on June 19, a welcome break for everyone. You can now sign contracts, reserve a plane ticket, pack your bags and get out of town! If you've been embroiled in communication snafus, those problems now even out and then vanish altogether.

Mark June 26. Uranus turns retrograde that day in Pisces, your twelfth house. This transit brings about insights into the workings of your own unconscious. You may attract unusual experiences and individuals who, in some way, help you to understand yourself better. This retrograde movement lasts until November 27, so use this time to get to know yourself.

Dates to watch for: Between June 20 and 26, the opposition between Mars in Leo and Neptune in Aquarius is either exact or very close. Oppositions emphasize the need for balance in our lives and usually involve a kind of grating tension that begs for resolution. This opposition impacts your fifth house of romance and your house of friends. One possible interpretation? You get involved with a friend, and because you have many mutual friends you can't be open about your relationship.

Best dates: June 4–8. During this time, Venus in Gemini and Mars in Leo are forming exact angles to each other that benefit your love life! In fact, your new partner could be someone who lives in your neighborhood—maybe as close as next door! This combination of planets also favors any kind of creative work you do. You may get help and support from siblings and relatives.

Aries—July 2008

It's a busy month, Aries, and the better informed you are, the happier you'll be. This month's notable dates start on July 1, with Mars entering Virgo, your sixth house of health and work. Mars is linking up with Saturn in this house, so you're a regular workhorse during this transit. You may be working longer hours and have greater responsibility. The Mars transit is terrific for getting yourself in shape. If you don't have a regular exercise routine yet, create one that you know you'll stick to.

July 2 features a new moon in Cancer, your fourth house. The effects of a new moon can be felt for four days on either side of the date given, and this one signals a new chapter for your home life. You may be moving, or someone will be moving in with you—or moving out. You may be expanding your house, adding on a room, or perhaps converting a room to an office or converting an office to a bedroom. You get the idea. It's a new chapter involving home and family.

Mercury enters Cancer and your fourth house on July 10, underscoring the energy of the new moon. There's lots of discussion at home during this Mercury transit, which lasts until July 26, and it seems to revolve around the positive changes taking place in your family life. Then, when Mercury enters Leo on July 26, forming a beautiful angle to your sun, your passions are revved up and you're ready to dive into a new romance. Mercury in Leo should also send your muse into high gear, urging you to get down to work on your creative projects.

On July 12, Venus enters Leo and your fifth house, preparing the way for the Mercury transit that begins on July 26. Venus's transit is one of the best all year for romance. If you're not involved with anyone at the beginning of the transit, you probably will meet someone before it ends on August 5. If you're in a relationship, then things should hum along quite nicely, with the emotions deepening and commitment levels rising.

Dates to watch for: The last week of the month should really add pizzazz to your love life and to your creativity. Another notable day for romance? Mark July 5, when the moon in Leo transits your fifth house of love.

Best dates: July 25–28 feature expansive Jupiter forming a nice angle to transiting Mars in Virgo. Even though Jupiter is retrograde, you'll reap some sort of career benefit. Pay close attention to details during this period.

Aries—August 2008

Batten down the hatches, Aries. The heavens are rocking and rolling this month and it starts on August 1, with a solar eclipse in your sign. This eclipse signals a beginning or ending to something in your personal life. Usually, solar eclipses trigger external events that allow us to see something that we didn't perceive before.

Two weeks later, on August 16, there's a lunar eclipse in Aquarius, your eleventh house. An emotional issue surfaces related to friends, groups, or to wishes and dreams that you have.

Long before the lunar eclipse, however, Venus enters a new sign—Virgo, on August 5. This transit, which lasts until August 30, could bring about an office flirtation or romance. It also signals a rather smooth time at work and a concern with your appearance. If you don't belong to a gym, now would be a good time to join. You may find yourself shopping for new clothes, in a style totally unlike your present style, or having dermatological work done.

On August 10, Mercury joins Venus in Virgo, in your sixth house. Saturn is also here and the combination of these planets emphasizes an office romance in which communication, structure, and responsibilities are paramount. You won't be looking for something casual during this transit. If you're committed already, then this combination of planets may indicate an abundance of discussions concerning a new creative project at work. You and your team may be brainstorming for the right structure for this project.

Mars enters Libra and your fourth house on August 19. This galvanizes your relationships, your sex life, and prompts you to actively seek out business partners and associates. You can aggressively negotiate contracts now, and don't hesitate to ask for what you feel you desire. You've never been the hesitant type or shy about expressing what you want, but now this is taken to the nth degree. The Mars transit lasts until October 3.

On August 28, Mercury joins Mars in Libra, adding sharp communication to your professional and personal partnerships. A meeting of the minds will be extremely important to you during this transit, which ends on November 4. A long transit for Mercury, but that's because it's moving retrograde between September 24 and October 15. Read more about that under the September roundup.

On August 30, Venus joins Mercury and Mars in Libra, your seventh house. This many planets in a single sign puts a lot of pressure on the affairs of that sign and house. Your relationships become paramount now and you have a deep need for balance and fairness. On this same day, there's a second new moon—in Virgo, your sixth house. This new moon should open up new vistas and opportunities in your daily work and in your health. You may want to perform some small, symbolic rituals on August 30 that encompass all your desires for the next month.

Dates to watch for: Around August 16, Mars in Virgo and Pluto in Sagittarius form a difficult angle to each other—a square. Expect tension related to your daily work and health and your worldview, education, and overseas travel. Try not to speed between August 10 and 18. You may get a ticket!

Best dates: In addition to the transit dates mentioned above, here are some other dates to mark on your calendar. August 8–9: Mercury and Pluto form very positive angles to each other, in fellow fire signs. Even though Pluto is retrograde, the powerful combination of these two planets transforms the way you think about your beliefs and worldview, your romantic relationships, and your creativity.

Aries—September 2008

September isn't quite as busy as August was. Two planets are turning direct this month, which is always good news. On September 7, Jupiter turns direct in Capricorn, your tenth house. Anything in your career that has been delayed should now move forward rather quickly. Think of this movement like that of a stone released from a slingshot. So as Jupiter now zips through your tenth house, your career opportunities come fast and furiously.

On September 8, Pluto turns direct in Sagittarius, your ninth house. If you're a writer in search of an agent or publisher, this movement may be just the thing to get you and your manuscript where you want to be. If you're starting college or graduate school, this movement certainly eases your adjustment.

The full moon in Pisces on September 15 should bring to light something that is hidden or secret. It may be related to a long-buried issue from your childhood, a past life, or might concern power you have disowned over the course of your life. This would be a good time for therapy and meditation.

Venus enters passionate Scorpio and your eighth house on September 23. Any romantic relationship that begins under this transit—which lasts until October 18—is apt to be intense. It also could be a past-life connection, so you'll be working out issues from other lives.

September 24 marks the beginning of the last Mercury retrograde this year. This retrograde occurs in Libra, your seventh house. A Mercury retrograde in your seventh house can play havoc with your communications with partners, so until October 15, when Mercury turns direct again, be very precise in your communication with your partners. You'll be striving to balance all the demands in your life, and while that will be challenging, you'll achieve it nonetheless.

The new moon in Libra on September 29 brings new opportunities related to your personal and professional partnerships. Since Mercury is still retrograde on September 29, it's to your advantage to be very clear about what you would like to achieve between now and the next new moon. Write out your goals. Create a strategy for attaining them.

Date to watch for: September 23. Mercury and Mars are dancing together and your attraction to another person begins with a meeting of the minds.

Best dates: For most of the month, Mercury, Venus, and Mars are traveling together in Libra, your seventh house. From September 13 to 20, they are so close together that their combined energies are amplified. Your love life perks up, your conscious mind is energized, and your sexuality is stimulated.

Aries—October 2008

Mark October 3 on your calendar. Mars enters Scorpio and your eighth house. This transit galvanizes your interest in the paranormal, life after death, reincarnation, and anything that goes bump in the night! Between October 3 and November 16, when Mars enters Sagittarius, your heightened sexuality may tempt you to get involved with someone who may not be right for you. Be sure to listen to your intuition about this person.

Mercury turns direct again on October 15, which is always good news, but it's especially positive for your love life. It's great to travel now and to sign contracts. Get busy, Aries!

On October 18, Venus enters Sagittarius, your ninth house. If you're traveling overseas, this transit should be enormous fun. Your plans unfold without a hitch and romance certainly is a distinct possibility. In fact, if you can find it, you may want to check out an Audrey Hepburn classic, *Two for the Road*. It will whet your appetite for overseas adventures.

The new moon on October 28 falls in Scorpio, your eighth house. This new moon should usher in new opportunities for loans, mortgages, insurance, wills, and inheritances. It can also trigger a quest of some kind related to the really big cosmic questions: What happens when we die? Can the dead communicate with the living? And who are you in the larger scheme of things?

Date to watch for: October 14, the full moon in Aries. This full moon should be especially good for those of you born between April 10 and 14. You should expect insights into your own personality and the culmination of something that has been in the works for a while.

Best dates: October 2–3 look very good for relationships. If you're overseas during this period, then the ante rises considerably. Mars in Libra and Pluto in Sagittarius are in perfect harmony. This can be a powerful combination of planets, but it's important not to overstep boundaries—either yours or someone else's. Also great? October 5–6, when Venus and Jupiter, the two best planets in the zodiac, are walking hand in hand in Scorpio and Capricorn. Even though neither of these signs is compatible with your sun, they are compatible with each other. Other people's resources are available to you on these dates, especially as those resources relate to your career.

Aries—November 2008

The month gets off to an intense start on November 4, when Mercury enters Scorpio and your eighth house, underscoring the themes of last month's new moon in the same sign. You're looking for the bottom line now, Aries, and you have the resources and knowledge to know where to go to find the information you need. Research and investigation are highlighted between November 4 and 23.

Lovely Venus enters Capricorn and your tenth house on November 12. Prepare for this one, Aries. It's a window of opportunity in which you can advance your career agenda, whatever that agenda may be. You're in a great place now to plan and lay down a strategy. Think in terms of six-month goals, yearly goals, a five-year plan. This transit can signal a romance with a peer or boss, too. It won't come as a big surprise if it happens. It's been in the works for a while now—secret looks, innocent flirtations, a kind of visceral attraction.

The full moon on November 13 falls in Taurus, your second house. Something about your finances or values is brought into stark relief. If you *don't* like what you see, decide how you can change it. If you *like* it, figure out how you can maintain this status quo.

Mars, your coruler, enters Sagittarius on November 16. This transit forms a beneficial angle to your sun. Think of it as a booster rocket that gets you moving in a direction that benefits you personally. If you're a writer in search of a publisher, this transit helps you find what (and who) you need. If you're in the market for an overseas trip, this transit helps you get to the country of your choice.

Mercury, symbolic of your conscious mind, enters Sagittarius on November 23, joining Mars in your ninth house. Your head now spins with ideas, visions. The impossible is possible. Four days later, on November 27, the new moon in Sagittarius adds fuel to his already very large and powerful fire.

Dates to watch for: November 1–2 present an intriguing combination of planets that form beneficial angles to each other. Mars in Scorpio, Jupiter in Capricorn, and Saturn in Virgo are not compatible with your sun sign, but they sure do love one another. Your resources, career, and daily work routine come together in a supportive team effort that forces your Aries sun to reconsider a particular path. The end result could be better than anything you ever imagined.

On November 26, Pluto enters Capricorn, where it will be until 2024. Take note of any events that occur around this date. They may provide insights into how Pluto's transit through your tenth house will unfold.

Best date: November 12. Venus and Pluto link up in Sagittarius, your ninth house. You're in the driver's seat, Aries. In romance, you hold the upper hand. How will you wield your power?

Aries—December 2008

As you enter the last month of the year, you're busier than usual, but in a good way, Aries. With Venus entering Aquarius and your eleventh house on December 7, the time you spend with friends is important. Whether you're partying with these people or just hanging out, new relationships are forged. One group that you belong to may undertake a charity or volunteer project for the holidays.

Two events occur on December 12. Mercury enters Capricorn and your tenth house and there's a full moon in Gemini, in your third house. The first transit, which lasts through the end of the year, indicates a lot of activity connected to your career. You may be traveling on business, having discussions concerning some new project or direction for your company, or you may be in discussions with another company for a possible job change.

To some extent, the activity suggested by Mercury could be triggered by events that occur around the full moon. It's possible that you'll be gathering information and facts so that you can make an informed decision about a career matter. With Pluto now transiting your tenth house with expansive Jupiter, profound change in your professional path is in the air, and however it unfolds, you will benefit.

December 27 is the next date that's important. Again, it features two astrological events—a new moon in Capricorn, your tenth house, and Mars entering Capricorn. This powerful combination of events brings new career opportunities, the ability to make long-range plans, and a steady physical energy that sustains you through the holidays!

Dates to watch for: For the first nine or ten days of December, Jupiter in Capricorn and Saturn in fellow earth sign Virgo travel at beneficial angles to each other. Your daily work provides you with the structure you need for career changes that are coming up.

Best date: December 27. Venus and Neptune meet up in Aquarius, stimulating your idealism. You and a partner may realize that you can't live without each other.

Brainstorming

Envision yourself a year, two years, or four years from now. What is your life like? Where do you live? Is your work satisfying to you? Are you single, married, a parent? Are you happy? Do you have enough money? Is your health good? What are your spiritual beliefs? Are you a vehicle for change in your family or community? In the space below, describe the life you would like to be living a year or two or four up the line. Be as outrageous, creative, and wild as you want. After all, it's *your* life. If you can imagine it, then you can create it.

MY LIFE IN _____ (choose a year)

_____
_____
_____
_____
_____
_____
_____
_____
_____
_____
_____
_____
_____

HAPPY 2009!

The Big Picture for Taurus in 2008

For 2008, Taurus, think creative, imaginative, optimistic. If you already work in a creative field, then this year you reap the benefits of your long, hard work. If you dislike your job, you will have opportunities to find something that suits you much better and provides that creative outlet you will need and crave this year.

If you're a writer, in the publishing field, or are involved in education, the travel industry, religion, or politics, then buckle up on January 1 because 2008 holds major, positive change for you. Even if you don't work in any of those industries, your worldview and beliefs are going to expand like crazy this year and undergo profound and permanent change.

You have two major hitters in fellow earth signs to thank for that—Pluto, the great transformer, and Jupiter, the planet of expansion and success, in Capricorn. You may feel compelled to work and live in ways that are more in line with your belief system and will attract opportunities and people who will help you do exactly that.

In addition to Pluto and Jupiter in earth signs, forming harmonious angles to your sun, Saturn is in Virgo all year, forming another beneficial angle to your sun. Since Saturn is the planet that symbolizes karma, rules and restrictions, and governs our physical lives, it's always best to have this planet on the plus side! Until the fall of 2009, Saturn will be in your fifth house of creativity, children, romance and love. It will help you find the proper structures in all of these areas. If you get involved in a romantic relationship this year, then the person may be older than you. If you're already in a relationship, then you and your partner may take it to the next level and a deeper commitment.

Uranus, the planet that symbolizes sudden, unexpected change, is still in your eleventh house this year, forming a beneficial angle to your sun. Its position suggests that some of your dreams for yourself are now being realized and that your friends and any groups to which you belong are helpful.

Neptune continues its long transit of Aquarius and your tenth house. This transit certainly favors fiction writing, script writing, photography, dance, music, art—in short, any creative endeavor. It also suggests that you may have some blind spots regarding your career ambitions, but that you can draw on the energy of your higher self to resolve any dilemmas you encounter.

BEST TIME FOR ROMANCE

Mark the dates between April 3 and May 23, when Venus, your ruler, is in your sign. Your romantic quota soars. You're also more artistic then and others see you in a whole new light. You feel more confident and your sex appeal soars. Great backup dates for romance fall between August 5 and 29, when Venus is transiting your fifth house of love and forming a beautiful angle to your sun.

BEST TIME FOR CAREER DECISIONS

Make career decisions between February 17 and March 11, when Venus is transiting your tenth house of careers. Other good dates? May 11–13 and September 3–5, when the sun and Jupiter see eye to eye and there's a nice flow of energy between them.

MERCURY RETROGRADES

Every year, there are three periods when Mercury,

the planet of communication and travel, turns retrograde. During these periods, it's wisest not to negotiate or sign contracts, to travel, to submit manuscripts, or to make major decisions. Granted, we can't live our lives entirely by Mercury retrogrades! If you have to travel during the periods listed below, however, then expect changes in your plans. If you have to sign a contract, expect to revise it.

It's also a good idea to back up computer files before Mercury turns retrograde. Quite often, computers and other communication devices act up. Be sure your virus software is up to date, too. Pay special attention to the house in which Mercury retrograde falls because this will be the area where you are most likely to experience delays, changes, and snafus. The periods to watch for in 2008 are:

January 28–February 18: retrograde in Aquarius, your tenth house of career.

May 26–June 19: retrograde in Gemini, your second house of finances. In other words, if you're expecting checks, they may be delayed. Don't make investments. Don't buy and sell stocks. Lie low.

September 24–October 15: retrograde in Libra, your sixth house of health and work.

ECLIPSES

Every year, there are four eclipses, two solar and two lunar. Solar eclipses trigger external events that allow us to see something that eluded us before. When an eclipse hits one of your natal planets, it's especially important. Take note of the sign and house placement. Lunar eclipses bring up emotional issues related to the sign and house into which they fall.

Here are the dates to watch for:

February 6: solar eclipse at seventeen degrees Aquarius, your tenth house of career. Those of you born between May 5 and 9 are likely to feel the greatest impact, in a challenging way. But check your natal chart to find out if you have any planets at seventeen degrees.

February 20: lunar eclipse at ten degrees Virgo, in your fifth house of romance, love, and creativity.

August 1: solar eclipse, nine degrees Leo, in your fifth house of romance. If you were born between April 28 and May 1, this eclipse will impact you strongly, in a challenging way.

August 16: lunar eclipse at twenty-four degrees Aquarius, your tenth house of career.

LUCKIEST DAYS IN 2008

Every year, Jupiter forms a beneficial angle with the sun, usually a conjunction, when both planets are in the same sign. In 2008, the angle is a lovely trine and it occurs during two time periods: May 11–13 and September 3–5. If you're going to buy a lotto ticket, do it during these periods!

Now let's take a look at what 2008 has in store for you month by month.

Twelve Months of Predictions
for Taurus
January–December 2008

Taurus—January 2008

Cymbals and drum rolls, please. Your year starts on a fantastic note—a new moon in Capricorn in your ninth house on January 8. The moon promises fresh opportunities for the next two weeks in publishing, education, and long-distance travel. If you're a writer in search of an editor or agent, you find the person who is exactly right for you. If you're a student, you may get a chance to head overseas for a semester abroad. Your company expands its products and services overseas. You get the idea here, Taurus. Regardless of your circumstances, this new moon promises that you are now on a roll.

On January 8, expansive Jupiter is close enough to the new moon to bring about serendipitous happenings. You're in the right place at the right time. Remember, Jupiter is the Midas touch and seeks to expand everything it contacts. Between January 1 and 6, Mercury is also in your ninth house in Capricorn, so you're fired up about all the new possibilities and eager to talk about them.

Between January 7 and 27, Mercury transits your tenth house of career, in Aquarius. You may be traveling for business, involved in contract negotiations, or doing some public speaking. On January 28, Mercury turns retrograde for the first time this year, so tie up your contract negotiations before then and sign on the dotted line. If you have to travel, expect sudden changes in your itinerary and schedule. During this retrograde period, there could be some tension with bosses or other authority figures.

On January 24, Venus joins Jupiter in your ninth house. A day later, Pluto changes signs, a major event, moving from Sagittarius to Capricorn. You'll have the travel bug, for sure, and if you're overseas already, then romance may be just a heartbeat away. If you're at home, Venus in the ninth house portends romance with someone you meet in a workshop or class, at church, or even at some political gathering. Your worldview and personal philosophy are expanding by leaps and bounds and you encounter tangible evidence of these expanded beliefs without looking very hard.

Manifestation, Taurus. That's what you're learning this month.

With Mars retrograde in Cancer and your third house until January 30, you may be reevaluating a relationship with a neighbor or a sibling or may be revising a manuscript or communication project. Avoid confrontation. Once Mars turns direct on January 30, you're ready to move full speed ahead.

The full moon in Leo on January 22, in your fourth house, looks like a very fine time to cuddle up with the one you love. You may feel like beautifying your home office around this full moon. Perhaps a little feng shui is in order!

Dates to watch for: January 8 and the two weeks afterward: plant your seeds. On January 19–20, Saturn and Jupiter join hands to bring rewards in your publishing and educational endeavors. Reread the material on Mercury retrogrades and follow those guidelines between January 28 and February 18. On January 25, Pluto joins Jupiter in your ninth house, putting you squarely in the driver's seat. Another date? January 25, when Pluto moves into Capricorn. Although it will retrograde and slip back into Sagittarius at a certain point this year, this transit is big. Pluto will be in Capricorn until late 2024.

Best date: January 24, when Venus and Jupiter link up in your ninth house. This could be the day you hear from that editor or agent or confirm your travel plans for the dream trip overseas.

Taurus—February 2008

A solar eclipse at seventeen degrees Aquarius, in your tenth house, sets the stage for the month. Expect some sort of external event that will allow you to see something about your career that previously eluded you. Since retrograde Mercury is so close to this eclipse degree, you'll be rethinking a professional issue or revising a project.

The solar eclipse is followed in two weeks, on February 20, with a lunar eclipse in early Virgo, in your fifth house. Lunar eclipses tend to concern inner, emotional events, and this one will impact a romantic relationship or a creative project in some way. Since it occurs at a harmonious angle to your sun, it should be positive.

Your ruler, Venus, joins Neptune in Aquarius in your tenth house on February 17, a positive transit for you. It's now time to walk your talk. Your ideals are at an all-time high and you may be trying to figure out how to incorporate them more effectively into your professional life. During this transit, which lasts until March 17, a raise or promotion is possible. You may feel that things are going so smoothly in your career that you'll be tempted to kick back and chill. Resist that urge. This transit won't happen again this year until December 7, so make the best of it!

On February 18, Mercury turns direct, so save any work pitches, brainstorming sessions, and discussions until after that date. After February 18, start making your plans for travel, sign contracts, return phone calls, set up dates for meeting with clients.

Dates to watch for: February 6 (solar eclipse), 18 (Mercury direct), 20 (lunar eclipse).

Best dates: February 23–26, when expansive Jupiter and unpredictable Uranus form harmonious angles to each other and to your sun. Expect the unexpected and the news is positive! Another terrific date falls on February 29, when the sun and Uranus form a wide conjunction to each other. Your intuition is remarkable on this date and you get a major boost from an unexpected source.

Taurus—March 2008

The new moon in Pisces on March 7 promises new friendships and group activities and perhaps even the manifestation of a dream. Over the course of the next two weeks, you have an opportunity to take or teach a class or workshop and the opportunity seems to come out of the blue. Idiosyncratic and highly individualistic people enter your life, too, and they are helpful to you in the manifestation of your dream.

Then, on March 12, your ruler, Venus, enters Pisces and your eleventh house, and on March 14, Mercury follows. These two planets certainly support the themes of the new moon and suggest the possibility of a new romance with someone you meet through friends and lots of lively discussions with friends. You may be joining a political action group, too, Taurus.

You get an extra boost of energy on March 4, when Mars enters into compatible water sign Cancer and your third house. This is a great transit if you're a writer, in public relations, the travel industry, or in any facet of communication. Expect increased activity. You may be running around more than usual and some of these trips could involve your mother or another nurturing female.

The full moon in Libra on March 21 could bring about some tensions in your daily work, particularly if someone makes a power play. Best to stay out of it, if at all possible.

Dates to watch for: March 7 (that new moon!), 12, 14, 21.

Best dates: March 1–2. Mercury and Venus are in Aquarius, moving tightly together through your tenth house. You're able to communicate your ideas easily and smoothly and both bosses and peers are receptive.

Taurus—April 2008

There's a lot of activity this month and it starts on April 2, when Mercury enters Aries and your twelfth house. You're now in a kind of preparatory stage for when Mercury enters your sign on April 17. Any work you do in seclusion and solitude should be beneficial now. If you're a writer, this transit gives you the space and privacy you need to start or finish a project. If you're a student, you may be part of a small study group that's focusing on a particular course or topic. This is a good time for therapy, too, if you're so inclined. Issues and concerns that have been buried in your unconscious now surface and it's easier to talk about them.

The new moon in Aries on April 5 gives you the opening to do exactly what the Mercury in Aries transit promises. You may get an opportunity to work behind the scenes in some capacity. It's also possible that you'll be visiting someone who is confined in a hospital, nursing home, or similar facility. The next two weeks are the perfect time to delve into who you are, to reclaim personal power that you have disowned, and to explore your dreams. Meditation would be helpful now.

On April 6, Venus joins Mercury in Aries, in your twelfth house. This transit is ideal for a secret romance. You and your partner spend a lot of time alone, conversing, getting to know each other. If the relationship begins in secret, however, that won't last. By the time Mercury enters your sign on April 17 or when Venus enters Taurus on April 30, you'll be itching to tell the world your good news.

After April 17, your communication skills are well honed and you could probably sell just about anything to anyone. If you have your natal moon or sun rising in Taurus, then your skills are enhanced even more. If you're involved in a contract negotiation during this period, you get exactly what you ask for, so don't be shy!

The full moon in Scorpio on April 20 occurs in your seventh house of partnerships, opposite your sun sign. Full moons often bring about certain tensions, and this one ends a path that you've been on. You may finish a project, tie up contract negotiations, or even end a romantic or business partnership that has served its purpose but can't be taken any further.

April 30 to May 23 marks one of the most romantic periods in 2008 because Venus, your ruler, is in your sign. If you're not involved with anyone when this transit starts, chances are good that you will be before the transit ends. If you're in a committed relationship when this transit begins, then the relationship may enter a whole new level. You and your partner could move in together or perhaps tie the knot.

Dates to watch for: April 5 (that new moon in Aries), 17, 30. Also, April 1–10, when expansive and lucky Jupiter teams up with unpredictable Uranus to bring in some marvelous surprise!

Best dates: April 1–2, when Mercury and Venus are snuggling up to each other in Pisces, your eleventh house. This suggests that someone you think is a friend turns out to be something much more than that. Or, you meet a romantic partner through a group activity.

Taurus—May 2008

The best news this month is the new moon in your sign on May 5. This moon happens only once a year and hurls open doors to new opportunities in all areas of your life. Since this moon receives positive energy from Uranus, the opportunities that come to you during the next few weeks come unexpectedly and are undoubtedly terrific surprises.

The full moon on May 19, in Scorpio, is opposite your sign, at a very late degree. Although every Taurus will feel the tension of this full moon, those of you born around May 28–29 will feel it the most.

Saturn, the planet that symbolizes the rules and parameters by which we live our physical lives, turns direct on May 2, in Virgo, your fifth house. This is very good news for your love life, Taurus. Your romantic relationships now find the appropriate structures and boundaries. Your creative projects suddenly seem to fall into place and your ideas flow.

Mars, the planet that rules our physical and sexual energy, enters Leo and your fourth house on May 9. Buckle up, Taurus, because your home life is about to blast off. In fact, your home and family may be showcased in some way now. You may decide to move, so your house goes on the market and is showcased to prospective buyers. Even if you aren't planning to move, there's more activity at home. Your kids and their friends come and go at all hours, you have friends over, your parents arrive. Busy, right?

Mercury enters Gemini, the sign that it rules, on May 2, energizing your second house of finances. This transit should bring news about checks that are owed to you—or could bring the checks themselves. Your daily life, at least for the next few weeks, revolves around what you earn and spend. You may be thinking quite a bit about how you earn your living—is it in line with your beliefs? Then, on May 26, Mercury turns retrograde. Check out the material on Mercury retrogrades in the overview section to find out how this impacts you. Hint: if the checks haven't arrived by May 26, they probably won't arrive until after June 19, when Mercury turns direct again.

On May 24, Venus joins Mercury in Gemini and your second house. Venus's transit through your house of money can work either for or against you. Your earning capacity may rise, but you may be spending more, too!

Dates to watch for: May 3, 9 (Jupiter turns retrograde, so its expansiveness is turned inward), 24, 26.

Best dates: May 23–30, Mercury, Jupiter, and Uranus will be in compatible angles to each other, adding excitement, unpredictability, and expansion to your life.

Taurus—June 2008

June 3 features a new moon in Gemini, your second house, so be prepared for your finances to take a definite upswing. You'll have new opportunities to make more money, perhaps by changing jobs or landing a project that seems to come to you with almost no effort on your part. Thank Venus for that. It's very close to this new moon, within two degrees, and its proximity helps to facilitate the flow of energy inherent in this moon.

The full moon on June 18 is in Sagittarius, your eighth house. Its proximity to Pluto—by one degree— suggests the power inherent in this moon. You may be locked in a struggle with someone over resources you share. If you're in the midst of a divorce, for instance, your soon-to-be-ex may give you trouble about dividing your assets. There could be challenging issues with insurance companies or taxes. You do get help from expansive Jupiter, however, particularly if your rising, natal moon or sun is between eighteen and twenty degrees Taurus. For an eighteen-to-twenty-degree sun, it means you were born between May 8 and 10.

On June 18, your ruler, Venus, enters Cancer, a sign more compatible with your own. It's possible that between now and July 12 a friendship with a neighbor heats up and becomes something more. Whether it's just a flirtation or becomes a relationship depends on where you are at that point in your life and what you're seeking in a relationship.

Mark June 19 on your calendar. Mercury turns direct and now your checks start arriving, your finances turn around, it's safe to travel again without unexpected snafus and delays. Well, it may not be that dramatic all at once, but things are definitely improving from here on out (until the next Mercury retrograde!).

Dates to watch for: In addition to the dates already mentioned, June 26 marks the beginning of a Uranus retrograde in Pisces that lasts until November 27. This retrograde impacts your friendships and any groups to which you belong. Expect some bumps and bruises and perhaps misunderstandings.

Best dates: June 4–8, when your ruler, Venus, and Mars are moving in a harmonious angle to each other. This combination certainly spices up your love life, your sex life, the money sector of your chart, and your home life.

Taurus—July 2008

The astrological weather this month is spectacular—and active. On July 1, Mars enters Virgo and joins Saturn in your first house. One of the things this transit does is activate your love life. Suddenly, you're all about pleasure and romance—finding it, experiencing it, soaking it up. Saturn may try to hold you back or may make you more cautious than you need to be, but when Mars is itching to move forward, you move. This transit lasts until August 19.

On July 10, Mercury enters Cancer again after its retrograde took it back into Gemini for a while. This is a more comfortable position for you, in a compatible water sign and your third house. It's excellent for all kinds of communication and for travel.

Your ruler, Venus, enters Leo and your sixth house on July 12. Even though Venus is now square to your sun, it may be doing very nice things for an office flirtation. Whether this relationship goes beyond the flirtation stage is up to you and depends on what you're looking for at this point in your life.

July 26 has Mercury joining Venus in Leo, your sixth house. Now you're really chatting it up over the water cooler and the lunch table. There may be some gossip about you and your new partner, too. You could be feeling an internal pressure to improve your physical appearance in some way. Perhaps a gym membership is in the offing?

The new moon on July 2 is in Cancer, your third house. Once again, new doors open according to the sign and house placement of the new moon and this one is compatible with your earth sign sun, so expect opportunities in communication, travel, and with siblings and neighbors. Even if you haven't planned on moving this year, this new moon may prompt you to start looking at other neighborhoods to get a sense of what you would like if and when you do move.

The full moon on July 18, in Capricorn and your ninth house, sheds light on a situation, individual, or event connected to overseas travel, education, politics or spirituality, and/or your worldview.

Dates to watch for: The last week of the month, when Mars is in Virgo and retrograde Jupiter is in Capricorn, should be quite exciting for you. Both of these planets form a beneficial angle to your sun and to each other, invigorating your love life, your worldview, and your ego!

Best date: July 25 features Venus and retrograde

Jupiter traveling in a beautiful angle to each other and to your sun sign. Romance, the arts, and creativity all are enhanced.

Taurus—August 2008

August has its share of astrological changes and it all begins on the first, with a solar eclipse in Leo, your fourth house. External events help you to see something about your home and family life that has escaped you before. Those of you born between April 29 and May 1 will feel this eclipse most strongly. It's in a difficult angle to your sun. But forewarned is forearmed!

Two weeks later, on August 18, the lunar eclipse in Aquarius occurs in your tenth house. This triggers some sort of internal process that prompts you to re-think your career goals and objectives. Or, it may simply be that you want to move in a new direction and your feelings help you to do it.

There are two new moons in August—the first a solar eclipse (above) in Leo, and the second, a new moon in Virgo, your fifth house. Now *this* one should be extremely pleasant for you, Taurus, bringing about new opportunities in romance and in all your creative endeavors.

Venus enters Virgo (joining Mars there) and your fifth house on August 5, one of those romantic periods mentioned in the big picture for you for 2008. This transit lasts until August 30. If you're not involved when it starts, you will be by the month's end, particularly with that second new moon also in your fifth house, bolstering the love theme. If you work in a creative field, then the combination of the new moon and the Venus transit in your fifth house certainly bodes well for new contracts and creative opportunities.

On August 10, along comes Mercury in Virgo, another emphasis on the fifth house theme. August shapes up to be one of your most creative and romantic months in a long time! Any relationship that begins under all this activity will have to be one in which communication is honest, flowing, a meeting of the hearts and minds.

Then everything shifts from Virgo and your fifth house to Libra and your sixth, daily health and work. On August 19, Mars enters Libra and your sixth house, followed by Mercury on August 28 and Venus on August 30. It's as if your romantic and creative lives now shift into a daily routine. It's possible that you and your partner move in together, go into business together, or work on a creative project together.

Dates to watch for: the three lunation dates—1, 16, 30. The period when the planets shift into your sixth house and Libra. Pay attention to any events that occur around these days; they are harbingers of what's in store for you for the rest of the year.

Best dates: August 16–18, when Venus and Jupiter retrograde form beneficial angles to each other and to your sun. Romance, creativity, and overseas travel figure prominently in the events of these three days.

Taurus—September 2008

Consider September a relatively quiet month, astrologically speaking. There are only two new transits and, of course, one new moon and full moon. Even so, let's take a look at what you can expect.

The full moon on September 15 should be pleasant for you. It's in Pisces, your eleventh house, where Uranus has been hanging out for quite a while now. You may have a completely different take on a particular dream or wish that you have and see it in a whole new light. Your friends and any groups to which you belong won't be a source of mystery and secrecy anymore. Everything will be out in the open. This moon will be within three degrees of Uranus, the planet that symbolizes the unpredictable, so there may be some big surprises in store for you related to friends. Things that happen seem to come at you out of nowhere. But these events and situations are positive. You may finally appreciate your own genius, Taurus, and honor it.

Your ruler, Venus, is in Libra, seeking balance and harmony in the workplace, until September 22. Then, on September 23, it enters passionate Scorpio, your seventh house, opposite your sun. A Venus opposition to the sun can bring about excessive spending or, with Scorpio, an emphasis on sex and getting to the absolute bottom line concerning a relationship or business partnership. Nonetheless, your relationships have quite an intriguing spin.

Mercury turns retrograde for the last time this year on September 24, in Libra, your sixth house. So before this date, make sure you have all your delegated responsibilities lined up, have your personal list of priorities, that you're organized. And then be prepared to revise, rethink, rewrite, and revisit issues you thought were solved.

On September 29, the new moon is in Libra, your sixth house. This should bring a new path related to work and your daily health. You may decide to treat yourself to a spa, join a gym, take up yoga, get a face-lift . . . you get the idea. It's time to beautify yourself. To make time for yourself. To indulge yourself.

Dates to watch for: In addition to the dates above, be aware that the three outer planets—Uranus, Neptune, and Pluto—are all retrograde now. Their energy doesn't work as effectively. But because these planets are slow-moving, you won't notice the effects as much as a retrograde of one of the faster-moving planets, like Mercury.

Best dates: September 22–23, when Mercury and Mars are conjunct or closely conjunct in Libra, your sixth house. During this period you are all about forceful communication and the search for balance. From September 13 to 20, Mercury, Venus, and Mars are traveling together, holding hands, in Libra, your sixth house. Again, the emphasis here is on relationships, mitigation of arguments, and seeking the right balance for all parties involved in a situation or discussion.

Taurus—October 2008

October is a relatively quiet month with the stars. Two planets change signs, and Mercury turns direct. Let's take a look at how you're affected.

Mark October 3. Mars enters Scorpio, your opposite sign today. This can lead to contention with romantic and business partners, but can also heat up a relationship. Your sex life should pick up, Taurus! And once Mercury turns direct on October 15, any challenges you've been experiencing at work should ease.

Venus moves into Sagittarius and your eighth house on October 18. Between then and November 12, you're in a strong position to obtain mortgages, loans, insurance settlements, even tax refunds. It's possible that you could meet someone through a seminar or workshop you take (or teach) on esoteric topics. Other people readily share their resources with you during this Venus transit.

The full moon in Aries on October 13 occurs in your twelfth house. Childhood issues, or issues you pushed aside or buried, may surface. You may visit someone in a nursing home or hospital. If people seem to be on the warpath around the time of this full moon, blame the sign: Aries is the warrior. During this full moon period, you may be playing around with new ideas for a creative project that requires research. The Internet is your favorite resource and there's no limit to what you may come across. Some obscure article or piece of news may seize you in a particularly strong way and you run with it.

The new moon in Scorpio on October 28 occurs in your seventh house. This bodes well for new relationships, contracts, and business partnerships. If you've been dissatisfied with a partnership, this new moon gives you an opportunity to find a partner whose beliefs and goals are more in line with your own.

Date to watch for: October 15: Mercury turning direct.

Best dates: October 2–3, Mars in Libra and Pluto in Sagittarius are traveling at complementary angles to each other and bring a certain tension to your activities. You must think and act quickly, decisively. On October 5–6, Venus and Jupiter are in beneficial angles to each other and to your sun and shower you with love and success. Sounds like a fortune cookie!

Taurus—November 2008

All right, this is the month to cast your vote and make it count. If you're ready to embrace change, to end corruption in government, to make the United States a government by the people, for the people, then vote for the party that represents that. Don't get suckered in by slick ads and empty promises. Vote your conscience, your heart—and don't vote out of fear.

Three of the faster-moving inner planets change signs this month, two turn direct, and Pluto moves back into Capricorn again. In other words, November is hectic. On November 4, Mercury enters Scorpio and your seventh house. This transit sets the stage for honest discussions with partners about where the relationship is, where it's going, and your mutual goals. In a romantic relationship, Mercury in Scorpio seeks the bottom line—who feels what and why and is the relationship on an equal footing?

Your ruler, Venus, enters Capricorn and your ninth house on November 12, a superb transit for overseas travel, education, and publishing endeavors. If you're a writer in search of an editor or agent, this transit steers you toward the right individuals. You get the break you've been hoping for. If you're off to college next fall, this transit brings good news, perhaps about early acceptance or even scholarship opportunities.

Four days later, on November 16, Mars enters Sagittarius and your eighth house, energizing everything connected to joint resources, taxes, and inheritance. You may be revamping your will or insurance policies and pursuing different loan and mortgage possibilities. You also may be taking a workshop in a metaphysical subject.

On November 23, Mercury joins Mars in Sagittarius, your eighth house. Lots of talk now, Taurus, about joint assets, insurance, and mortgages. If you're in debt, you and your partner are brainstorming for ways to get out of debt. You may be looking at end-of-the-year tax breaks, too.

What about November's moons? The full moon on November 13 is in your sign, a once-a-year event. Romance, finances, and your personal needs are highlighted under this moon. Plan something special for you and your partner. Four days on either side of this moon is when the energy is strongest, so you may get an inkling about what's in store for you as early as November 9.

On November 27, the new moon in Sagittarius underscores the eighth house themes you've been experiencing this month. New opportunities and pathways open up in terms of joint resources. Your partner may get a promotion or raise and you may have an opportunity to travel overseas, for either business or pleasure. With Mercury moving direct for the rest of the year, it's time to get out and see the rest of the world!

Dates to watch for: November 1–2. Mars in Scorpio, Jupiter in Capricorn, Saturn in Virgo, and Uranus in Pisces are all traveling in very close proximity to each other and—except for Mars—forming easy angles with your sun. Expect the unexpected during these two days, a sudden turn of events, the sudden appearance of an individual you haven't seen for a while, a sudden bonus. Sudden and positive: those are the operative words.

Best dates: November 12–13. Jupiter in Capricorn and Saturn in Virgo form a nice angle to your sun. The expansiveness that's going on in your life now finds exactly the right niche.

Taurus—December 2008

December 12 looks like the kind of day you'll remember. First, there's a full moon in Gemini, your second house of finances. So, for several days on either side of this date, your finances and your personal values will be highlighted in some way. Saturn will also form a difficult angle to this moon, suggesting that you may have to pull in your spending, establish a budget and stick to it, and save more of what you earn.

Also on December 12, Mercury enters Capricorn and your ninth house, joining Pluto there. This combination confers powerful communication skills. If you're in politics, in the public eye, or have a product to pitch, today is the day to do it. Get out there and be heard!

Five days earlier, on December 7, Venus enters Aquarius and your tenth house, joining Neptune there. Venus's presence in any house usually brings ease and comfort, so this should be a pleasant transit for professional matters. It lasts into the new year. With Neptune also sharing this house, your ideals are quite strong now and you are learning to integrate them into your professional endeavors.

The new moon in Capricorn on December 27 certainly bodes well for you for the new year, particularly in publishing, education and overseas travel. If you're self-employed, your product or service could expand to overseas markets. If you're a writer, you find the publishing house/editor/agent who supports your work. If you're in college, new opportunities come your way, perhaps in terms of courses or a semester abroad.

Also on December 27, Mars enters Capricorn, joining Pluto and Jupiter. This concentration of planets, plus the new moon, packs quite a positive and life-altering wallop.

Dates to watch for: On New Year's Eve, Saturn turns retrograde in Virgo, your fifth house. This could put something of a damper on your New Year's plans. In fact, for the next few months, you may be scrutinizing your romantic relationships in terms of whether they fit your needs. Try not to obsess about this. Saturn in the fifth house also can be helpful in terms of your creative work.

Best date: December 25, when Venus and Neptune form a beautiful angle to each other and to your sun. Ease, idealism, comfort, romance. Does it get any better than this for Christmas? Also, not a single planet is retrograde!

Brainstorming

Envision yourself a year, two years, or four years from now. What is your life like? Where do you live? Is your work satisfying to you? Are you single, married, a parent? Are you happy? Do you have enough money? Is your health good? What are your spiritual beliefs? Are you a vehicle for change in your family or community? In the space below, describe the life you would like to be living a year or two or four up the line. Be as outrageous, creative, and wild as you want. After all, it's *your* life. If you can imagine it, then you can create it.

My Life in _____ (choose a year)

_____
_____
_____
_____
_____
_____
_____
_____
_____
_____
_____
_____
_____

HAPPY 2009!

The Big Picture for Gemini
in 2008

Welcome to 2008, Gemini! It's your year for laying foundations and building on them. Your communication skills are as strong as usual and you get help from Saturn in Virgo, your fourth house. This planet helps to structure what you want to say, how you say it, and aids you in finding the right venue. Your home life may be a bit more structured now, too.

Saturn left Leo late last year. Even though it forms a challenging angle with your sun now, you need the structure and the restrictions that it brings. You may feel at times that you're burdened in some way by your family, one of your parents, or your personal environment. You eventually get used to whatever Saturn brings, however, but to make this transit more positive, meet your obligations and responsibilities.

At the tail end of 2007, lucky and expansive Jupiter entered Capricorn and it will be there through the end of this year, in your eighth house. This transit indicates it's a good year to get a mortgage or car loan and that your spouse or partner may get a substantial raise or even a payout. You could find yourself signing up for workshops or seminars on esoteric topics. You may even be writing about some of these topics.

Pluto enters Capricorn on January 25, joining Jupiter in your eighth house. It then retrogrades for a while, going back into Sagittarius from mid-June to late November. During the months it's in Capricorn, it works to transform your joint finances. This can be good or bad, depending on the present state of the finances you share with a partner. Jupiter always seeks to expand what it touches, however, and Pluto always transforms.

While Jupiter and Pluto are forming this angle with your sun, you are called upon to adjust your attitude about joint finances. In fact, the sooner you adjust, the happier you'll be.

Neptune continues its lengthy transit through Aquarius and your ninth house. If you're a writer or involved in the publishing industry, law, or higher education, this transit has been adding spiritual insights to your work. Your compassion has accelerated. But since Neptune also represents our blind spots, the areas represented could cause you to feel disillusioned or victimized. The most positive way to handle this energy is to do things for others, without expecting compensation, and to deepen your spiritual practice, whatever it is.

Uranus continues its transit through Pisces and your tenth house. Because it is the planet that symbolizes sudden, unexpected change, your career and professional life have been going through a lot of abrupt changes and upsets in the last few years. But you get bored easily, anyway, Gemini, so this isn't necessarily a bad thing. Use Uranus's energy to attract unusual and idiosyncratic people into your professional life.

BEST TIME FOR ROMANCE

You'll enjoy the period between June 5 and July 18, when Venus is in your sign. Your love life picks up big time, your creativity picks up speed and momentum, and others see you much differently. Another great time for romance falls between August 30 and September 23, when Venus transits through Libra, your fifth house of love.

BEST TIME FOR CAREER DECISIONS

With Uranus creating unpredictability in your career, timing is everything. With Jupiter forming a favorable angle to Uranus, however, mark the following dates for making career decisions: between January 1 and May 9, and between September 7 and the end of the year. During these periods, Jupiter is moving direct and its energy flows nicely with that of Uranus.

MERCURY RETROGRADE

Every year, your ruler, Mercury, turns retrograde three times. During these periods, it's wise not to negotiate or sign contracts, to travel, to submit manuscripts, or to make major decisions. Granted, we can't live our lives entirely by Mercury retrogrades! If you have to travel during the periods listed below, however, then expect changes in your plans. If you have to sign a contract, expect to revise it. Communications are bumpy, it's easy to be misunderstood. It's a good time to revise, review, and rewrite.

During these periods, it's a wise idea to back up computer files before Mercury turns retrograde. Quite often, computers and other communication devices act up. Be sure your virus software is up to date, too. Pay special attention to the house in which Mercury retrograde falls. It will tell you the area of your life most likely to be impacted. The periods to watch for in 2008 are:

January 28–February 18: retrograde in Aquarius, your ninth house of long-distance travel.

May 26–June 19: retrograde in Gemini, your sun sign and first house of self.

September 24–October 15: retrograde in Libra, your fifth house of love and creativity.

ECLIPSES

Every year, there are four eclipses, two solar and two lunar. Solar eclipses trigger external events that allow us to see something that eluded us before. Solar eclipses are sometimes challenging, depending on the sign and where it impacts your natal chart. When an eclipse hits one of your natal planets, it's especially important. Lunar eclipses bring up emotional issues related to the sign and house into which they fall. If you have your birth chart, check to see if the eclipses hit any natal planets. If they do, pay special attention to events that occur for up to six months after the eclipse.

Here are the dates to watch for:

February 6: solar eclipse at seventeen degrees Aquarius, your ninth house of long-distance travel, higher education, and worldview. Those of you born between June 6 and 10 are likely to feel the most positive impact of this eclipse.

February 20: lunar eclipse at ten degrees Virgo, in your fourth house of home and family. An emotional issue surfaces related to your family and one of your parents.

August 1: solar eclipse, nine degrees Leo, in your third house of siblings, community, and your conscious thoughts. If you were born between May 28 and June 1, this eclipse will impact you strongly, in a positive way.

August 16: lunar eclipse at twenty-four degrees Aquarius, your ninth house of long-distance travel, higher education, and worldview.

LUCKIEST DAYS IN 2008

Every year, Jupiter forms a beneficial angle with the sun, usually a conjunction, when both planets are in the same sign. In 2008, the angle is a lovely trine and it occurs during two time periods: May 11–13 and September 3–5. If you're going to buy a lotto ticket, do it during these periods!

Now let's take a look at what 2008 has in store for you month by month.

Twelve Months of Predictions
for Gemini
January–December 2008

Gemini—January 2008

The year starts off with the planets aligned in your favor. Your ruler, Mercury, enters Aquarius and your ninth house on January 7. A trip may be in the offing until January 28, and it could be to an overseas destination. It's also possible that your product or service expands to an overseas market. If you're a college-bound student, then Mercury brings news about college acceptances and/or scholarship possibilities. If you're a writer in search of an agent or publisher, this Mercury transit brings positive news!

If you're pitching a product or a manuscript or even just an idea, do it before January 28, when Mercury turns retrograde for the first time in 2008. The retrograde occurs in your eighth house, making it unwise to apply for mortgages or loans until the planet turns direct again on February 18. Also, don't make any changes to your insurance coverage or will during this period.

January 8 features a new moon in Capricorn, your eighth house. New opportunities surface concerning your partner's earnings. He or she may get a job offer or raise. You could get an insurance or tax refund. You have an opportunity to teach or take a seminar or workshop in an esoteric topic. An inheritance is possible, too.

The full moon on January 22 in Leo, your third house, brings a project to a culmination point. If you're a writer, you finish your manuscript or screenplay. If you're in the travel business, you tie up a deal. This full moon, plus several days on either side, could take you on a trip to see a sibling or other relative or may launch your search for a new neighborhood.

On January 24, Venus enters Capricorn, another eighth house signature for the month. Again, this facilitates getting mortgages and loans and indicates that if you're in the midst of a divorce, the division of assets goes smoothly.

Mars, which started the year in retrograde motion, turns direct on January 30.

Dates to watch for: January 8 and the two weeks afterward: plant your seeds. On January 19–20, Saturn and Jupiter join hands in Capricorn to bring rewards in joint resources. Reread the material on Mercury retrogrades, however, and follow those guidelines between January 28 and February 18. Another date to watch for is January 25, when Pluto changes signs and enters Capricorn—and your eighth house. Take a look at the big picture for Gemini to see what this will entail over a long period of time. Although it will retrograde and slip back into Sagittarius at a certain point this year, this transit is big. Pluto will be in Capricorn until late 2024.

Best date: January 24, when Venus and Jupiter link up in your eighth house. This could be the day you hear about a mortgage or loan or about an inheritance.

Gemini—February 2008

Your ruler, Mercury, turns direct on February 18, so that's a great piece of news for this month. Pack your bags, sign your contracts, contact everyone on your e-mail list. Life will be running more smoothly now.

That said, though, there's a solar eclipse on February 6, in Aquarius, your ninth house. Something related to your belief system, education, or an overseas trip now becomes glaringly apparent. If a challenge surfaces, deal with it. This eclipse occurs at a positive angle to your sun, however, so it should bring about positive results related to all ninth house endeavors and to any group activities in which you're involved. It will impact those of you born between June 6 and 8 most strongly.

Two weeks later, on February 20, the lunar eclipse in Virgo impacts your fourth house of home and family. Expect some sort of emotional reaction to events involving your family, parents, home, and/or personal environment.

On February 17, Venus enters Aquarius and your ninth house. This lovely transit indicates smoothness in publishing activities and anything related to overseas travel and education. If you're traveling overseas when this transit occurs, it certainly favors romance in a foreign country. Or, another possibility, romance with a foreigner (so you don't even have to be traveling!).

Some of the other planets' positions have a bearing on your chart this month, Gemini. Lucky Jupiter, for instance, is still transiting Capricorn and your eighth house, making it easier than usual to obtain mortgages and loans. Once Mercury turns direct on February 18, apply! Or, if you've applied already, you should hear after February 18.

Uranus is still transiting your tenth house, in Pisces, leading to sudden and unexpected twists and turns in professional matters. It's been in Pisces since March 2003, so you probably already know that it tends to attract unusual individuals into your life.

Dates to watch for: both eclipse dates—February 6 and 20—and the date that Mercury turns direct, February 18.

Best dates: February 23–26, when Jupiter in Capricorn and Uranus in Pisces form a very nice angle to each other, stimulating your eighth and tenth houses (shared resources and career).

Gemini—March 2008

March gets off to an intriguing start with the new moon in Pisces on March 7. This new moon should open up new possibilities and opportunities in your career. You land the job of your dreams, sell a book or manuscript for more money than you've gotten before, meet the right people at the right time, and your professional options expand. A raise or significant promotion could be in the offing! In fact, on March 4, Mars enters Cancer and your second house of finances, triggering activities related to earning and spending, so a raise may be a significant part of the evolving opportunities. The theme of this moon is bolstered by Mercury and Venus also entering Pisces.

On March 12, Venus enters Pisces, indicating a certain smoothness to professional endeavors. Your intuitive connection to what's going on around you professionally is strong. Two days later, on March 14, Mercury joins Venus in your tenth house, suggesting a lot of discussion concerning your new opportunities and a promotion or raise. Around or on either of these two days could be when you hear the news about your promotion or raise.

The full moon on March 21 brings a creative project to a culmination. This moon should be quite pleasant for your love life, too, because it occurs in your fifth house—love, romance, and creative endeavors.

Dates to watch for: In addition to the dates mentioned above, mark the first two weeks of the month, when Neptune will be forming a nice angle with your sun. It's especially important for those of you born between June 12 and 14. Your idealism is pronounced during this time.

Best dates: March 1–2, when Venus and Mercury

are in Aquarius, your ninth house. This combination should stimulate activities related to publishing, overseas travel, education, and your worldview. If a relationship begins in early March, then the chances are quite good that the attraction, for you, will have to begin with a mental chemistry.

Gemini—April 2008

April's astrological weather is furiously busy! It begins on April 2, when Mercury enters fiery Aries and your eleventh house. This transit, which lasts until April 17, stimulates a lot of communication and activities with friends and groups. You may join a theater or writing group or travel with a group of friends and/or acquaintances.

On April 6, Venus joins Mercury in Aries in your eleventh house. A friend or someone you meet through friends may turn out to be something much more. If a romantic relationship starts under this transit, it's likely to be quite passionate. Your friendships tend to run more smoothly now, too, at least until April 30, when this transit ends. You may be doing more with groups of people whose interests are in line with yours. It's a terrific time for publicity and promotion, too, so if you've got a product to pitch to the public, get out there and do it!

In between these two transits, on April 5, there's a new moon in Aries, your eleventh house. This moon certainly supports the themes above dealing with friends and groups, with new people entering your life and new opportunities that involve the manifestation of your wishes and dreams. New moons are for planting the seeds of what you want and hope for, so get busy, Gemini. This new moon receives nice energy from Mars in Cancer, which suggests an intuitive connection with what's going on. Listen to your hunches around the new moon.

The full moon in Scorpio on April 20 occurs in your sixth house of health and work. Expect passions to fly at the office water cooler, Gemini, and the attention may surprise you. What you considered to be a harmless flirtation with a coworker could turn into a passionate affair. Saturn sends positive beams to this full moon, which suggests that you find the right structure for your daily work routine, and any relationship that begins under this moon may have very definite parameters.

Dates to watch for: The first ten days of the month feature a harmonious angle between Jupiter in Capricorn and Uranus in Pisces. For you, this indicates unusual and expansive experiences related to your career and to other people's resources. Unusual and gifted individuals appear just when you need them most and are readily able and willing to share their resources with you. Sounds like a run for political office, Gemini.

Best dates: April 1–2. Mercury and Venus are conjunct in Pisces, your tenth house. These two days hold career news—a reward or professional recognition is possible.

Gemini—May 2008

This could be one of your best months all year. The action begins on May 2, when your ruler, Mercury, enters your sign. Your mind is so finely tuned now that thoughts literally hum along, collecting and gathering information, facts, and ideas, then leap to something else at the speed of light. This is a terrific transit if you're a writer, in public relations, sales, or the travel business. It's also excellent for teaching and learning. Also on May 2, Saturn turns direct in Virgo, your fourth house. It's been retrograde since late 2007 and its direct motion is good news for your home and family life. You won't feel quite as restricted now in your home life and can find the proper structures and venues for your family activities.

On May 9, Mars enters Leo and your third house, another awesome transit. It acts as a booster rocket for your communication abilities and bolsters your energy even on a rare slow day. You can burn your candle at both ends, meet deadlines with ease, raise funds for your favorite charity or political candidate, sell, pitch, and generally wow everyone around you. If your natal Mars is in Leo, then this transit is known as a Mars return and is always an especially powerful time. This transit lasts until July 1 and is sure to trigger a lot of daily activity—short trips, sightseeing, increased contact with neighbors, siblings, and relatives. If you've been thinking about moving, then you may be checking out neighborhoods to find one that appeals to you.

Venus enters your sign on May 24, joining Mercury in your first house. This beautiful transit is one of the more romantic periods this year. Your sex appeal soars, your magnetism deepens, you're the life of the party. Any relationship that begins under this transit will be unusual and lively, but for sexual chemistry to exist, there must be a meeting of the minds between you and your partner.

Now let's look at this month's new and full moons. The new moon on May 5 is in Taurus, your twelfth house. This moon brings opportunities to work behind the scenes on creative projects, gives you the opportunity for solitude that you need to meet deadlines, and is especially good for therapy, if you're so inclined. You may be visiting hospitals, nursing homes, even jails and prisons, perhaps for some sort of charity work or for research. This moon also favors new opportunities to delve into who you really are—separate from your family and friends and other people who define and inhabit your world. You may have an opportunity for a past-life regression, for instance, that helps you get to the root of a long-standing issue or concern. Or,

75

you meet someone from a past life and your mutual recognition is immediate.

The full moon two weeks later, on May 19, is in passionate Scorpio and your sixth house. And passions certainly run high at work for several days on either side of this moon. The motives of coworkers and employees are glaringly obvious to you now. You're after the absolute bottom line in whatever you tackle.

On May 26, Mercury turns retrograde and everything slows down again. You will be rewriting, revising, rethinking your positions. The retrograde ends on June 19. Read through the advice for Mercury retrogrades in the overview section.

Dates to watch for: May 3–25, when Mercury is moving direct through your sign.

Best dates: May 23–30, when Mercury, Jupiter, and Uranus are in harmonious angles to each other, bringing unexpected opportunities that expand and enhance your life in some way. Even though both Mercury and Jupiter are retrograde, circle these dates.

Gemini—June 2008

Whenever your ruler, Mercury, is moving retrograde, you spend several weeks in a spin, trying to keep things on an even keel. The hassles end on June 19, when Mercury turns direct again, so your month improves immeasurably after that.

Before that, on June 3, there's a new moon in your sign, something that happens only once a year. This is the best new moon for you all year, promising new opportunities in many areas of your life. Several days before this new moon, write down your wishes and dreams. Be clear and concise about what you want for yourself over the next year. Each month, focus on your list, post it where you can see it often.

Both Venus and Mercury are close to this moon, making it likely that romance, communication, and travel are part of the package deal. If you're dissatisfied with your job, then this moon helps to attract opportunities for a new job that is more in line with your personal beliefs and interests. If you're a writer who needs an agent or editor, this moon could bring both.

Two weeks later, on June 18, the full moon in Sagittarius should be quite romantic for you and your partner. Pluto is at a one-degree conjunction with this moon, indicating that you're in the driver's seat, Gemini. Just don't get into power plays—that is, don't misuse your power!

When Venus enters Cancer and your second house on June 18, your finances begin to smooth out considerably. You may be spending more, too, however, so be sure that the checks have cleared before you shop! Also, Venus's transit through your second house suggests the potential for a romantic relationship with someone who shares your values. You'll share a deep intuitive connection with this person.

Dates to watch for: June 20–26, when Mars's opposition to Neptune is exact. This can be a difficult period because it pits energetic Mars against inspirational Neptune. The best way to navigate it is to follow the flow of your intuition. Don't throw up walls of resistance. June 13: Pluto, after retrograding back through Sagittarius, now enters Capricorn and your eighth house again. Around or shortly after this date, your spouse or someone else with whom you share finances and resources may get a raise or promotion. If you're in debt when this transit begins, set up a budget and stick to it!

Best dates: June 4–8, when Venus and Mars form a harmonious angle to each other and to your sun. This combination spices up your love life and brings you and your partner closer together.

Gemini—July 2008

On July 1, Mars enters Virgo and your fourth house. This transit energizes everything to do with your home life, family, and personal environment. You may be spending more time with one or both of your parents. They may need help getting to and from doctor or dentist appointments or perhaps they're in the midst of a move and need help getting settled.

The new moon on July 2 is in Cancer, your second house, and is within six degrees of Venus, indicating some very nice financial events for you. You'll have an opportunity to earn more money, doing work that you enjoy. It could be a part-time job that comes to you exactly when you need it or you start an entirely new job with better money and more benefits. Eight days after this new moon, on July 10, Mercury enters Cancer and your second house, underscoring some of what the new moon promises. Between July 10 and 26, you may be traveling—for an interview?—or could be in contract negotiations about this new opportunity.

The full moon on July 18 is in Capricorn, your eighth house. You see where your insurance needs may be lacking and take steps to rectify the situation. Also, if you've applied for a mortgage or loan, you close the deal on July 18 or several days to either side of it.

When Venus enters Leo and your third house on July 12, it forms a harmonious angle with your sun and could bring about a romance with someone you meet through neighbors or through a sibling. It's even possible that the romance is with a neighbor or someone who lives in your immediate community. There's a lot of warmth and passion associated with Venus in Leo, and any relationship that starts under this transit will be fun and romantic.

On July 26, Mercury joins Venus in Leo. You and your partner communicate well under this combination of planets. You may take a lot of short trips together, get involved in a joint writing or public relations project, or could head up a community project together.

Dates to watch for: The whole month is a mixed bag. Four planets are retrograde—Jupiter, Uranus, Neptune, and Pluto—which means their energy is dormant. But the last week or so of the month should be pleasant, with retrograde Jupiter in Capricorn forming a beneficial angle with Mars in Virgo. Translation? Lots of activity and positive experiences related to your home and family life.

Best dates: July 14, when you uncover the perfect structure for a writing project, and July 25, when retrograde Jupiter and Venus form a beautiful angle to each other, bringing harmony to your love life.

Gemini—August 2008

Two eclipses are the biggest news this month. The solar eclipse on August 1 is in Leo, your third house, and triggers events that allow you to see a relationship with a sibling or relative in a much clearer light. The eclipse could also stimulate travel—weekend trips to a nearby place, as opposed to a trip to Europe.

Two weeks later, on August 16, the full moon in Aquarius lights up your ninth house. Neptune falls very close to the full moon, suggesting a romantic, perhaps even inspirational evening with your partner, perhaps in an overseas port. This full moon is also a lunar eclipse, which indicates that an emotional issue may surface related to your personal philosophy and beliefs. Someone may challenge what you believe and you'll feel compelled to defend those beliefs. There's always choice involved, however, and you may decide that an argument isn't worth it!

The new moon on August 30—yes, there are two of them this month—is in Virgo, in close proximity to Saturn. This new moon brings fresh opportunities related to your home and family. If you've considered a move, this new moon could bring the chance to make one. You may decide to set up a home office or to move your office to another location in your house, or you may hire someone to help you out in your home-based business.

Venus enters Virgo and your fourth house on August 5. Very nice for your love life at home and for the smooth functioning of your family life in general. You may be spending money on the beautification of your home—or your home office—and it could be something as simple as fresh paint for a room.

Mercury, your ruler, enters Virgo and joins Venus in your fourth house on August 10. This transit, which lasts until August 28, should stimulate all home and family activities. People are coming and going at all hours, you may be doing more running around than usual, and your in-box fills with e-mails. Touch base with your clients, editors, agents, and anyone else who is involved in your livelihood. And while you're at it, plan a long weekend trip for yourself and your family.

Mars also changes signs this month—entering Libra and your fifth house on August 19. This transit does wonderful things for your love life and urges you to balance your needs against those of a romantic partner. You're seeking peace and harmony now and may be visiting museums, seeing art films, attending concerts, and doing anything and everything that stimulates your creative side.

On August 28 and 30, Mercury and Venus respectively join Mars in your fifth house. Your muse should be screaming in your ear now. There's no better time to dust off that manuscript or screenplay, to review your portfolio, or to audition. With these three planets stacked up in your fifth house, you're on a major creative roll. Hardships you've experienced, challenges you've faced, now should melt away. The Venus transit, which lasts until September 23, signals the best time this year for romance. If you're involved already, then things may crank up quickly to the next level.

Date to watch for: August 16 could be challenging. Mars in Virgo and Pluto in Sagittarius, your opposite sign, form a square to each other, indicating some possible tension at home, with your partner.

Best dates: Despite the warning above, August 16–18 feature a beautiful angle between Venus and retrograde Jupiter, which should mitigate some of the challenges mentioned above.

Gemini—September 2008

September is a quiet month with the stars. The last Mercury retrograde of the year begins on September 24, in Libra, your fifth house of love and romance. This may create some communication issues between you and your partner, so be very clear in what you say and how you say it. Mercury turns direct again on October 15.

The day before Mercury turns retrograde, Venus enters Scorpio and your sixth house. Expect lots of activity in your daily work routine for the next couple of weeks. A flirtation with a coworker may heat up, and you could get a raise, a promotion, or be recognized for your contributions. Since Mercury does retrograde during this period, be sure that your communications with employees and coworkers is clear and direct, that you hold off signing contracts and submitting manuscripts for consideration.

The full moon on September 15 is in Pisces, your tenth house. A professional issue or relationship is the focus of this moon. Since Uranus (unpredictable events) is very close to the moon, it's possible that an unexpected event throws career matters into stark relief so that you can see exactly what's going on and make an informed decision.

The new moon on September 29 is in Libra, your fifth house. Does it get any better than this for new romantic opportunities? Not much! Your love life suddenly pops open and you're besieged with choices. This new moon also promises a major creative opportunity.

Dates to watch for: September 22–23, when Mercury and Mars are conjunct in Libra. You and your partner are involved in very lively discussions about your relationship.

Best dates: September 13–20. Mercury, Venus, and Mars are holding hands in Libra, your fifth house. This trio definitely spices up your love life and your creativity.

Gemini—October 2008

Your ruler, Mercury, turns direct on October 15, a day to celebrate, always! This was the last Mercury retrograde of the year, too, Gemini, so you're in the clear until next year. When it turns direct, it's in Libra, your fifth house, and is stoking the fires of your creativity. So if you spent the retrograde period rewriting, revising, and rethinking your position, you should now have an excellent grasp of the issues and be able to move ahead.

October 3 is the day that Mars enters Scorpio and your sixth house. This transit, lasting until November 16, energizes your daily work routine and galvanizes you to complete something you started a while back. Be careful that you don't become impatient with coworkers and employees. Or, if you do, bite your tongue and keep your irritation to yourself.

On October 18, Venus enters Sagittarius and your seventh house. Even though Venus is now opposite your sun, this transit should ease any tension you've experienced recently with your partner. It's also excellent for the negotiation and signing of contracts.

The full moon on October 14 is in fiery Aries, your eleventh house. It forms a wide angle (a trine, positive) with Pluto in Sagittarius, suggesting that some of the events may have to do with personal power. One thing is for sure, a friendship or the motives of a group to which you belong will become much clearer to you.

The new moon on October 28 is in Scorpio, your sixth house. Expect new opportunities and experiences in your daily work. This could be a new job, new responsibilities, even new employees and coworkers to deal with. It's also an excellent time to join a gym, go on a diet, or start an exercise routine.

Date to watch for: October 26 could feel strange. Mercury is at sixteen degrees Libra (fifth house), Mars is at fifteen degrees Scorpio (sixth house), and Jupiter is at sixteen degrees Capricorn (eighth house). Mercury in Libra is certainly compatible with your sun and sharpens your communication skills. And although Mars and Jupiter in their respective signs are compatible with each other, they aren't compatible with your sun sign or with Mercury. So there could be some tensions related to romance and daily work. Perhaps the crux of the matter is a romance at work?

Best dates: October 2–3, when Mars in Libra and Pluto in Sagittarius form harmonious angles to each other and to your sun sign. These two days are wonderful for partnerships and romance.

Gemini—November 2008

The most important thing you can do this month is to vote. Don't allow yourself to be motivated by fear or fearmongering in the media. Vote your conscience. Ask yourself what kind of world you want for these next critical four years.

On November 4, Mercury enters Scorpio, your sixth house. This transit sharpens your communication and intuitive skills in your daily work environment. You enlist the aid of a group of coworkers for a research project and the higher-ups applaud your efforts.

Lovely Venus enters Capricorn and your eighth

house on November 12. If ever there is a time to apply for a mortgage, refinance your house, and update your insurance, this is it. Venus smoothes over any rough spot you may encounter in these various processes. You may have to adjust your attitude somewhat about some of these issues, but Venus promises success.

Mars enters Sagittarius and your seventh house on November 16. Sexual chemistry is a given with this transit. But the mutual attraction between you and your partner shouldn't prevent you from discussing the relationship's bigger picture. Do you both hold the same goals and hopes for the relationship? Find out how your partner feels about where things are going.

On November 13, the full moon in Taurus sheds light on something hidden. It may be an issue from your childhood that you've buried deep within, a secret relationship, your own or someone else's real motives. It could be that you finally understand a particular dream or series of dreams you've had that alter your life in some way. Uranus forms a nice angle to this moon, so there will be an unexpected element to your discoveries.

The new moon on November 27 is in Sagittarius, your seventh house. This should be quite an interesting couple of weeks for you, Gemini. A new relationship is in the offing—or a current relationship reaches a newer, deeper level of understanding and commitment. This new moon also bodes well for any work you do with a partner—a joint project or business venture, for instance.

Dates to watch for: November 1–2, when four planets—Mars, Jupiter, Saturn, and Uranus—are all in angles compatible with each other, in either earth or water signs. These four planets are in a challenging angle to your sun, however. The areas impacted are your home and personal life, resources you share with someone else, and your career.

Best date: that new moon on November 27!

Gemini—December 2008

December shapes up as a very pleasant month. Every planet is moving in direct motion, so they're all functioning the way they should. Then, on December 31, Saturn turns retrograde, which could mess up your New Year's plans in some way. Before we reach that point, however, let's look at what changes lie in between.

On December 7, Venus enters Aquarius and your ninth house. Very nice for romance overseas or with a foreign-born individual. This transit also favors publishing and education endeavors. It's an excellent time to submit your manuscript, to expand your company's services and products overseas, and to generally feel good about life, Gemini!

On December 12, there are two events worth noting. The first is that your ruler, Mercury, enters Capricorn and your eighth house. Okay, so Capricorn can make you feel somewhat uncomfortable, unless you happen to have your natal moon or rising in that sign. But the truth is that it helps you build structures, to condense your resources, and move steadily toward a goal. In your eighth house, this could refer to building an impressive financial portfolio!

Also on December 12, there's a full moon in your sign! You're not only onstage now, you're loving it. People notice you, your self-confidence soars, and you and your partner should enjoy a romantic evening together. Neptune forms a harmonious angle to this moon, suggesting that your ideals are running high. Are you walking your talk?

On December 27, Mars joins Mercury in Capricorn, your eighth house. Remember that portfolio? Well, now you have the energy of Mars behind you, shoving you forward along the path of your financial goals.

Plan for New Year's ahead of time and make up your list of resolutions. Even if everything changes at the last moment, you're better off because you have a plan, an agenda, a definite direction.

Dates to watch for: December 1–7, when Jupiter and Saturn form a beautiful angle to each other and urge you to expand your goals, to tend to details at home, and to rid yourself of any and all fears!

Best date: December 12. That full moon in your sign, plus a great angle between Mercury (your conscious mind) and Pluto (power).

Brainstorming

Envision yourself a year, two years, or four years from now. What is your life like? Where do you live? Is your work satisfying to you? Are you single, married, a parent? Are you happy? Do you have enough money? Is your health good? What are your spiritual beliefs? Are you a vehicle for change in your family or community? In the space below, describe the life you would like to be living a year or two or four up the line. Be as outrageous, creative, and wild as you want. After all, it's *your* life. If you can imagine it, then you can create it.

MY LIFE IN _____ (*choose a year*)

_____

_____

_____

_____

_____

_____

_____

_____

_____

_____

_____

_____

HAPPY 2009!

The Big Picture for Cancer in 2008

Welcome to 2008, Cancer! It promises to be an intriguing year, so let's take a closer look.

In late 2007, Saturn left Leo and your second house of finances and moved into your third house. You learned a lot about your beliefs concerning money while Saturn was in Leo and also became more aware of discipline and responsibility concerning your finances. Now Saturn is in Virgo, where it will transit for two and a half years.

During Saturn's transit through Virgo, your conscious thoughts will become more structured and disciplined. You may feel burdened at times, particularly if you have siblings. A brother or sister, for instance, may need your help and emotional support. You may encounter restrictions or delays in terms of your community or neighborhood. Your communication ability will be more focused and organized.

Jupiter, the planet that symbolizes expansion and success, entered Capricorn and your seventh house at the end of 2007 and will remain there until early 2009. During this transit, your partnerships—both romantic and professional—expand and broaden. A deeper commitment in a relationship is possible. On January 25, Pluto enters Capricorn, joining Jupiter in your seventh house. Throughout the year, Pluto moves back into Sagittarius when it turns retrograde, then finally enters Capricorn again in late November. The combination of Jupiter and Pluto suggests that a romantic or business partnership will transform your life profoundly, in a positive sense. This partnership could be with a foreign-born individual or someone who works in the law, higher education, or in publishing.

Uranus, the planet symbolic of sudden, unexpected change, continues its transit through Pisces and your ninth house, forming a beneficial angle to your sun. You may be traveling overseas this year and the opportunity could come up suddenly. Make sure you have a bag packed and ready to go for most of the year and that your passport is in order! Uranus also attracts unusual individuals who are often brilliant, idiosyncratic, or unusual in some way. If you get involved with someone while traveling overseas, the relationship will be exciting, for sure, but may not last forever.

Neptune continues its long transit through Aquarius and your eighth house. By now, you should have a pretty good idea what kinds of experiences Neptune attracts—the strange, mystical, and spiritually inspired. There could be some confusion concerning your spouse's income or any resources you share with others.

BEST TIME FOR ROMANCE

Mark the dates between June 18 and July 12, when Venus is in your sign. Your romantic quota soars. You're also more artistic then and others see you in a more flattering light. You feel more confident and your sex appeal rises. Great backup dates for romance fall between September 23 and October 18, when Venus is transiting your fifth house of love and forming a beautiful angle to your sun.

Other excellent dates for romance fall between May 11 and 13 and September 3 and 5, when the sun and Jupiter see eye to eye and there's a nice flow of energy between them.

BEST TIME FOR CAREER DECISIONS

Make career decisions between April 4 and 30, when Venus is transiting your tenth house of careers.

This should be quite a smooth time professionally. In fact, things may be going along so smoothly that you'll be tempted to kick back and relax. Don't. Seize the opportunity.

MERCURY RETROGRADES

Every year, there are three periods when Mercury, the planet of communication and travel, turns retrograde. During these periods, it's wisest not to negotiate or sign contracts, to travel, to submit manuscripts, or to make major decisions. Granted, we can't live our lives entirely by Mercury retrogrades! If you have to travel during the periods listed below, however, then expect changes in your plans. If you have to sign a contract, expect to revise it.

It's also a good idea to back up computer files before Mercury turns retrograde. Quite often, computers and other communication devices act up. Be sure your virus software is up to date, too. Pay special attention to the house in which Mercury retrograde falls. It will tell you the area of your life most likely to be impacted. The periods to watch for in 2008 are:

January 28–February 18: retrograde in Aquarius, your eighth house of shared resources.

May 26–June 19: retrograde in Gemini, your twelfth house—what's hidden, the personal unconscious, karma.

September 24–October 15: retrograde in Libra, your fourth house of home, family, your parents.

ECLIPSES

Every year, there are four eclipses, two solar and two lunar. Solar eclipses trigger external events that allow us to see something that eluded us before. When an eclipse hits one of your natal planets, it's especially important. Take note of the sign and house placement. Lunar eclipses bring up emotional issues related to the sign and house into which they fall.

Here are the dates to watch for:

February 6: solar eclipse at seventeen degrees Aquarius, your eighth house of shared resources, taxes, insurance, and esoteric topics. Those of you born between July 7 and 11 are likely to feel the greatest impact. Check your natal chart to find out if you have any planets at seventeen degrees.

February 20: lunar eclipse at ten degrees Virgo, in your third house of communication, siblings, and the conscious mind.

August 1: solar eclipse, nine degrees Leo, in your second house of finances. If you were born between June 29 and July 3, this eclipse will impact you strongly.

August 16: lunar eclipse at twenty-four degrees Aquarius, your eighth house of shared resources.

LUCKIEST DAYS IN 2008

Every year, Jupiter forms a beneficial angle with the sun, usually a conjunction, when both planets are in the same sign. In 2008, the angle is a lovely trine and it occurs during two time periods: May 11–13 and September 3–5. If you're going to buy a lotto ticket, do it during these periods!

Now let's take a look at what 2008 has in store for you month by month.

Twelve Months of Predictions
for Cancer
January–December 2008

Cancer—January 2008

Since the moon rules your sign, you're particularly sensitive to the new and full moons that happen every month. The first lunation in January is a new moon on January 8, in Capricorn, your seventh house. This one should bring in a new relationship, if you're so inclined, and new opportunities in partnerships generally. Uranus forms a harmonious angle with this new moon, indicating there's a suddenness and unpredictability to the events. Go with the flow, Cancer.

The full moon on January 22 is in Leo, your second house. For several days on either side of this moon, you'll have a much better grasp of your finances—where your money is going, how much you earn, what goes to taxes, what you pay into FICA. Romantically, this could be a great time for you and your partner, with a lot of warmth and lively discussion. If you're not involved, you could meet someone who shares your values.

The year begins with Mercury in your opposite sign, Capricorn, suggesting that you and your partner are involved in a lot of discussion and chatter about your relationship. This is a good thing, Cancer, since you sometimes have difficulties expressing the myriad emotions that ebb and flow through you in a given day.

On January 8, Mercury enters Aquarius and your eighth house. Expect news concerning a mortgage or loan application. If you haven't heard by January 28, when Mercury turns retrograde, then news probably won't arrive until after February 18, when Mercury turns direct again.

On January 24, Venus enters Capricorn, joining Jupiter in your seventh house. The combination of the two most beneficent planets in the zodiac in your house of partnerships suggests a successful period for both personal and professional partnerships. If you're in a committed relationship already, then you and your partner may move in together or even tie the knot. If you're not involved with anyone, then you probably will be before the Venus transit ends on February 17.

Mars started the year in retrograde motion, in your sign. This indicates bumps and nicks in your personal life, things that don't move as quickly or as directly as you like. On January 30, Mars turns direct again and the flow returns to your life.

January 25 marks a significant transit—Pluto, the slowest-moving planet in the zodiac, enters Capricorn and your seventh house. Expect profound change to unfold in the area of partnerships over the course of 2008. Also, reread the introductory section at the front of the book to understand Pluto's important role in world affairs. Throughout the year, Pluto will retrograde back into Sagittarius and your sixth house, touching off work and health issues that you've experienced the last several years. But by the end of the year, the planet is firmly in Capricorn.

Dates to watch for: January 24, when Venus enters your seventh house; January 25, when Pluto joins it; and January 28, when Mercury turns retrograde.

Best date: January 24 is a day to plan something special with your partner. Venus and Jupiter are conjunct in Capricorn, your seventh house.

Cancer—February 2008

February features two eclipses—a solar eclipse on February 6 and a lunar eclipse on February 20. The solar eclipse at seventeen degrees and forty-four minutes Aquarius impacts your eighth house. Expect events that provide you with greater insight concerning resources you share with someone else—a spouse, for instance, or a parent or child. If you're in the midst of a divorce, this eclipse brings the financial issues into stark relief. Mercury is close to the eclipse degree, indicating a lot of discussion and debate concerning the issues that surface. This eclipse will have the greatest impact on Cancers born between July 8 and 11.

The lunar eclipse on February 20 is at one degree and fifty-three minutes of Virgo, in your third house. Saturn is at a close degree to this moon. Emotions run high concerning a relationship with a sibling, a relative, or a neighbor. You find the proper structure for a communication project you're working on, and even though you may balk at it initially, you come to the realization that it works well. This eclipse could feature some short trips—weekend getaways, perhaps, or just more running around than usual—and more communication than usual through e-mail. Those of you born between June 21 and 24 will feel this most strongly.

If you're planning a trip, don't travel until after February 18, when Mercury turns direct. But if you have to travel, expect changes in your itinerary and schedule.

Now that Venus has brought a smoothness to your partnerships, it enters Aquarius and your eighth house, underscoring some of the same themes as the solar eclipse. Venus now facilitates your decisions and any processes you have to go through as a result of what you learn or discover because of the solar eclipse. Your spouse or partner may get a raise or a promotion. Also, you may take a workshop in an esoteric subject that interests you.

Dates to watch for: the eclipse dates, of course, but also February 22, when Venus in Aquarius and Saturn in Virgo (your eighth and third houses respectively) form an exact and challenging angle to each other. Your partner may be overly critical today, so just let it flow over you and try not to make a big deal out of it.

Best dates: February 29, when the sun and Uranus are widely conjunct each other, in Pisces, a sign compatible with yours. Expect the unexpected. It may concern overseas travel, an expansion of your business overseas, or be connected to education or the law.

Cancer—March 2008

The new moon on March 7 is in Virgo, your third house. You'll find this new moon very much to your liking, with new opportunities opening up in several areas. If you've been considering a move, this new moon may prompt you to get out and look at different neighborhoods to get a sense of what you're searching for. It also opens up new opportunities with travel— weekend trips or short business trips, as opposed to long, overseas trips.

The full moon on March 21 is in Libra, your fourth house, and is exactly square to Pluto, in your seventh house. There could be some tension at home—with a parent, partner, or anyone else within your immediate environment. Try to balance the demands in your life around this time. The Libra full moon, however, can be quite romantic if your life is already balanced, so plan something special with a partner and avoid direct confrontations.

Mars enters your sign on March 4 and stays there until May 9. Since Mars energizes everything it touches, your personal life suddenly slams into overdrive. You may be working longer hours to meet a deadline and your sex life heats up, especially after

March 12, when Venus enters compatible Pisces and your ninth house. In fact, on March 14, Mercury joins Venus in Pisces, emphasizing the possibility of romance with someone from another country.

With the three inner planets working in your favor, it's possible that your business or product expands to overseas markets, that you sell your manuscript, or that your worldview is suddenly front and center of your life. If you've been hoping to travel overseas, now is the time to plan the trip. Go online to search for package deals.

During March, Uranus is continuing its journey through Pisces and your ninth house, adding an unpredictable and exciting flavor to both Mercury and Venus and to Mars's transit through your sign. Some possibilities? A romance that begins—or ends—suddenly, business opportunities that fall in your lap with almost no effort on your part, or a run for political office. Keep your options open and go with the flow, something at which you always excel.

Dates to watch for: the lunar dates—March 7 and 21—but also March 22, when Mercury and Venus are conjunct in Aquarius, emphasizing your need for honest communication with a partner.

Best date: March 21. Despite the tension that often accompanies a full moon, March 21 promises to be quite interesting, when Mars in Cancer and Uranus in Pisces form a beautiful angle to each other and to your sun. Expect the unexpected and express your gratitude for what comes your way.

Cancer—April 2008

Mercury's transit through Aries and your tenth house begins on April 2, marking an important time in your career. Expect travel related to your career and professional matters and lots of brainstorming and discussion about your ideas and projects. Even though

Mercury now forms a challenging angle to your sun, your mind and communication skills are sharp and you have the ambition to do what it takes to get to where you want to go professionally.

On April 6, Venus joins Mercury in Aries, your tenth house. Aren't you the lucky one! Mercury provides you with the mental agility and foresight you need now and Venus comes right along, assuring you that the process will go smoothly. Your bosses and peers will be receptive to your ideas and initiatives and you may receive a reward, a promotion, or even a raise between now and July 12, after Venus has finished transiting your sign. It's as if Venus's transit of your tenth house gets the ball rolling.

On April 17, Mercury enters Taurus and your eleventh house, and on April 30 Venus follows. The combination livens up your friendships and group activities, and focuses your attention on your wishes and dreams. Are you happy with the way your life is going? Are you happy in your relationships, job, career? These questions are the types you'll be asking yourself now.

Now let's take a look at the new and full moons for the month. April 5 features a new moon in Aries, which underscores the activity this month in the career sector of your chart. It ushers in new opportunities for all professional matters. If you're discontent with your career, this new moon brings a chance to change career paths. If you feel you deserve more recognition or pay for what you do, this new moon brings ample opportunities to be paid what you deserve.

On April 20, the full moon in Scorpio happens in your fifth house, at a positive angle with your sun and with Saturn. A romantic relationship reaches a culmination—you commit to each other or go your separate ways. You finish a creative project or see something about one that you know you can improve and dive back into it again. If research is your passion, then this full moon could bring the answers you've been seeking.

With energetic Mars still in your sign until May 9

and forming a beneficial trine with Uranus, sudden, unpredictable events will continue into May. The combination also attracts unusual, idiosyncratic people who have unique perspectives, belief systems, and insights that can be helpful to you in some way. During this period, don't judge people by how they look. Just listen.

Dates to watch for: The first two weeks of the month feature Jupiter and Uranus in beneficial angles to each other. Your partnerships expand in some way and the people who enter your life during this period are certainly not business as usual!

Best dates: April 1–2, when Mercury and Venus are conjunct in Pisces, your ninth house. Sudden insights are possible with political issues, spiritual beliefs, even foreign governments and policies. Once again, anytime Uranus is tossed into the mix, things are never predictable.

Cancer—May 2008

There's a lot of activity in the stars this month and it begins on May 2, when Mercury enters Gemini, one of the signs that it rules. With the planet of communication in your twelfth house, it's a great time for getting to the root of long-standing issues. Therapy is one option. If that doesn't interest you, meditation or some sort of mind-body discipline like yoga or tai chi could prove beneficial.

On May 26, Mercury turns retrograde and doesn't go direct again until June 19. By now, you should know the drill on this one: rewrite, revise, rethink, reevaluate—those are the buzzwords for Mercury retrograde periods. If you have to travel, don't be surprised if your flight is canceled, your schedule changes, or you miss a flight. It's all part of the Mercury retrograde package. Be sure to back up computer files before May 26, to confirm all appointments, and to communicate clearly with everyone to diminish the possibility of being misunderstood.

Another noteworthy event happens on May 2: Saturn turns direct in Virgo for the first time this year. Its direct motion, in your third house, indicates that the parameters and boundaries that appeared last September in your relationships with siblings, relatives, and neighbors are clearer to you now. These parameters could include your insistence that family members notify you before they just show up on your doorstep for a prolonged stay or that you would prefer that they call before just dropping by.

On May 9, Mars enters Leo and your second house. This transit, lasting until July 1, stimulates the financial sector of your chart. Suddenly, it seems that you're working longer hours, but checks you're owed start arriving and will continue to do so until Mercury turns retrograde on May 26. If you're challenged about your values, you will defend them vigorously and convincingly. Mars loves a fight, after all, and when it's in Leo, you aren't the least bit afraid of standing up for yourself.

Venus enters Gemini on May 24, joining Mercury in your twelfth house. Secret romance? An affair? Or are you just spending more time with the one you love? All are possible under this transit. If the relationship is supposed to be a secret, however, that probably won't last beyond June 18, when Venus enters your sign, or June 19, when Mercury turns direct again. The Venus transit also suggests that you may be working on a creative project of some kind that requires a lot of solitude.

This month's new moon on May 5 is in a compatible earth sign, Taurus, your eleventh house. Expect new friends, more involvement in group activities, opportunities to promote and publicize your product or company, and perhaps some sort of financial break that comes to you through friends. This new moon forms a wide and beneficial angle with Uranus, indicating that whatever happens around the time of the new moon will be unpredictable and exciting.

The full moon on May 19 is in Scorpio, a water sign compatible with your sign, so expect one of those aha! moments concerning a romantic relationship or a creative project. Your emotional intensity leads you down some very strange paths, Cancer, so listen to your intuition on and around the date of this full moon.

Dates to watch for: Three planets turn retrograde this month: Mercury, on May 26, which we've already discussed; Jupiter, on May 9; and Neptune, on May 26. With both Mercury and Neptune changing directions on May 26, this could be a challenging day. You're suddenly quite the introvert, mulling over your ideals and puzzling through how they fit into the way you live your life. The Jupiter retrograde turns this planet's expansive energy inward, urging you to examine your spiritual beliefs and how or if they fit into a current relationship or partnership.

Best dates: May 1–2, when Mars in Cancer and Uranus in Pisces are moving in harmonious angles to each other and to your sun. Expect the unexpected and don't be surprised at how quickly events change from one thing to another.

Cancer—June 2008

There are two news flashes this month. The first, on June 18, is when Venus enters your sign, one of the most romantic periods for you this year. Your sex appeal gets a major boost, you're suddenly in demand socially, and your love life flourishes. If you're not involved when this transit begins, you may be by the time it ends on July 12. And if you're not, it won't matter because you'll be so busy with so many people that a committed relationship may not hold the same appeal for you.

The second news flash happens on June 19, when

Mercury turns direct again in Gemini. From this point to July 10, Mercury rushes toward its appointment with your sign. So finish up your creative work, because once July 10 rolls around, your schedule fills quickly and you're out in the public more frequently. It's interesting to note that the Venus transit and the change in Mercury's direction happen within just a day of each other. It's as if one sets the stage for the other.

This month's moons may not be your favorites, but there are ways to utilize this energy, as you'll see. The new moon on June 3 is in Gemini, your twelfth house. This moon is very close to both Mercury and Venus, indicating a lot of discussion and communication with a romantic partner or with someone who shares your creative and artistic passions. Fresh opportunities surface to delve into your own motives, dreams, even your past lives. It's possible that within the next few weeks you meet someone you have known in another life or realize that someone involved in your current life is a past-life lover, friend, or family member. Meditation would be beneficial to you around the new moon and also for the next two weeks leading up to the full moon. Keep track of your dreams, too. They may hold important information and insights about an issue that concerns you.

The full moon in Sagittarius on June 18 lights up your sixth house. Your daily work routine and health are in the spotlight now. This full moon is within one degree of Pluto, indicating that power issues and profound transformation are part of the picture. Are you or is someone in your daily work environment involved in power plays? Are you ready to take control of your health? If so, this is a good time to start a regular exercise routine, hire a trainer, or take up yoga or some other discipline that involves the mind-body connection.

Dates to watch for: Between June 20 and 26, Mars and Neptune are opposite each other, in Leo and Aquarius respectively. This can lend itself to confrontations with people who don't share your beliefs. Your wisest move in such situations is to decide whether an argument or debate will change anyone's mind. Think before you speak.

Best dates: June 4–8, when Venus and Mars form harmonious angles to each other, facilitating relationships with the opposite sex.

Cancer—July 2008

July 1 the action begins when Mars enters Virgo and your sixth house. This transit lasts until August 19 and triggers a lot of activity related to your daily work and health. For instance, you now stop procrastinating about seeing a dentist or doctor and schedule the appropriate appointments. You may try out alternative treatments like acupuncture, massage, even nontraditional healing methods, such as Reiki or reconnective therapy (see the book *The Reconnection* by Eric Pearl). At work, you pay closer attention to details and don't hesitate to delegate when you're swamped.

Mercury enters your sign on July 10, heightening your communication skills. It's likely that you're more intuitive now and synchronicities may proliferate at an astonishing rate, indicating that you're on the right track toward achieving a goal or dream. You could be traveling for either business or pleasure, but there will be an underlying quest that is entirely personal. This transit lasts until July 26.

Improved finances should come about under a Venus transit through Leo and your second house, which begins on July 12 and lasts until August 5. You may be spending a lot of money, too, perhaps on a big-ticket item. Just be sure the checks have cleared before you make your purchase. A romance is possible with someone who shares your values or, if you're involved already, you may buy an expensive gift for this person.

July's moons should be pretty spectacular for you, particularly the new moon in your sign on July 2. This one happens only once a year and attracts new opportunities, people, and situations in all areas of your life. Venus forms a wide conjunction with this moon, of six degrees, but that's close enough to suggest a new romance or a creative breakthrough.

The full moon on July 18 is in Capricorn, your opposite sign, and your seventh house. Expect revelations about a romantic or business partnership. Due to the positive angle that Uranus forms to this full moon and to your sun, the revelations are sudden and unexpected.

Date to watch for: July 5, when Mars and Saturn are conjunct in Virgo, your third house. You either put the brakes on a situation involving siblings or neighbors or on a communication project, or you've got the physical stamina to work long and hard to complete something.

Best date: July 25, when Venus and retrograde Jupiter form a beneficial angle to each other. This combination enhances your love life and brings your muse to full attention, ready and willing to serve *you*.

Cancer—August 2008

August features the second set of eclipses for the year, a second new moon as well as four transits, so it's a hectic month. On August 1, the solar eclipse at nine degrees, thirty-four minutes of Leo impacts your second house. A financial issue snaps into clarity for you. Once you see what, you can take corrective measures. Your values may come into play during this eclipse as well. Mercury is within three degrees of this moon, indicating debate and conversation about the issues involved. Those of you born between June 30 and July 3 will feel the effects of this eclipse most strongly.

The lunar eclipse on August 16 is at twenty-four

degrees, fifty-four minutes Aquarius. An emotional issue surfaces concerning your career or a professional issue or relationship. Neptune is within two degrees of this moon, suggesting that you may not have the full story or all the facts.

The new moon on August 30 is in Virgo, your third house. Saturn is within three degrees of this moon, suggesting that the opportunities that arrive during the next month are solid and grounded. These opportunities concern writing and communication, siblings, neighbors and neighborhoods, and travel. The opportunities this new moon attracts revolve around your daily life.

Venus enters Virgo on August 5, conferring an ease and smoothness in your relationships with siblings, relatives, neighbors. If you're a writer or in the communication or travel business, then things certainly look up during this transit. It's also possible that a neighbor or someone you meet through a sibling or relative becomes a romantic interest, surprising both of you! Venus's transit through your third house underscores some of the themes of the new moon in Virgo on August 30. Venus enters Libra on the same day as the new moon, enhancing a smooth flow of events at home and suggesting that your love life with your spouse or partner picks up.

On August 10, Mercury joins Venus in Virgo and your third house. Any relationship that begins when these two planets are so close indicates that communication will be the major attraction initially in the relationship. Can you bare your soul to this person? This transit ends on August 28, just before the new moon in Virgo, but bolsters the themes of the new moon. When it enters Libra on August 28, things at home become much more lively, with a lot of discussion about equality among family members. You may be in the mood to beautify your home in some way, too.

On August 19, Mars enters Libra and your fourth house. This means that at some point between August 10 and 30, all the inner planets will be in Libra, placing a lot of pressure on family members to coexist peacefully. Your home may be the favored spot for parties and gatherings. Your parents will figure into the equation as well.

Date to watch for: August 16, when Mars in Virgo and Pluto in Sagittarius form a challenging angle to each other. Power issues surface between you and a coworker or employee or between you and a sibling or neighbor. Or all of the above! Tread lightly.

Best dates: August 17–18, when Venus and Jupiter, the two best planets in the zodiac, form a harmonious angle to each other, smoothing over the disagreements on August 16 and lending a rather pleasant energy to your relationship with your romantic or business partner.

Cancer—September 2008

You should enjoy the full moon on September 15. It's in Pisces, a sign compatible with your sun, and your ninth house, and Uranus is within three degrees of it. Something concerning your educational goals, spiritual or political beliefs, or foreign travel is highlighted under this moon. Your perceptions and imagination are exceptional and there's an air of excitement and unpredictability that you undoubtedly sense shortly before the full moon. It may concern a personal relationship and whether it has been taken as far as it can go. Decisions, decisions. Make them before Mercury turns retrograde on September 24.

The new moon in Libra on September 29 occurs in your fourth house. Doorways open related to your home, family, and personal environment. You may set up a home office, start searching other neighborhoods or cities for a possible move, or someone may move in with your family. Art and music are both highlighted here, so this new moon could bring something as wonderful as a new piano, a piece of art you've coveted, or some new insight into your relationships with your family members.

Jupiter turns direct on September 7, in your seventh house. This is very good news for your personal and business partnerships. After months of Jupiter's expansive energy being turned inward, it now blossoms outward, enriching your relationship with your spouse or partner and helping the growth of your business partnership.

On September 23, Venus enters Scorpio, and your fifth house, marking the start of one of the most romantic periods this year. If you're not involved when this transit begins, you probably will be when it ends on October 18. Regardless, this is a time when you have several options in terms of romance and your sex life is likely to be active. Creatively, you'll be hooked into an intuitive flow in your current project.

The next day, September 24, Mercury turns retrograde for the last time in 2008, in Libra, your fourth house. By now, you know the drill on Mercury retrogrades. Since this one is in Libra, however, you should be especially careful to communicate with your family—spouse, kids, parents—as clearly as possible. Also, if your appliances go berserk during this period, don't freak. Just get them fixed. Be sure to back up your computer files ahead of time.

Dates to watch for: September 22–23, when Mercury and Mars are conjunct in Libra. You'll be struggling to keep things at home in balance. Your mind is especially sharp now.

Best dates: September 13–20. Mercury, Venus, and Mars are conjunct in Libra. So now there's another planet to confuse the picture! But it shouldn't be all that confusing. You're in the mood to talk with the ones you love, many of your activities involve your family during this period, and there's a certain aesthetic and artistic texture to your lives.

Cancer—October 2008

The full moon on October 14 is in Aries, your tenth house. Both Pluto and Neptune form harmonious angles to each other and to the moon, but not to your sun sign. This full moon may present challenges in terms of your career or with a boss or peer. Part of the problem may be a lapse in communication, which will be rectified after October 15, when Mercury turns direct again in Libra. Then the harmony you're seeking is within your reach.

On October 28, the new moon in early Scorpio falls in your fifth house, promising a new romantic relationship, new creative opportunities, and a new chapter in your relationship with your kids. This moon forms a harmonious angle with your sun sign so the results should be extremely positive for you.

There are several other dates to make note of this month. On October 3, Mars enters Scorpio and your fifth house. This transit offers a harbinger of what the new moon brings and looks very promising for a heated affair. There's chemistry in this relationship! Also, you're on a creative roll with this transit, which lasts until November 16, able to meet deadlines and get to the bottom line of anything you're researching or investigating. Your intuition also deepens under this transit, particularly as it pertains to your children and romantic partners. Until October 18, Venus shares the house and sign with Mars, doubling the emphasis on a relationship. Whether you're looking for sex, companionship, or just someone to have fun with, it's all there.

If you're currently involved with someone, then Venus and Mars paired up in your fifth house is the classic combination for a romantic and sexually charged period in your relationship.

Dates to watch for: October 2–3, when Mars in Libra and Pluto in Sagittarius form harmonious angles to each other but challenging angles to your sun. Be careful that power plays don't surface at home, with your family, and in your workplace, with employees and coworkers.

Best dates: October 19–31, when Saturn in Virgo forms a harmonious angle with your sun. This combination strengthens your communication skills. It's terrific if you're a writer, in public relations, advertising, or the travel industry because you find the right structure for whatever you're doing.

Cancer—November 2008

Batten down the hatches for November, Cancer. In addition to the Thanksgiving holiday, there's plenty going on in the stars and it starts on November 4, when Mercury enters Scorpio, joining Mars in your fifth house. This combination emphasizes your need for open and honest communication with a romantic partner with whom you also share a deep physical attraction. This combination is also excellent for all creative work that you do within the next few weeks, allowing you to enter the intuitive flow from your higher mind. Your muse isn't just in attendance; she's speaking 24/7.

On November 23, Mercury enters Sagittarius and your sixth house. You have more contact with employees and coworkers now, perhaps even contact at social events because of the holidays. You're looking for the bigger picture in your daily work environment, and one way of finding it is communicating more with the people around you. Thanks to Pluto's retrograde motion, it's back in Sagittarius and your sixth house until November 26. So between November 23 and 26, draw on Pluto's power in all your communications.

On November 12, Venus enters Capricorn, your opposite sign, and your seventh house. Despite the opposition to your sun, this transit should light up your relationship with a spouse or romantic partner. It should also be good for business partnerships, conferring smoothness and ease. On November 26, when Pluto enters Capricorn and joins Venus in your seventh house, you're in the driver's seat where all partnerships are concerned. There may be some power struggles. You've also got Jupiter in Capricorn in the seventh, so expect expansion in your partnerships, and permanent change.

A Pluto opposition to your sun brings profound and transformative change to your personal life. And since Pluto is going to be in Capricorn until 2024, you're in for a long haul, Cancer. It may not be the smoothest road you've ever traveled, but one thing is for sure: it will never bore you.

Mars enters Sagittarius on November 16, providing a booster rocket for your daily work. Deadlines that once seemed challenging now look like child's play. You may not have much patience with coworkers or employees, but don't make the mistake of believing you must do everything yourself. Delegate.

The full moon on November 13 is in Taurus, an earth sign compatible with your Taurus sun. This moon receives positive beams from both Uranus and Saturn, bringing a certain excitement and strangeness to events and situations. Overall this full moon should be good for you.

The new moon on November 27 is in Sagittarius and underscores some of the themes mentioned above. Since new moons symbolize new paths according to sign and house, however, you can expect fresh opportunities in your daily work routine and health. You may join a gym or take up some other form of regular exercise. If you've been hoping to change jobs, this new moon could bring an opportunity to do so. Both Mercury and Mars are close to this moon, indicating a lot of discussion (perhaps about the new job offer?) and decisive action.

Dates to watch for: November 26–28, when Pluto enters Capricorn. The first few days surrounding a change in signs for one of the outer planets can sometimes be the most intense.

Best date: November 17, when Mercury in Scorpio, Jupiter in Capricorn, and Saturn in Virgo form harmonious angles to each other. You may be on a quest of some kind, and if you follow the serendipitous signs you find what you're looking for.

Cancer—December 2008

As you enter the final month of the year, every planet is moving in direct motion—that is, functioning as it's supposed to. On December 7, Venus enters Aquarius and your eighth house. This transit, which lasts through the end of the year, indicates that your mortgage comes through, you get your car loan, your insurance matters are humming along smoothly. Your partner or spouse may get a raise and you may attend a workshop on an esoteric topic that interests you. In short, things in your house of shared resources are looking up!

On December 12, there are two noteworthy events. First, Mercury enters Capricorn, joining Pluto and Jupiter in your seventh house. Your partnerships become the focus of your attention. You're seeking open communication, equality, and expansion. You and your partner are now able to build a mutual foundation for your relationship and may decide to move in together or get married.

Also on December 12, the full moon in Gemini, your twelfth house, sheds light on a long-buried issue or secret. If you don't like what you find, just deal with it and get things out into the open. This moon has some stressful aspects to it, so your best bet is to go with the flow, if possible, and tackle whatever challenges surface.

December 27 also features two events—Mars enters Capricorn, joining Mercury, Pluto, and Jupiter in your seventh house. This concentration of planets in the partnership sector of your chart really brings on the pressure to understand your closest relationships in romance and business and to deal with the issues, whatever they are, in ways that benefit everyone involved. These themes are repeated with the new moon in Capricorn, also on December 27. But because new moons promise new paths and opportunities, it appears that everything concerning you about relationships now begins to work out in your favor. You have ample opportunities for new relationships—or a new chapter in a current relationship. It's a nice harbinger for the New Year!

Date to watch for: December 31, when Saturn turns retrograde in Virgo, your third house. This could play havoc with your New Year's plans, particularly if you've been run-down or tired lately. You may not feel up to par. Or, if you've planned some big bash at a place that demands a permit or some sort of official permission slip, it may not come through in time. Best to stick close to home and have friends and family come to your place to see in 2009.

Best date: December 25, when Venus and Neptune form a harmonious angle to each other, bringing an idealism into your love life!

Brainstorming

Envision yourself a year, two years, or four years from now. What is your life like? Where do you live? Is your work satisfying to you? Are you single, married, a parent? Are you happy? Do you have enough money? Is your health good? What are your spiritual beliefs? Are you a vehicle for change in your family or community? In the space below, describe the life you would like to be living a year or two or four up the line. Be as outrageous, creative, and wild as you want. After all, it's *your* life. If you can imagine it, then you can create it.

MY LIFE IN _____ (*choose a year*)

_____

_____

_____

_____

_____

_____

_____

_____

_____

_____

_____

HAPPY 2009!

The Big Picture for Leo in 2008

Welcome to 2008, Leo! It's going to be a fascinating year. Saturn left your sign late last year, which was probably a distinct relief! It's now going to spend two and a half years in your money house, urging you to bring structure and discipline to your earning and spending. But Saturn is just a small part of the picture.

Jupiter, the planet of success, luck, and expansion, entered Capricorn and your sixth house late last year. This yearlong transit should bring great expansion in responsibility and opportunities in your daily work life. Since the sixth house also represents daily health, you may expand your regular exercise routine (or start one) by adding aerobics, yoga, or a gym workout. Sometimes, Jupiter's transit through the sixth spells a weight gain, so pay special attention this year to exercise, diet, and nutrition.

Neptune, the planet of higher inspiration—but also of illusions—continues its transit through Aquarius and your seventh house. The impact of this transit is subtle, unfolding over a long period of time. That said, you probably have noticed that you tend to idealize your partner, or marriage and intimate partnerships generally. Your partner may inspire you in some way—spiritually, creatively—and you share a strong bond.

Uranus, the planet of sudden, unexpected change, continues its transit through Pisces and your eighth house. This transit has been going on since 2005, so you're familiar with its energy by now. You can expect more unexpected events and situations surrounding resources that you share with others. Your partner or spouse may get a sudden raise and promotion—or be fired. It can be as black and white as that. Your interest in metaphysics and esoteric topics deepens. You're urged to pay close attention to things like insurance and wills. You get the idea here, Leo. The eighth house is one of dichotomies, covering mundane details and encompassing esoterica as well.

Pluto, the planet of transformation, starts the year in Sagittarius, your fifth house. But on January 25, it enters Capricorn and your sixth house. On April 2, however, it turns retrograde and moves back into Sagittarius. On September 8, it turns direct again, and then on November 26 enters Capricorn once more. Pluto will be in Capricorn for a very long time—until late 2024—and will transform your daily work routine.

BEST TIME FOR ROMANCE

Look for a pleasurable time between July 12 and August 5, when Venus will be in your sign. Your love life picks up, your popularity increases, and your self-confidence soars. In addition, there's a new moon in your sign on August 1, which signals new beginnings in your personal life. But the August 1 new moon is also part of a solar eclipse. Check the Eclipses section below to find out what that could mean for you.

Another good time for romance falls between October 18 and November 12, when Venus is in Sagittarius, transiting your fifth house of romance. On December 27, there's a new moon in your house of romance, so look to that day for something utterly divine in romance.

BEST TIME FOR CAREER DECISIONS

On May 5, there's a new moon in Taurus and your tenth house of career. This moon indicates new beginnings and opportunities related to professional matters. You'll have a month or so to launch a new business, land a dream job, or change jobs. You get help from Venus during this period, which is traveling at a wide conjunction to the new moon. This opportunity could involve the arts, music, or a creative project that is dear to you.

The full moon in Taurus on November 13 should bring a culmination to something you've worked on very hard in the past months.

MERCURY RETROGRADE

Every year, Mercury, the planet of communication and travel, turns retrograde three times. During these periods, it's wisest not to negotiate or sign contracts, to travel, to submit manuscripts, or to make major decisions. Granted, we can't live our lives entirely by Mercury retrogrades! If you have to travel during the periods listed below, however, then expect changes in your plans. If you have to sign a contract, expect to revise it. Communications are bumpy, it's easy to be misunderstood. It's a good time to revise, review, and rewrite.

During these periods, it's a wise idea to back up computer files before Mercury turns retrograde. Quite often, computers and other communication devices act up. Be sure your virus software is up to date, too. Pay special attention to the house in which Mercury retrograde falls. It will tell you the area of your life most likely to be impacted. The periods to watch for in 2008 are:

January 28–February 18: retrograde in Aquarius, your seventh house of partnerships.

May 26–June 19: retrograde in Gemini, your eleventh house of friends.

September 24–October 15: retrograde in Libra, your third house of communication.

ECLIPSES

Every year, there are four eclipses, two solar and two lunar. Solar eclipses trigger external events that allow us to see something that has eluded us. When an eclipse hits one of your natal planets, it's especially important. Take note of the sign and house placement. Lunar eclipses bring up emotional issues related to the sign and house into which they fall. If you have your birth chart, check to see if the eclipses hit any natal planets. If they do, pay special attention to events that occur for up to six months after the eclipse.

Here are the dates to watch for:

February 6: solar eclipse at seventeen degrees Aquarius, your seventh house of partnerships. Those of you born between February 4 and 8 are likely to feel the most challenging impact of this eclipse.

February 20: lunar eclipse at ten degrees Virgo, in your second house of finances.

August 1: solar eclipse, nine degrees Leo, in your first house. If you were born between July 30 and August 4 or have other planets in Leo, you'll feel this eclipse most strongly in a positive way.

August 16: lunar eclipse at twenty-four degrees Aquarius, your seventh house of partnerships.

LUCKIEST DAYS IN 2008

Every year, Jupiter forms a beneficial angle with the sun, usually a conjunction, when both planets are in the same sign. In 2008, the angle is a lovely trine and it occurs during two time periods: May 11–13 and September 3–5. If you're going to buy a lotto ticket, do it during these periods!

Now let's take a look at what 2008 has in store for you month by month.

Twelve Months of Predictions
for Leo
January–December 2008

Leo—January 2008

The first new moon of 2008 occurs on January 8, in Capricorn, your sixth house. It brings new opportunities related to your daily work routine—a new job, perhaps, that is more in line with what you want to do; greater responsibilities in your present job; or a promotion. If you would like to open your own business or become self-employed, this new moon attracts opportunities to do so. As with any opportunity, though, you have to be ready to jump on it and do your part.

The full moon on January 22 is in your sign and will have the most impact if you're born early in the Leo cycle, between July 23 and 25. You may experience some tension with a personal or professional partner, but otherwise this full moon should bring a fresh perspective to a personal issue or concern.

What about planetary transits this month? Look to January 7 for Mercury's transit into Aquarius, your seventh house. You and a partner (romantic or professional) are chattering away about the relationship and your individual and joint needs. You may be in contract negotiations for your business. Don't hesitate to ask for everything you feel you deserve. Be sure to sign before Mercury turns retrograde on January 28 or after it turns direct again on February 18.

And while we're on the subject of Mercury retrograde, turn to the big picture for Leo this year and read over the section on Mercury retrogrades—the dos and don'ts.

On January 24, Venus enters Capricorn and your sixth house, underscoring some of the themes of the new moon in Capricorn. A flirtation with a coworker or employee now heats up. Are you interested because this person bolsters your ego or is there really an irresistible attraction?

January 25 marks a significant transit, when Pluto enters Capricorn and your sixth house. Take a look at the introduction to see what this means on a global scale. For you personally, this transit is going to transform your daily work routine and your health maintenance. It's a long transit, too, lasting until 2024, so the changes will be subtle, taking place over time. Throughout the year, Pluto will retrograde back into Sagittarius and your fifth house, touching off romantic and creative issues that you've dealt with before. But by the end of the year, the planet is firmly in Capricorn.

Mars started the year in retrograde motion, stirring up things behind the scenes and possibly creating some bumps and bruises in friendships. On January 30, it turns direct again, in Gemini, your eleventh house, setting the stage for next month's social activities.

Dates to watch for: January 24, when Venus enters your sixth house; January 25, when Pluto joins it; and January 28, when Mercury turns retrograde.

Best date: January 24 is a day to plan something special with coworkers or employees. Venus and Jupiter are conjunct in Capricorn, your sixth house.

Leo—February 2008

There are two eclipses this month to watch for. The solar eclipse on February 6 is in Aquarius, your seventh house. Mercury is very close to this moon, indicating that you may be in contract negotiations to expand your business or company services overseas. If you're a writer, you could get an offer on your manuscript or may have an opportunity to travel overseas, perhaps for research. If you're born in the middle of the Leo cycle—between August 9 and 11—you'll feel this eclipse most strongly.

The lunar eclipse in Virgo on February 20 impacts your second house. An emotional situation surfaces at home that concerns your family or one of your parents—someone in the family may need more emotional support from you. Roll with the punches, Leo. Let your compassion shine.

On February 17, Venus enters Aquarius and your seventh house, emphasizing some of the same themes as the solar eclipse in Aquarius. A romantic relationship is now possible with a foreign-born individual or in a foreign place, if you're traveling overseas. If you do get involved under this transit, the person is likely to be idiosyncratic or visionary in some way. This trait appeals to the part of you that enjoys the unusual.

A day later, Mercury turns direct again. So after that date, it's time to pack your bags, sign your contracts, and send off your manuscripts. Life is back on a more even keel. In fact, until March 12, Mercury and Venus travel in the same sign and house, accentuating your need to communicate openly with your partner.

Dates to watch for: The eclipse dates, of course, are ones to watch for. Also, February 22, when Venus and Saturn are square to each other, but Venus forms a harmonious angle to your sun. You persevere through whatever challenges the day tosses your way.

Best dates: February 23–26, when Uranus and Jupiter form a harmonious angle to each other. Your checks arrive!

Leo—March 2008

March is busy, Leo, so buckle up and make note of the specific dates. The action begins on March 4, when Mars enters Cancer and your twelfth house. You'll be spending time alone to complete a project or meet a deadline. If you're involved in a relationship, then things heat up under this transit. You and your partner may be spending a lot of time together, in private, perhaps in secrecy. The secrecy won't last forever, though. Once Mars enters your sign on May 9, the truth gets out.

March 7 features a new moon in Pisces, your tenth house. The opportunities this moon brings span the spectrum—from a new career path, to a promotion or raise, to some sort of reward or peer recognition for the good work you've done. Since Uranus is within a degree of this moon, expect the opportunities to come suddenly, unexpectedly, out of the blue.

The full moon on March 21 is in Libra, a sign compatible with yours, and in your third house. Romance, romance, Leo! But only if you overcome any power issues that surface between you and your partner.

Date to watch for: March 7, which not only features the new moon in your tenth house but also has Mercury and Venus holding hands in your ninth house. This combination suggests that you and your partner may have a meeting of the minds. Your worldviews are similar.

Best dates: The first two weeks of March have Venus and Neptune forming harmonious angles to each other and to your sun. Your idealism isn't just talk. You're learning to integrate it into your most personal relationships and into your creative projects.

Leo—April 2008

You'll love the new moon in Aries on April 5. If you've been hoping to travel overseas, this new moon may bring the opportunity to do so. Also, your business or product may expand to an overseas market, or a foreign-born individual is helpful to you now. If you're a college student, this new moon could bring the opportunity for a semester abroad. If you're headed for college in the fall, this new moon helps you decide which college you would like to attend. If you're a writer in search of a publisher, then you may get an offer on your manuscript. In other words, Leo, the news is uniformly good, regardless of your situation.

On April 20, the full moon in Scorpio lights up your fourth house. This moon is opposed to the career sector of your chart, so you may experience a tug-of-war between your responsibilities to your family and your responsibilities to your boss and career. One solution is to work more out of your home over the next month. Saturn forms a harmonious angle with this moon, indicating that a raise is possible. Try to follow the hints the universe throws your way in the form of synchronicities—seemingly random coincidences that do have an underlying order and meaning.

On April 2, Mercury enters Aries and your ninth house, repeating some of the new moon themes. You're quite vocal now about your personal philosophy and beliefs, and if you're in politics, then this transit helps you state things clearly. Four days later, on April 6, Venus joins Mercury in Aries, adding a kind of insurance policy that all ninth house endeavors will run smoothly. Remember: the ninth house governs education, law, politics, your worldview and spiritual beliefs, long-distance travel, publishing, and foreign cultures and countries.

On April 17, Mercury enters Taurus and your tenth house. There's a lot of socializing now with peers and bosses and you may be pitching ideas, business plans, even debating about why you deserve a raise. There may be some travel related to business over the next two weeks. On April 30, Venus follows Mercury into your tenth house, setting the stage for a romance with a peer in May.

Dates to watch for: For the first ten days or so of the month, Jupiter and Uranus travel in harmonious angles to each other, triggering unexpected events and situations related to your daily work and resources you share with others. You might, for instance, find that your responsibilities increase and you must enlist the help of others in your office to get the job done.

Best dates: April 1–2, when Mercury and Venus are conjunct in Pisces. You'll be talking about wills, inheritances, and taxes.

Leo—May 2008

The new moon in Taurus on May 5 attracts opportunities related to your career. Some of the possibilities are a complete change in your career path, a new job with better pay and benefits that's more in line with your interests, a new boss, or a promotion and a raise. The area of your career that has captured your focus since the New Year is where things start happening and shifting. Jupiter forms a wide but beneficial angle to this moon—a six-degree trine—indicating expansion and success.

The full moon in Scorpio on May 19 is in a very late degree—nearly thirty—and Uranus forms a wide trine to it. This moon may cause some tension at home. Passions are running fast and furiously and everyone seems to be searching for their version of what's true. Uranus brings about an unexpected event that snaps everything into clarity for you.

On May 2, Mercury enters Gemini, a sign that it rules, and your eleventh house. This transit should be fun, with lots of socializing with friends and groups who share your interests and passions. If you're a writer, then chances are good that you'll be working on a project with a friend. If you're in the travel business, you may get a group of friends together for a cruise or some other kind of trip. This transit also favors promotion and advertising.

Even more fun starts on May 9, when Mars enters your sign, Leo, firing up your libido and your physical energy in general. Think of this transit, which lasts until July 1, as your booster rocket.

Venus enters Gemini and your eleventh house on May 24, so that romance is quite likely with someone you considered to be a friend. Or, it may be someone you meet through a group to which you belong—a theater group, for example, or a writers' or bridge group. Then on May 26, everything seems to slow down when Mercury turns retrograde for the second time this year. This one hits you in the eleventh house of friends and happens while Venus is still in that house. The entire three weeks may feel like you've put your foot in your mouth unless you are very careful about what you say, when you say it, and how you say it.

Dates to watch for: Saturn turns direct in your sign on May 2. This is wonderful news, even if the impact isn't immediate. You're now able to use Saturn's energy to find the correct structure and goals for your personal life. On May 9, Jupiter turns retrograde, so its expansive energy is driven inward, urging you to examine your spiritual beliefs and worldview.

Best dates: May 23–30, when Mercury and Jupiter form a harmonious angle to each other. From May 26 onward, however, Mercury is retrograde. The combination of these two planets should bolster your daily work routine and career.

Leo—June 2008

On June 3, the new moon in Gemini is in your eleventh house. This moon should attract new friends, opportunities to join groups that support your varied interests, and highlights the wishes and dreams you have for yourself. The moon shares a close conjunction with Venus, indicating that women are helpful to you now and that romance with someone who has been a friend or with someone you meet through friends is a distinct possibility. Also, Mercury forms a five-degree conjunction to this moon—somewhat wide—but this indicates lively discussions with friends or even that other people are talking about *you*.

The full moon on June 18 is in Sagittarius, a fellow fire sign, and your fifth house. Since your fifth house deals with love, this moon should be quite romantic for you. You're able to grasp the emotional complexities of your most intimate relationship and finally have the larger picture you've been looking for. Also on June 18, Venus enters Cancer, your twelfth house. This transit takes you behind the scenes of your own life, into the watery realms of your unconscious. It's a good time to enter therapy, if you're so inclined, or to take up meditation. Another thing this transit suggests is a secret love affair.

Mars continues its transit through your sign, providing you with all the physical energy you need. Your sex appeal is on a definite upswing and your life is extremely busy, in a positive way!

June 19 is a day to celebrate! Mercury turns direct again in Gemini, your eleventh house. So any misunderstanding you've had with friends should begin to clear up. It's safe to travel again, so pack your bags, Leo, and head for the nearest airport.

Dates to watch for: June 26, Uranus turns retrograde in Pisces. The effects of this retrograde are more subtle than a Mercury retrograde and occur over a longer period of time (until November 27). That said, it impacts your eighth house of shared resources. If you're in the midst of a separation or divorce, for instance, it could affect what you get in your settlement. Or your partner may experience a sudden change in his or her income. From June 20 to 25, Mars and Neptune are opposed to each other. This could create some tension between you and your partner, but keep your optimism on a high note and you'll get through it just fine.

Best dates: June 4–8, when Venus and Mars form harmonious angles to each other and to your sun. Sparks fly between you and your partner, the chemistry is just about perfect.

Leo—July 2008

The new moon on July 2 is in Cancer, your twelfth house. This provides you with ample opportunities to extend yourself to people in hospitals, nursing homes, or similar institutions. You may also have a chance to do exciting work behind the scenes, perhaps working with your intuition or dreams. Since Venus is within six degrees of this moon, there's a chance that romance blossoms in secrecy. Or, you meet someone when and where you least expect it! Consider this new moon preparation for next month's new moon (and solar eclipse) in your sign.

The full moon on July 18 is in Capricorn, your sixth house. There could be some tensions with coworkers or employees. But overall you're in a good position now to understand how you can build your company or business for the long term. Jupiter forms a wide—ten degrees—conjunction with this moon, indicating a positive outcome. It would be better if Jupiter were closer, but take the ten degrees!

July 1 brings activity and energy surrounding your finances because Mars moves into your second house of finances until August 19. Take advantage of this transit by studying the stock market, investing in products that you use, stashing some money away in your IRA. You may be spending more, too, however, so just be sure the checks have cleared before you hit the mall.

Mercury enters Cancer on July 10, emphasizing some of the themes of the new moon. This transit is great if you're a writer—you've got the solitude, the peace and quiet you need to complete a project. It also favors strong dream recall and lots of conversation in private, perhaps with your partner or the new romantic interest in your life.

On July 12, you enter one of the most romantic periods this year, when Venus enters your sign. This transit lasts until August 5, so if you're not involved with anyone and want to be, get out and be seen. Accept invitations. Get around. If you're involved already, then this transit signals a smooth and romantic period in the relationship. Since Venus also rules the arts, this transit signals breakthroughs and opportunities related to your artistic projects and goals. All Leos have a dramatic streak, and if you're in the entertainment business you're in for a very pleasant period.

On July 26, Mercury enters your sign, signaling the beginning of an intellectually stimulating couple of weeks. The transit doesn't end until August 10, so it coincides with the solar eclipse in Leo on August 1. More on that under August's activities.

Date to watch for: July 5, when Mars and Saturn are conjunct in Virgo, your second house. Mars craves action, Saturn demands restraint. The tug-of-war could be problematic. Don't make any financial decisions until later in the month, when the two planets are separating from each other.

Best date: July 12, when Venus enters your sign.

Leo—August 2008

August is a major month for you, Leo, and it all starts with the solar eclipse in your sign on August 1. Those of you born between July 30 and August 3 are going to feel the impact more strongly, but every Leo will experience the effects. For starters, during the next six months you'll be scrutinizing yourself and your life through a series of external events that will prompt you to do this. Mercury is within two degrees of this eclipse, indicating that a lot of talk and chatter occurs over the next six months that deals with your personal transformation and changes.

On August 16, there's a lunar eclipse in Aquarius, your opposite sign, and seventh house. This eclipse brings up an emotional issue related to a romantic or business partnership or with friends. Neptune is close to this moon, suggesting that you may not have the full picture or all the details.

On August 30, there's a second new moon—in Virgo, your second house. This one is sure to stimulate your finances. You have an opportunity to earn more money or to find the right investments for your situation and tax bracket or both.

Look to August 5 for the beginning of a good financial period. Venus enters Virgo and your second house, bringing an easy flow of money—but the flow moves in both directions! You may want to buy a big-ticket item, or your kids may need new wardrobes for the upcoming school year. Rather than rack up credit card bills, pay cash. On August 10, Mercury follows Venus into your second house. Now there's a lot of talking about money—how to earn more, spend less, save more, and what investments might be good. Pay close attention to financial details now—check your bank statements carefully, stay on top of where your money goes.

Mars enters Libra and your third house on August 19, bringing lots of activity in your community, neighborhood, or with siblings and relatives. This transit, which lasts until October 3, is in a sign compatible with your own, so things should go pretty smoothly. You could be involved in a community beautification project or feel the urge to spruce up your own surroundings.

This theme is underscored by two more transits into Libra—Mercury on August 28 and Venus on August 30. Romance and love may be on your mind, too, however, and it's possible that you meet a romantic interest through a sibling or neighbor. If so, communication will be a vital part of the relationship. If you're involved already, then the combination of these two planets portends a strong period for the relationship.

Dates to watch for: In addition to the eclipse dates, August 16 could be problematic, when Pluto and Mars form a challenging angle to each other. Power issues may surface.

Best dates: From August 12 to 16, Venus and Jupiter form a harmonious angle to each other—but not to your sun. Still, these four days are noteworthy, triggering activity related to finances and your daily work and health routine.

Leo—September 2008

Two planets turn direct this month—Saturn in Virgo on September 2 and Jupiter in Capricorn on September 7. Saturn's change in direction should be beneficial to your finances and Jupiter's change should smooth things over at work. In fact, if you've been hoping for a raise at work, it could come after September 7 and before Mercury turns retrograde on September 24. More on Mercury in a moment.

The full moon in Pisces on September 15 affects the shared resources sector of your chart. Other people's money, insurance, and tax matters are highlighted under this full moon. Be sure that your insurance payments are up to date, and if you've applied for a loan or mortgage, check in with the bank to see where things stand. It's wise to look for end-of-the-year tax breaks now—business equipment you might need, a research trip, a new computer or printer. Uranus is in close proximity to this moon, indicating that whatever comes to light will do so suddenly, unexpectedly, and catch you by surprise.

The new moon on September 29 is in Libra, your third house. This moon ushers in opportunities concerning your community and neighborhood. If you've been contemplating a move to another area, then you may be traveling to other cities and towns, seeking the perfect spot for you and your family. There may be a reconciliation with a brother, sister, or other relative.

On September 23, Venus enters Scorpio and your fourth house. This transit lasts until October 18 and spells a romantic time with your spouse or partner. If you and your partner don't live together, then you may decide to take the plunge. Or you may decide to get married. Scorpio is a passionate, intensely emotional sign, so regardless of what transpires under this transit, it could be an emotional and sexual roller coaster.

Now back to the Mercury retrograde, which begins on September 24, in Libra, your third house, and continues until October 15. This retrograde impacts your relationships with siblings and other relatives, neighbors, and your daily conscious routine. If you're a writer, plan on revising, rewriting, and rethinking your project. You won't even have to travel very far for this retrograde to affect you. You may be out running errands and have a flat. Or your battery dies. Small but annoying events.

Date to watch for: September 24, when the retrograde begins.

Best dates: September 22–23, when Mercury and Mars are conjunct in Libra, your third house. This should spice up your daily life, with lots of lively discussions and debates. You'll be striving for balance and harmony, and the best way to find it is to listen to music that uplifts your soul, visit museums, and take in some new films.

Leo—October 2008

Mars enters Scorpio and your fourth house on October 3, kicking your libido into high gear until November 16. This transit in your fourth house indicates that your sex life at home picks up, and sometimes that can help the romantic part of the relationship. Also, since it's in Scorpio, a sign that it corules, you may be doing investigative research out of your home office, perhaps in preparation for a creative project or even in anticipation of an eventual move. The impetus to move, in fact, is strong during the Mars transit.

The full moon on October 14 is in Aries, a fellow fire sign, and your ninth house of careers. Something reaches a culmination point pertaining to education, publishing, overseas travel or markets, or your spiritual and personal beliefs. Pluto forms a wide and harmonious angle to this moon, which is excellent for you because that planet is also in a fire sign. You'll be in the driver's seat with this full moon, Leo, particularly as it pertains to love and romance. Just don't let it go to your head.

The new moon on October 28, several days before Halloween, is in Scorpio, colliding with Mars's transit through the same sign and house. Wow. The combination of the new moon and the Mars transit indicates that your home life heats up. If you're uninvolved at the end of October, that probably will change by the end of November.

In between these two moons comes a cause for celebration—Mercury turns direct again on October 15, in Libra. This movement should help to clear the air in your neighborhood and with your siblings. If you've got the travel itch, then get online and figure out where you want to go!

Date to watch for: Neptune turns direct in Aquarius on Halloween. Even though you may not notice the immediate impact of this movement, things should now straighten out with a romantic or business partner. You may find yourself investigating the occult or other esoteric topics.

Best dates: October 2–3, when Mars and Pluto form harmonious angles to each other and to your sun.

Leo—November 2008

November is a busy month astrologically, with some potentially odd weather. On November 4, Mercury enters Scorpio, joining Mars in your fourth house. Now you and your spouse or partner have a chance to talk about the bottom line: Are you destined for each other? Do you want to stay together? What are your individual needs? You may be actively looking for a new home, too. But unless things unfold effortlessly, it may be best to wait.

Venus enters Capricorn and your sixth house on November 12. Between now and December 7, when Venus enters Aquarius, things at work are all about building a plan and working toward a goal. That effort unfolds smoothly. An office flirtation now heats up and the only question you have to ask yourself, Leo, is what you're looking for in a relationship. Commitment or just fun?

The next day, November 13, the full moon in Taurus highlights your career house. Make some preparations for this one. While you don't want to start anything new, bring professional projects to a close, clear your desk. You could be up for a raise or promotion, so show your best side.

On November 16, Mars enters fellow fire sign Sagittarius, a transit that will surely please you! Your love life picks up—sexual chemistry is the dominant theme—and your creativity soars. Take advantage of this transit, which lasts until December 27.

Now, the new moon on November 27, in Sagittarius, your fifth house. If ever there's a moon that portends love and romance, this moon is it. Expect the best for yourself in terms of romance and visualize what you want in a partner. Or in a creative project.

Dates to watch for: November 1, when Uranus turns direct in Pisces, your eighth house. Again, the effect is subtle, but once Uranus makes this turn, mortgages and loans are easier to obtain. And if you've been investigating the occult or other esoteric topics, this movement brings the teacher or mentor or direction you need. And it happens unexpectedly. On November 26, Pluto enters Capricorn again, for good, for a very long transit through your sixth house. The impact will be subtle because that transit lasts until 2024, but your daily work routine undergoes a slow and permanent transformation.

Best date: the new moon on November 27.

Leo—December 2008

As you head into the last month this year, an odd and wonderful thing has happened—every planet is moving in direct motion. That means they're all functioning at peak capacity.

On December 7, Venus enters Aquarius and your seventh house, a very nice transit for bolstering all partnerships, both romantic and professional. Even though Venus is now opposed to your sun, you can deal with it.

On December 12, there are two celestial events worth mentioning. Mercury enters Capricorn and your sixth house, indicating lots of conversation and discussion, perhaps concerning upcoming projects. You may have more social interaction now with employees and coworkers. Even though you will have to adjust your thinking or attitude about a particular detail, this should be a productive period for your daily work.

Also on December 12, the full moon in Gemini lights up your eleventh house. It's a social time, and you'll be hanging out with friends and any groups to which you belong. You may find yourself in a bookstore around this full moon or with a group of friends whose interests and passions are the same as yours.

The new moon in Capricorn on December 27 is in your sixth house and helps to set the work tone for the New Year. Opportunities now come to you in terms of your daily work. If you don't like your job, then the New Year may bring you new job offers. If your health has been iffy, the New Year brings healing. Pluto is within five degrees of this moon, indicating that you're entering a period of profound transformation in how you earn your daily bread, Leo. Perhaps in 2009 you get the break you've hoped for.

Date to watch for: December 31, Saturn turns retrograde. Okay, so it's not a great thing for your New Year's celebrations. Someone may try to put a damper on your festivities. But you're the eternal optimist, Leo, and somehow always land on your feet. The cat with nine lives! Roll with the punches and make adjustments. Don't let this spoil your celebrations for the New Year.

Best date: December 25. Aside from the fact that it's Christmas, Venus and Neptune are conjunct in Aquarius, so your romantic life is filled with idealism and great hopes.

Brainstorming

Envision yourself a year, two years, or four years from now. What is your life like? Where do you live? Is your work satisfying to you? Are you single, married, a parent? Are you happy? Do you have enough money? Is your health good? What are your spiritual beliefs? Are you a vehicle for change in your family or community? In the space below, describe the life you would like to be living a year or two or four up the line. Be as outrageous, creative, and wild as you want. After all, it's *your* life. If you can imagine it, then you can create it.

MY LIFE IN _____ (*choose a year*)

_____

_____

_____

_____

_____

_____

_____

_____

_____

_____

_____

_____

HAPPY 2009!

The Big Picture for Virgo
in 2008

Welcome to 2008! The year has much in store for you, Virgo, and most of it will be to your liking. Let's start with Saturn in your sign—not just for this year, but for the next two and a half years. Of all the signs that experience Saturn, it should cause the least problems for you, mainly because you're already a responsible, disciplined, and task-oriented individual. If anything, Saturn will bring you the means to create the proper structures in all areas of your life. You will learn, if you don't already know, what's really important to you and will be able to reach for your dreams and manifest them more easily.

You'll be getting plenty of help from Jupiter, which is now in compatible Capricorn, your fifth house of creativity and romance. In fact, your creativity should practically burst at the seams all year. New opportunities come to you that allow you to stretch your creative muscles. Your creative schedule may change. If, for instance, you've been doing your best creative work during the day, you may now try to do your creative work at night.

On the romantic front, Virgo, it should be an incredible year. If you're involved with someone at the beginning of 2008, then the relationship may deepen throughout the year, culminating in whatever you both are looking for. Whether that means living together, marriage, or starting a family, it's all possible. If you're not involved at the beginning of the year, you certainly will be by year's end. Jupiter seeks to expand whatever it touches, bringing happiness and good luck to whatever area of the chart it transits.

In addition to this, Pluto enters Capricorn on January 25, joining Jupiter in your fifth house. Pluto is about profound and permanent transformation, so you can expect monumental changes in your love life! Pluto retrogrades back into Sagittarius and your fourth house through the year, then finally enters Capricorn for good on November 26.

Uranus continues its journey through Pisces, in opposition to your sun, in your seventh house. Uranus oppositions can be troubling, upsetting, and challenging precisely because they shake up the status quo. If you're a person who doesn't adhere to the status quo, who embraces change, this lengthy transit won't be as disturbing to you. But you'll find that exciting and idiosyncratic people are entering your life frequently now. They are teachers, mentors, individuals whose insights teach you something. This transit can also result in the sudden, unexpected beginning or ending to relationships.

Neptune, the planet that symbolizes our highest inspiration as well as our illusions and blind spots, continues its very long transit through Aquarius and your sixth house. This transit brings a certain confusion, perhaps to your daily work, or it infuses your daily work with a spiritual quality. If you get any negative health reports under this transit, be sure to get a second opinion. Neptune can confuse even the best-intentioned doctors!

BEST TIME FOR ROMANCE

Mark the dates between August 10 and 28, when Venus is in your sign. Your romantic quota soars. You're also more artistic and others see you in a more flattering light. You feel more confident and your sex appeal rises. Great backup dates for romance fall between January 24 and February 17 and November 12 and December 7, when Venus is transiting your fifth house of love and forming a beautiful angle to your sun.

Other excellent dates for romance fall between May 11 and 13 and September 3 and 5, when the sun and Jupiter see eye to eye and there's a nice flow of energy between them.

Overall, 2008 is likely to be one of your most romantic and creative years.

BEST TIME FOR CAREER DECISIONS

Make career decisions between May 24 and June 18, when Venus is transiting your tenth house of careers. This should be quite a smooth time professionally. In fact, things may be going along so smoothly that you'll be tempted to kick back and relax. Don't. Seize the opportunity. There will be a lot of traveling, coming and going, during this period. Communication will be vital.

MERCURY RETROGRADES

Every year, there are three periods when Mercury— the planet of communication and travel—turns retrograde. During these periods, it's wisest not to negotiate or sign contracts, to travel, to submit manuscripts, or to make major decisions. Granted, we can't live our lives entirely by Mercury retrogrades! If you have to travel during the periods listed below, however, then expect changes in your plans. If you have to sign a contract, expect to revise it.

It's also a good idea to back up computer files before Mercury turns retrograde. Quite often, computers and other communication devices act up. Be sure your virus software is up to date, too. Pay special attention to the house in which Mercury retrograde falls. It will tell you the area of your life most likely to be impacted. The periods to watch for in 2008 are:

January 28–February 18: retrograde in Aquarius, your sixth house of health and work.

May 26–June 19: retrograde in Gemini, your tenth house of careers.

September 24–October 15: retrograde in Libra, your second house of finances.

ECLIPSES

Every year, there are four eclipses, two solar and two lunar. Solar eclipses trigger external events that allow us to see something that eluded us before. They can bring about beginnings and endings. When an eclipse hits one of your natal planets, it's especially important. Take note of the sign and house placement. Lunar eclipses bring up emotional issues related to the sign and house into which they fall.

Here are the dates to watch for:

February 6: solar eclipse at seventeen degrees Aquarius, your sixth house of health and work. You'll be able to see something about your daily work routine or health that you haven't perceived before. It's time to start a regular exercise routine, if you don't have one already. If you've considered getting another job, this solar eclipse could bring about the opportunity for a new job. Those of you born between September 8 and 12 are likely to feel the greatest impact. Check your natal chart to find out if you have any planets at seventeen degrees.

February 20: lunar eclipse at ten degrees Virgo, your sun sign! This one is very important for you, especially if you're born between September 1 and 5. Expect external events to reveal something about yourself or your early childhood.

August 1: solar eclipse, nine degrees Leo, in your twelfth house. Since this house symbolizes what is hidden, an issue may surface that reveals something about your early childhood or power you have disowned.

August 16: lunar eclipse at twenty-four degrees Aquarius, your sixth house of daily health and work.

LUCKIEST DAYS IN 2008

Every year, Jupiter forms a beneficial angle with the sun, usually a conjunction, when both planets are in the same sign. In 2008, the angle is a lovely trine and it occurs during two time periods: May 11–13 and September 3–5. If you're going to buy a lotto ticket, do it during these periods!

Now let's take a look at what 2008 has in store for you month by month.

Twelve Months of Predictions
for Virgo
January–December 2008

Virgo—January 2008

The first new moon of 2008 occurs on January 8, in Capricorn, your fifth house, a wonderful portent for a new romance and a major boost in your love life. This new moon also stimulates your creative adrenaline and brings opportunities for you to indulge in your creativity. Perhaps that manuscript you sent off months ago now sells or your home-based business now takes off in a major way. This new moon is trine to your sun, a harmonious angle, so the news can only be positive.

The full moon on January 22 is in Leo, your twelfth house. It illuminates something that was hidden in your life or some long-standing issue that it's now time to confront and resolve. If you have the time and patience, you might want to consider therapy for whatever this issue is. Your dreams around this full moon are apt to be vivid and you'll be able to recall them easily. Insight comes to you through these dreams, so be sure to record them.

What about planetary transits this month? Look to January 7 for Mercury's transit into Aquarius, your sixth house. This transit, which lasts into February, stimulates discussions and activities with coworkers and employees. You may be involved in pitching ideas at work, assigning people to teams for a particular project, or even socializing more with people from work. Then, on January 28, Mercury turns retrograde for the first time this year. So, from that date to February 18, when Mercury turns direct again, don't start anything new at work. Revise, reevaluate, and rethink your current projects. Since your sign is one that Mercury rules, any Mercury retrograde has an impact on your activities.

On January 24, Venus enters Capricorn and your fifth house, underscoring the themes of the new moon in this house. Romance, romance. If you're not involved when this transit begins (or at the time of the new moon in this sign), you will be before the transit ends on February 17. Or, you'll be having so much fun, with so many options for romantic involvement, that you won't be thinking about one partner or relationship. This transit should benefit your creative life tremendously, particularly if you have a natal rising or moon in Libra or Taurus, which Venus rules. Your muse is at your beck and call. Use this transit to finish your novel or screenplay, to get your portfolio together, to schedule and perform auditions.

January 25 marks a significant transit, when Pluto enters Capricorn, joining Jupiter in your fifth house. Talk about a lineup of astrological factors in your love and creativity house! Take a look at the introduction to see what this means on a global scale. For you personally, this transit is going to transform your love life and your creative endeavors. It's a long transit, too, lasting until 2024, so the changes will be subtle, taking place over time. Throughout the year, Pluto will retrograde back into Sagittarius and your fourth house, touching off family issues you've dealt with before. By the end of the year, the planet is firmly in Capricorn.

Mars started the year in retrograde motion, stirring up activities with friends and groups. On January 30, it turns direct again, in Gemini, your tenth house of career, setting the stage for next month's focus on professional issues.

Dates to watch for: January 24, when Venus enters your fifth house; January 25, when Pluto joins it; and January 28, when Mercury turns retrograde.

Best date: January 24, when Venus and Jupiter link up in Capricorn, your fifth house. Plan something special with your partner. Romance is a given today.

Virgo—February 2008

Buckle up, Virgo. It's a busy month, with two eclipses, the first pair of the year. The solar eclipse in Aquarius on February 6 occurs in your sixth house, indicating events that allow you to see something about your daily work routine in a more lucid light. Mercury is within a degree of this moon, so there's apt to be a lot of discussion about the revelations associated with this eclipse. Also, Venus in Capricorn and Uranus in Pisces each form a semi-sextile to this moon, a minor aspect that often feels like an itch you can't scratch. You know something is there, just beneath the surface, but you can't quite see what it is. Uranus brings an element of surprise to this eclipse and Venus indicates that it may involve a relationship or creative project.

Two weeks later, the lunar eclipse occurs in Pisces, your opposite sign, in your seventh house. This eclipse may bring up emotional issues related to relationships—romantic and professional. You can handle anything that comes up, just be prepared. Check any planets in your natal chart that lie at one degree—those will feel the impact of the lunar eclipse more strongly.

On February 17, Venus enters Aquarius and your sixth house, emphasizing some of the same themes as the new moon. Since it forms a quincunx to your sun, though, you may have to make attitude adjustments concerning an employee or coworker. A flirtation with a coworker may become something else under Venus's transit. Is this just a harmless flirtation for you or are you looking for something deeper, Virgo?

Finally, on February 18, Mercury turns direct again in Aquarius, your sixth house. Anything at work that has been confusing now clears up. And if you live in a cold climate and have been hankering to escape the February blues, it's safe to travel again!

Dates to watch for: both eclipse dates.

Best date: February 1, when Venus and Jupiter are holding hands in Capricorn, your fifth house of romance. Any time the two most beneficent planets in the zodiac link up, it's a day to remember.

Virgo—March 2008

March is busy astrologically and it all begins on March 4, when Mars enters Cancer and your eleventh house. This transit should galvanize your social life, with invitations pouring in for parties, group activities, perhaps even publicity events and promotions for your company or your own creative endeavors. Your intuition is strong during this transit, so don't hesitate to follow your hunches. This transit lasts until May 9.

The new moon in Pisces on March 7 is in your seventh house of partnerships. If you're not involved now, then this moon brings ample opportunities to meet people. With Mars in your eleventh house, some of those opportunities come through friends or groups with which you work. If you are involved in a relationship, this new moon may take things to a deeper, more committed level. Also, new business partnerships are possible now. You find a partner for your home-based business, you get a contract for a manuscript or screenplay, your company finds the investor it needs. Uranus is very close to this new moon, suggesting an element of unpredictability to the events that unfold. Expect the unexpected, Virgo!

Venus enters Pisces and your seventh house on

March 12. This transit, which lasts until April 6, should stimulate your love life. If you're not involved with anyone when the transit begins, you probably will be seeing someone before the transit ends. If you're involved in a relationship, then things pick up in a positive sense. This transit also favors business partnerships. You now find the manager or business partner who supports your vision and goals. If you would like to be involved in an artistic partnership of some kind, this transit presents you with the opportunities you need.

On March 14, Mercury enters Pisces and joins Venus in your seventh house. The combination of these two planets, plus the new moon in this house, underscores similar themes: new opportunities in romance, communication, travel, and partnerships. Your spouse or partner may need more of your support and nurturing at this time, which you're delighted to provide.

March 21 brings a full moon in Libra, your second house. This romantic moon attracts someone who shares your values and interests. It also illuminates a financial issue, so that you're armed with full information now and can make a decision.

Dates to watch for: the eclipse dates, naturally!

Best date: March 29, when Venus and Uranus are holding hands in your seventh house and Jupiter in your fifth house forms harmonious angles to both planets and to your sun. Talk about an awesome day for romance and creativity!

Virgo—April 2008

April features a number of transits and a full moon in a compatible water sign that should prove quite pleasant for you. Let's take a closer look.

On April 2, Mercury enters Aries and your eighth house. Between now and April 17, you may be dealing with wills, tax matters, and inheritances. Since tax day is coming up very quickly, be sure you've got all your paperwork in order and have claimed every deduction to which you're entitled. Also on April 2, Pluto turns retrograde in Capricorn, your fifth house. The effects of this movement will be subtle, but since they impact your love life, avoid power issues and struggles.

When Mercury enters Taurus on April 17, you suddenly have a yen for travel, and the more exotic the locale, the better. Be sure to schedule your trip either before May 26 or after June 19, when Mercury will be moving retrograde. If you're a writer in search of a publisher or an agent, this Mercury transit could open some doors. Be alert for signs that nudge in one direction or another.

On April 30, Venus follows Mercury into Taurus and your ninth house. This very nice transit promises romance abroad or with someone from a foreign country. It's also possible that your business expands into overseas markets, that your books sell to a foreign country, or that your screenplay is sold to a foreign distributor.

The new moon in Aries occurs on April 5, in your eighth house. This could portend good fortune with taxes and inheritances or with the study of esoteric subjects. This new moon also opens a different kind of door—to the unexplored, the uncharted. Ghosts, reincarnation, mediumship, and communication with the dead are all part of eighth house matters. So, buckle up for the ride, Virgo!

On or around the full moon in Scorpio on April 20, your passions are rising, your libido is kicking into high gear. You may realize that the chemistry you feel with a neighbor or someone you've met through a relative is mutual and undeniable. The big question now? What're you going to do about it?

Saturn in Virgo forms an exact sextile with this moon, bringing a curious ease and structure to a special relationship.

Dates to watch for: April 1–2, when Mercury and

Venus are conjunct in Pisces, your seventh house. Look for honest and open communication with a romantic or business partner.

Best dates: For the first ten days of the month, expansive Jupiter and unpredictable Uranus are conjunct in your seventh house. This curious combination could result in some surprisingly positive events with you and a partner.

Virgo—May 2008

Your ruler, Mercury, enters Gemini and your tenth house on May 2, galvanizing the career sector of your chart. If you travel under this transit, it will be for business rather than pleasure, although you're sure to enjoy yourself regardless. Try not to travel between May 26 and June 19, when Mercury is moving retrograde. During this retrograde period, make an attempt to communicate clearly with peers and bosses because the propensity for being misunderstood will be high.

May 5 features a new moon in compatible earth sign Taurus, in your ninth house. This moon should bring opportunities related to education, publishing, and long-distance travel. If you're a high school student narrowing the field of possible colleges, this new moon helps point you in the right direction. If you're a writer in search of a publisher, this moon could attract the company or individual you need. Uranus forms a wide (five degrees) sextile to this moon, suggesting that events happen suddenly, unexpectedly, and have an air of excitement about them.

The full moon in Scorpio two weeks later, on May 19, occurs in your third house. The period on or around this date has a passionate feel about it. Your emotions are running high and there could be some tension concerning your neighborhood or community or with a sibling. If you've thought about moving, this full moon may find you scoping out neighborhoods.

Mars enters Leo and your twelfth house on May 9. For the next couple of months, you may be spending more time in solitude. This certainly doesn't imply that you'll be lonely; in fact, you need this period to accomplish goals and complete projects that you've been working on for some time. This would be an excellent time to start a regular exercise program if you don't have one already and to work with dream recall.

On May 24, two days before Mercury turns retrograde, Venus enters Gemini and your tenth house. You'll enjoy this transit specifically because it facilitates everything in your career. You may feel that things are going so smoothly that you'll be tempted to kick back or take time off. Try to avoid that. Consider this transit a window of opportunity to forward your agenda.

Dates to watch for: May 26, when Mercury turns retrograde, and May 9, when Jupiter turns retrograde in your fifth house. The Jupiter retrograde could impact your love life, but in a subtle way because its energy is turned inward. You're scrutinizing what you really want in a partner during this retrograde, which lasts until September 7. On May 2, Saturn turns retrograde in your sign. Again, the effects of this movement are subtle, but there could now be delays or restrictions in your personal life.

Best dates: May 1–2. Mercury and Jupiter form a harmonious angle to each other and to your sun sign during these two days. Take advantage of the expansive mental energy available to you now.

Virgo—June 2008

The new moon in Gemini on June 3 looks extremely promising for your career. Whether it's a new job or even a new career altogether or a raise and significant promotion, you're in the driver's seat for the next thirty days. This new moon happens only once a year, so take advantage of it, Virgo. If you have new ideas or projects to pitch, wait until after Mercury turns direct on June 19. In the meantime, get your priorities lined up. You get help from Venus's proximity to this new moon (within two degrees) and also from Mercury's nearness to this moon, within five degrees. Both of these planets suggest ease, help from women, particularly women involved in the arts, and lots of discussions and debate.

The full moon on June 18 is in Sagittarius, your fourth house. Pluto is within a degree of this moon, indicating that power issues may surface at home. Or there could be a tug-of-war between your professional and family obligations. This full moon helps you grasp the larger picture of your home life and your career, however, and how you might combine the two—like through a home-based business, for instance.

Also on June 18, Venus enters Cancer and your eleventh house, stimulating activities and relationships with friends. Under this transit, you may join a political action group, offer your services to a charity, or get involved with some other group that supports your interests and passions. Try not to join anything, however, until Mercury turns direct on June 19. This Venus transit also opens up some intriguing possibilities with romance. You may meet someone who interests you through your friends or your group activities.

Mars continues its transit through Leo and your twelfth house, so you're paving the way for when Mars enters your sign on July 1. So clean up "internal debris," confront your demons, figure out your motivations, do whatever you need to do so that you begin with a clean slate on July 1.

Dates to watch for: Uranus, the planet of sudden, unexpected events, turns retrograde on June 26 in your seventh house. This retrograde movement has subtle effects on your partnerships. Between now and November 27, when Uranus turns direct again, you're scrutinizing what you want in your business and romantic partnerships. Between June 20 and 25, Mars in

Leo and Neptune in Aquarius are opposed to each other, creating tension between your daily work responsibilities and your need for solitude.

Best dates: on or around the new moon in Gemini on June 3.

Virgo—July 2008

There are four transits and two moons to watch for this month. It begins on July 1, when Mars enters your sign. This last happened two years ago, in July 2006, so look back to that time for any events or situations that stand out in memory. Some of the same patterns could be repeated. One thing this transit does is boost your physical energy. You suddenly can work longer hours, and seem more focused in everything you take on. If you're moving around too quickly, this Mars transit lends itself to clumsiness, so watch where you step!

The new moon on July 2 is in Cancer, your eleventh house. This moon brings opportunities to forge new friendships and to work with groups. If you're politically active, then this transit provides the opportunity to find like-minded individuals. If you've always wanted to join a writers' or theater group, the next thirty days bring a chance to find that group. This new moon is within six degrees of Venus, which suggests the possibility of romance with someone you meet through friends or through a group.

On July 10, Mercury enters Cancer, so some of the themes of the new moon are emphasized. Debate and discussion are hallmarks of this transit. You also should listen closely to your intuition during this time, particularly as it pertains to your family and one of your parents. On July 26, Mercury enters Leo and your twelfth house, suggesting that your daily life will be unfolding behind the scenes, perhaps in solitude. If you have deadlines to meet, this transit helps you meet them. It also favors therapy—but the therapist could be a trusted friend or partner.

The full moon on July 18 is in Capricorn, your fifth house. Talk about romantic! Make maximum use of this full moon by planning something special with your partner. If you're not involved, then get out and be seen. This moon also illuminates an issue related to one of your children—if not a flesh-and-blood child, then a child of your imagination, your creativity.

Date to watch for: July 3 could be challenging. Venus and Pluto form a wide trine to each other, but difficult angles to your sun. The challenges could surface at home, in your love life, or simply within.

Best dates: July 10–12, when Mars and Saturn are conjunct in your sign. If you use the energy right, this conjunction can help you find the proper structure for a personal project or issue. Follow your instincts on these days and you'll know exactly what to do and when to do it.

Virgo—August 2006

In addition to five transits this month, there are also another pair of eclipses and an extra new moon. In other words, Virgo, August is filled with activity, and things get off to a running start with a solar eclipse in Leo on August 1. This eclipse happens in your twelfth house, the house of what's hidden, the house of karma. It's possible that you now perceive some long-standing issue or concern in a completely different way. A past-life memory could surface as the result of an interaction with another person or spontaneously, perhaps as the result of a dream or insight. Mercury is close to this eclipse degree, suggesting discussion and debate.

On August 5, you enter one of the most romantic periods of this year, when Venus enters your sign. Your sex appeal soars, your creativity deepens, and if you're not involved, you probably will be before this transit ends on August 30. Then, on August 10, Mercury follows Venus into your sign. This combination of planets confers great facility and ease for communication in any form. You're able to talk openly with your partner, the two of you baring your souls without fear of reprisal. Mars is still in your sign at this time, too, so all the inner planets are stacked in your favor. If you're involved in a sexual relationship, then things are looking very positive.

August 16 features a lunar eclipse in Aquarius, your sixth house. Something emotional or intuitive surfaces that concerns your daily work or health. Be sure to follow your hunches around this time and to be vigilant for any hints the universe tosses your way. Synchronicities abound.

Mars enters Libra and your second house on August 19, galvanizing your finances. You either spend more or bring in more or both! You may be working two jobs to make ends meet, or, more likely, you're working harder to earn overtime for some special event. You may have an opportunity between August 19 and October 3 to change jobs—a job where you're offered more money. Mercury follows Mars into Libra and your second house on August 28, a transit that indicates discussion and debate about your finances—what you earn, what you spend, and your beliefs about money.

Then, on August 30, Venus enters Libra and your second house, too, so everything now is about money and your personal values. One possibility suggested by the combined energy of these three planets in your second house is that you and a partner go into business together and suddenly discover that you're making more money by integrating your individual skills than you ever did alone.

The second new moon this month occurs on August

30, in your sign. Saturn is within three degrees of this moon and strongly urges you to follow the rules in terms of any opportunity that comes to you in the next thirty days!

Date to watch for: August 16. Not only is it the day of the lunar eclipse, but Mars and Pluto are square to each other, suggesting power plays.

Best dates: August 12–18, when Venus and retrograde Jupiter form a beautiful angle to each other, expanding and blessing your love life.

Virgo—September 2008

You'll be glad to know that Saturn turns direct in your sign on September 2. Now you can begin reaping some of this planet's benefits—tangible results of any inner work you've been doing, for instance, or finding the proper structure for something in your personal life. It could be something as simple as getting organized or practicing feng shui on a particular area of your home.

Venus moves into passionate Scorpio and your third house on September 23. This transit is sure to bring about a new relationship if you aren't involved right now. This new romance could be with a neighbor or someone you meet through a community activity or organization in which you're involved.

September 24 marks the beginning of the last Mercury retrograde for the year. It occurs in Libra, your money house, so there may be delays related to all financial matters. During this retrograde period, someone may challenge you on your beliefs or values. The best way to deal with it is to not argue or debate the issue.

The full moon on September 15 is in Pisces, your opposite sign, and seventh house. It's a terrific moon for romance and imagination, but there could be a little tension because you feel torn between your responsibilities to a partner and your responsibilities to yourself. The new moon in Libra on September 29 marks the beginning of a propitious financial period, in which you have new opportunities for earning money.

Dates to watch for: Since most of the month's themes revolve around money, the dates to watch for include the beginning of Mercury retrograde, on September 24, and September 22–23, when Mercury and Mars are conjunct in your second house, bringing plenty of mental energy and brainstorming to the issue of money.

Best dates: September 13–20, when Mercury, Venus, and Mars are all gathered in your second house, urging balance and harmony where money matters are concerned. If there was ever a time when you hoped to find a way to earn money that's more in line with your beliefs and values, this trio provides the opportunity to do so.

Virgo—October 2008

The best news this month occurs on October 15, when your ruler, Mercury, turns direct again. Now that it's safe to invest and travel again, do both to your heart's content! There won't be any more Mercury retrogrades until 2009, Virgo, so you're in the clear!

On October 3, Mars enters passionate Scorpio and your third house. This transit may put you squarely in the middle of a community or neighborhood dispute. Rather than taking sides or engaging in debate or arguments, back off and become an observer. You'll learn more about the truth of the situation. This transit forms a harmonious angle to your sun and certainly can heighten your libido! If you're not involved with anyone when the transit starts, you may find yourself in a highly charged sexual relationship before the transit ends on November 16.

Venus enters Sagittarius on October 18. Your love

life at home picks up. You and a partner may decide to move in together if you aren't living with each other already or you could decide to buy a place together. Your artistic work either reflects your home life at this time or you now set up a studio or office at home that is reserved for your creative work. However this transit unfolds for you, be grateful for what you have. Sometimes, gratitude goes a very long way.

What about this month's moons? Of the two, you'll like the new moon best, but let's take a look first at the full moon in Aries on October 14. Around or on this date, you could experience tension related to resources you share with someone else—a partner, a child, or a spouse. Since Neptune forms a close and harmonious angle with this moon (but not with your sun sign), it could be that you have been trying to make decisions without having all the information. Well, Virgo, you'll have the full pot of information with this moon to make an informed decision.

The new moon on October 28 is in Scorpio, your third house. This moon forms a harmonious angle with your sun and suggests that you find the neighborhood where you would like to live, make new friends and acquaintances within your community, or discover that you're about to have a brother or sister. Since new moons represent opportunities related to house and sign, it's also possible that an opportunity for research or investigations comes your way or that you have the opportunity to heal a relationship with a sibling or neighbor.

Dates to watch for: October 2–3. A power struggle or power issues may surface at home.

Best dates: October 5–6, when Venus and Jupiter form harmonious angles to each other and to your sun. Pay close attention to everything that happens to you during this two-day period, especially where romance is concerned. It's your lucky day!

There's a lot of stuff going on this month, Virgo, and it all begins on November 4, when Mercury enters Scorpio and your third house. This transit should kick-start your communication talents, making it easier to meet writing deadlines, to touch base with your e-mail list of clients, and to do whatever you need to do to tie up loose ends at work. You may have more contact than usual with siblings and other relatives under this transit and may be taking several short-distance trips by car.

Venus enters Capricorn and your fifth house on November 12, one of the most romantic transits this year. The transit lasts until December 7, so take advantage of it. If you're not involved with anyone right now, get out and be seen, create more options for yourself. If you are involved, this period should be extremely pleasant for the relationship, particularly until November 16, when Mars in Scorpio is forming a harmonious angle to your sun and to transiting Venus.

The full moon on November 13 is in a compatible earth sign, Taurus, and your ninth house. This moon snaps elements of your worldview into clarity. You may have a better idea now how to deal with your deeper beliefs and understand how they help to create your reality. Take some time to read Masaru Emoto's book *The Hidden Messages in Water,* and then practice expressing love and gratitude.

There are some Sagittarius and home themes this month that begin on November 16, when Mars enters Sagittarius, continue when Mercury enters Sagittarius on November 23, and reach a pinnacle with the new moon in Sagittarius on November 27. So what does it all mean? Let's take a look at the transit of Mars, which remains in your fourth house until December 27. Expect lots of activity at home—people visiting, your family members coming and going at all hours, a lot of hustle and bustle. When Mercury is added to the mix, you're able to grasp the larger picture related to a personal or home issue. You may do more traveling under this transit, probably for pleasure, and could feel a stronger need to move elsewhere.

If you've thought about moving, the new moon in Sagittarius brings ample opportunities to explore the possibilities.

Date to watch for: November 12, when Venus enters Capricorn and your fifth house.

Best dates: November 12–December 7.

Virgo—December 2008

Taking stock at the beginning of the last month of 2008, all the planets are moving direct, so their energies are functioning as they should. The situation remains like that until New Year's Eve, when Saturn turns retrograde in Virgo. But more on that in a moment.

On December 7, Venus enters Aquarius and your sixth house, making a romance or flirtation at work very likely. It'll be up to you whether you want to take this relationship any further. Since Mars will still be moving through Sagittarius, forming a harmonious angle with Venus, a deepening of the relationship looks positive.

On December 12, there are two noteworthy events. Mercury enters Capricorn and your fifth house, and there's a full moon in Gemini in your tenth house. The first transit indicates that you'll be in a communicative mood, eager to get your point of view across. If you get involved in a relationship under this transit, the attraction, for you, will have to begin in the mind, in how well the other person understands you and communicates his or her feelings. This transit is terrific for writers or anyone in the public relations or advertising business. The full moon should be excellent for professional matters. A project or issue is brought to a culmination—you finish what you started. Don't start anything new under this full moon; tie up all loose ends. Get your desk cleared for the holidays.

On December 27, Mars follows Mercury into Capricorn and your fifth house. Your libido kicks into high gear and so does your creative drive. Perhaps they are one and the same for you now. You could be writing a romance or erotic novel or your life may read like an erotic novel. Mars combined with Mercury gives great energy to anything you say or write. Your energy and passion shine.

Date to watch for: December 31, when Saturn turns retrograde in your sign. This movement may mess up your New Year's Eve plans, perhaps through some restriction or delay. Perhaps your babysitter can't make it or the star of the festivities can't come. Best advice? Go with the flow and have contingency plans.

Best date: December 25, when Venus and Neptune are conjunct in your sixth house. Perhaps your office romance is more important than you think. It may speak to your ideas.

Brainstorming

Envision yourself a year, two years, or four years from now. What is your life like? Where do you live? Is your work satisfying to you? Are you single, married, a parent? Are you happy? Do you have enough money? Is your health good? What are your spiritual beliefs? Are you a vehicle for change in your family or community? In the space below, describe the life you would like to be living a year or two or four up the line. Be as outrageous, creative, and wild as you want. After all, it's *your* life. If you can imagine it, then you can create it.

My Life in _____ (choose a year)

_____
_____
_____
_____
_____
_____
_____
_____
_____
_____
_____
_____

HAPPY 2009!

The Big Picture for Libra
in 2008

Welcome to 2008, Libra! Let's start with the magnificent news first—and that's Jupiter in Capricorn, your fourth house, your home and family. Jupiter, as the planet of expansion, promises at least one of several possibilities: you move to a larger home or expand your existing home; your family grows—a baby or someone moves in with you; you gain a generally luckier feeling about your home life; or you purchase property, perhaps for investment purposes. Your connection to the collective unconscious deepens and grows in some way, perhaps through a creative project or through a broadening of your spiritual beliefs.

On January 25, Pluto joins Jupiter in your fourth house. Pluto is about profound and permanent transformation, so you can expect monumental changes in your home and family life. Pluto retrogrades back into Sagittarius and your third house through the year, then finally enters Capricorn for good on November 26. This means you'll feel Pluto's impact in your third house of communication off and on this year. But you already know what that means, since you have been living with it since 1995.

Saturn entered Virgo in the fall of 2007 and is now in your twelfth house, which governs all that is hidden in our lives. In a sense, for the next year you'll be clearing out long-standing issues so that you begin with a clean slate when Saturn enters your sign in the fall of 2009. Saturn governs the rules of physical existence—that's probably why it's known as the planet of karma!—so your exploration of your own unconscious should be put into some sort of context. Meditation, for instance. Or therapy. Or even just a trusted partner, friend, or family member in whom you can confide.

Uranus, the planet of sudden, unpredictable events, continues its transit of Pisces and your sixth house. The angle it forms to your sun indicates that you must make adjustments in your attitudes throughout the year when it comes to your daily work and health. Maybe a boss or coworker is driving you crazy. Rather than placing the blame on the other person, ask yourself what lesson you're supposed to learn from this individual. Chances are that once you learn the lesson, whatever it is, the problem will disappear. You, after all, are the consummate charmer of the zodiac and should be able to charm your way through any challenge.

Neptune is still transiting Aquarius and your fifth house, which it's been doing since 1998. Since it is the planet of higher inspiration—as well as illusion—you may not be seeing your romantic partners as they really are. You may put these people on pedestals or your idealism gets in the way of an honest relationship. Or, another possibility is that your idealism is what binds you to your romantic partners.

Neptune in the fifth house is excellent for artistic and creative projects—dance, art, music, fiction writing, photography, acting, moviemaking. If you have interests in any of these areas, dive in, Libra. Indulge yourself.

BEST TIME FOR ROMANCE

Mark the dates between August 30 and September 22, when Venus is in your sign. Your romantic quota soars. You're also more artistic and others see you in a more flattering light. You feel more confident and your sex appeal rises. Great backup dates for romance fall between February 17 and March 11, when Venus is transiting your fifth house of love and forming a beautiful angle to your sun.

Other excellent dates for romance (and just about anything else) fall between May 11 and 13 and September 3 and 5, when the sun and Jupiter see eye to eye and there's a nice flow of energy between them.

BEST TIME FOR CAREER DECISIONS

Make career decisions between June 18 and July 11, when Venus is transiting your tenth house of careers. This should be quite a smooth time professionally. In fact, things may be going along so smoothly that you'll be tempted to kick back and relax. Don't. Seize the opportunity. There will be a lot of traveling, coming and going, and socializing during this period. Communication will be vital.

MERCURY RETROGRADES

Every year, there are three periods when Mercury—the planet of communication and travel—turns retrograde. During these periods, it's wisest not to negotiate or sign contracts, to travel, to submit manuscripts, or to make major decisions. Granted, we can't live our lives entirely by Mercury retrogrades! If you have to travel during the periods listed below, however, then expect changes in your plans. If you have to sign a contract, expect to revise it.

It's also a good idea to back up computer files before Mercury turns retrograde. Quite often, computers and other communication devices act up. Be sure your virus software is up to date, too. Pay special attention to the house in which Mercury retrograde falls. It will tell you the area of your life most likely to be impacted. The periods to watch for in 2008 are:

January 28–February 18: retrograde in Aquarius, your fifth house of romance and creativity. Best course? Review and revise all creative projects and don't start a new relationship—unless it's with someone from the past who reappears in your life.

May 26–June 19: retrograde in Gemini, your ninth

house, your worldview. It definitely won't be a propitious time for overseas travel or for signing up for college or graduate school courses. Someone may challenge your beliefs. Defend yourself, but without being confrontational.

September 24–October 15: retrograde in Libra. Whenever Mercury turns retrograde in your own sign, your life feels like you're inside of a bumper car.

ECLIPSES

Every year, there are four eclipses, two solar and two lunar. Solar eclipses trigger external events that allow us to see something that eluded us before. They can bring about beginnings and endings. When an eclipse hits one of your natal planets, it's especially important. Take note of the sign and house placement. Lunar eclipses bring up emotional issues related to the sign and house into which they fall.

Here are the dates to watch for:

February 6: solar eclipse at seventeen degrees Aquarius, your fifth house of romance and creativity. You'll be able to see something about your romantic partnerships and creative projects that you haven't perceived before. A new relationship may appear, though, or new creative opportunities.

February 20: lunar eclipse at ten degrees Virgo, your twelfth house. Long-standing issues stir up emotions you thought you had conquered. You may spend time visiting someone in a hospital or nursing home. You may be spending time in solitude, too.

August 1: solar eclipse, nine degrees Leo, in your eleventh house. Something about a friend or a group to which you belong becomes glaringly obvious.

August 16: lunar eclipse at twenty-four degrees Aquarius, your fifth house of romance and creativity. This house seems to take a lot of hits this year, but roll with the punches, Libra, and you'll come out just fine.

LUCKIEST DAYS IN 2008

Every year, Jupiter forms a beneficial angle with the

sun, usually a conjunction, when both planets are in the same sign. In 2008, the angle is a lovely trine and it occurs during two time periods: May 11–13 and September 3–5. If you're going to buy a lotto ticket, do it during these periods!

Now let's take a look at what 2008 has in store for you month by month.

Twelve Months of Predictions for Libra
January–December 2008

Libra—January 2008

The first new moon of 2008 occurs on January 8, in Capricorn, and sets the tone for the month. This moon falls in your fourth house, so you can expect new opportunities in terms of your home and family. If you've thought about moving, now is the time to start looking at neighborhoods, houses, and property. Or, equally possible, your family grows—there's a birth, or a friend or relative moves in. It's also possible that you may be expanding your home in some way, perhaps by adding a room or remodeling.

The full moon two weeks later, on January 22, is in Leo, your eleventh house. Plan something special with friends on or around this date. This should be a festive time for you. The point of this full moon is to get out and be seen, Libra!

Your ruler, Venus, begins the year in Sagittarius, your third house. This transit probably has caused a flirtation with a neighbor or someone you met through a brother or sister to heat up considerably. You have to decide if you want just a flirtation or something more.

On January 24, Venus enters Capricorn and your fourth house, signaling a romantic and enjoyable time at home, with your partner. You may decide to create a home office for yourself, using colors and furniture

163

arrangements that enhance feelings of harmony and peace. Try putting in a small fountain. The sound of running water will facilitate your creativity.

Mercury begins the year in Capricorn, your fourth house. This suggests there's a lot of activity in your home during the first week of the year. Perhaps guests are leaving, kids are starting school, and you're on a fast track into 2008. On January 7, Mercury enters Aquarius and follows Venus into your fifth house, making it likely that communication will be vital in any of your romantic relationships. On January 28, Mercury turns retrograde for the first time this year, in Aquarius. This period may feel strange to you, with your social calendar changing constantly as appointments are broken or forgotten altogether. Read over the section on Mercury retrogrades in the big picture for Libra. The retrograde doesn't end until February 18.

Mars begins the year retrograde in Cancer, your tenth house. Since Mars represents our physical and sexual energy, you may be feeling overwhelmed at work. Don't pitch any new projects until after January 30, when Mars turns direct again, or, better yet, wait until after February 18, when Mercury will be moving direct, too. Once Mars turns direct, things you have put on hold in your profession will begin to move forward again.

Dates to watch for: January 24, when Venus enters your fourth house, and January 25, when Pluto joins it. The Pluto transit is especially significant. Over the next several decades, this planet's transit will cause profound and permanent changes in your home and family life.

Best date: January 24, when Venus and Jupiter link up in Capricorn, your fourth house. Plan something special with your partner. Romance is a given today.

Libra—February 2008

Buckle up, Libra. It's going to be a wild, bumpy month. On February 6, the solar eclipse in Aquarius, your fifth house, brings clarity to a romantic relationship, to a creative project, or to your relationship with your kids, if you have them. New opportunities may come up in all these areas. Mercury is within a degree of the sun during this eclipse, suggesting a lot of discussion and lively debate. Venus is exactly square to the eclipse degree, indicating that a source of possible tension is a romantic relationship.

. Two weeks later, on February 20, the lunar eclipse in Virgo occurs in your twelfth house. Emotions surface concerning something that has been hidden in your life. With Saturn so close to this moon, your emotions may be connected to an older individual who is in a hospital or nursing home.

On February 17, Venus enters Aquarius and your fifth house, signaling one of the most romantic periods for you this year. A day later, Mercury turns direct in Aquarius, so you're in very good shape with love and romance for the rest of the month. Your creative life takes on a new dimension, too, with greater insights into your own creative process.

Dates to watch for: the eclipse dates, for sure, and February 18, when Mercury turns direct. February 22 could be problematic with a relationship.

Best dates: February 23–26, when Jupiter and Uranus form a harmonious angle to each other, perhaps urging you to set up your home office or work more out of your home.

Libra—March 2008

The new moon in Pisces on March 7 brings new opportunities to your daily work. You may get a job offer that excites you. If so, it will arrive suddenly, unexpectedly, and you'll have to decide quickly about accepting it. With Uranus so close to this new moon, your usual work routine is sure to be disrupted in some way, but this will be an exciting time for you, Libra, so stay on your toes.

The full moon in your sign on March 21 brings to light something in your personal life that could be causing you tension. Pluto forms a difficult angle to this moon, indicating that power issues may be at the root of the tensions. If you can resolve this dilemma, the full moon turns out to be romantic!

Aside from the two moons this month, look to March 4 for a burst of energy related to your career. Mars moves into your tenth house, indicating a powerful period (until May 9) in which you're in the driver's seat. Your intuition is right on target now and you have the physical energy to complete projects and pitch new ideas. Peers and bosses should be receptive to your ideas.

On March 12, your ruler, Venus, enters Pisces, your sixth house, emphasizing some of the new moon themes. Your imagination is strong during this transit and you're able to apply some of your ideas to your daily work routine. You may be more concerned about your physical appearance during this transit, so if you don't already have a regular exercise routine, start one. This is also an excellent time to revamp your wardrobe.

Mercury follows Venus into your sixth house on March 14. Expect a lot of discussion and social activities with coworkers and employees during this transit. With both Mercury and Venus now in your sixth house, any flirtation or romance that develops through work will be based on solid, open communication.

Dates to watch for: March 28, when Venus and Uranus are conjunct in Pisces. Unpredictable events and situations surface in a relationship at work.

Best date: March 7, when Mercury and Venus are both in Aquarius, your fifth house. You and your partner may be spending late nights talking and cozying up!

Libra—April 2008

The new moon on April 5 is in Aries, your seventh house. This moon sweeps in new opportunities in partnerships—either romantic or professional. If you're not involved with anyone right now, you probably will be before April ends. It's not just a new moon in your seventh house that does it, but also the transits of Mercury and Venus in the same sign and house. The Mercury transit begins on April 2 (and ends on April 17) and the Venus transit goes from April 6 to 30. The combination of planets puts communication at the top of your list of needs in personal relationships. Without it, even your rushing passions won't be quite as heated.

The full moon on April 20 is in Scorpio, your second house. This moon brings to light a financial issue where your values may come into play. Due to the nature of Scorpio, you'll be investigating or researching money matters around or on this full moon. There could be some tensions with a partner over money. But no one dislikes confrontation more than you do, Libra, so you'll do everything you can to make sure the tensions dissipate.

On April 17, Mercury enters Taurus, your eighth house. Pay close attention to any events concerning shared resources that unfold over the next few weeks. These events may provide hints of the tensions that could surface around the full moon. You may be discussing things like wills and tax issues with an expert. And don't forget tax day on April 15!

On April 30, Venus joins Mercury in Taurus, setting the stage next month for an ease in obtaining mortgages and loans. Your spouse or partner could get a raise, too.

Dates to watch for: During the first ten days of the month, Jupiter in Capricorn and Uranus in Pisces are making a harmonious angle to each other but not to your sun. Any tension that develops between your home and work life looks worse than it is.

Best dates: April 1–2, when Mercury and Venus are in your sixth house, creating romantic sparks between you and a coworker.

Libra—May 2008

May looks like a busy and exciting month. The action gets off to a running start on May 2, when Mercury enters Gemini, one of the signs it rules, and your ninth house. This transit certainly puts you in a very good place if you're a writer or work in the publishing or travel industries. Business suddenly picks up and things seem to fall into your lap without much effort on your part. You've got no shortage of ideas.

On May 5, the new moon in Taurus occurs in your eighth house, alongside Venus. You're in a very good place now for obtaining mortgages and loans. Your partner's income may shoot up, which benefits you as well, and new opportunities arrive related to the investigation of esoteric topics. Maybe it's time you tried a past-life regression or visited a medium!

May 9 features a Mars transit into Leo, a fire sign compatible with your sign. It's in your eleventh house of friends. Between now and July 1, when Mars changes signs again, you can expect a lot of activities and social events with friends. You may join a political action committee or some other group whose focus fits your interests.

The full moon on May 19 is another one in Scorpio, so some of last month's full moon themes concerning money and finances may be repeating themselves. This moon is in the last degrees of Scorpio—twenty-nine degrees and fifty-six minutes—indicating an urgency to resolve the issues, whatever they are.

On May 24, Venus enters Gemini and your ninth house, emphasizing the themes of the new moon. Romance is possible with a foreign-born person or with someone you meet while traveling overseas. Mercury turns retrograde in Gemini on May 26, however, so the romantic interest could be with someone from your past who appears in your life again. If you're traveling overseas when this transit begins, expect changes in your schedule and try to be as flexible as possible. If you're not traveling yet, then delay it until after June 19, when Mercury turns direct again.

Dates to watch for: May 2, when Saturn in Virgo turns direct. The effects of this movement are subtle but impact your twelfth house. You now can move forward in your therapy, meditation, and dream recall. May 26, when Mercury turns retrograde.

Best dates: May 29–31, when Venus in Gemini and Mars in Leo make harmonious angles to each other and to your sun, firing up your love life. It's possible that you meet someone through friends or a group to which you belong.

Libra—June 2008

The new moon on June 3 should be a good one for you, Libra. It's in a fellow air sign, Gemini, and your ninth house, indicating new opportunities for foreign travel and investments, for expanding your business or product to an overseas market, and for romance with a foreign-born individual. Try not to start anything new until after June 19, however, when Mercury turns direct again. This new moon, by the way, is very close to Venus, indicating that romance is a distinct possibility. You may also get some sort of break in the arts.

The full moon on June 18 is in Sagittarius and Pluto is only a degree away. This moon occurs in your third house—siblings, relatives, neighbors, communication, and travel—and indicates that a power issue of some kind surfaces. Also on this date, Venus enters Cancer and your tenth house. This transit favors all professional endeavors. A raise or promotion could be right around the corner, particularly after June 19, when Mercury is moving direct again. Pitch your ideas and push your agenda—you've got the Midas touch until July 12, when Venus changes signs again.

A day after the full moon, Mercury turns direct in Gemini. Pack your bags, Libra, send out your e-mail newsletter, touch base with clients again, and let your life move into forward motion again.

Dates to watch for: June 19, when Mercury turns direct. June 20–26, when Mars is opposed to Neptune, creating a tension between your creative needs and those of other people.

Best date: the new moon on June 3.

Libra—July 2008

This month, the astrological weather is changeable, busy, and will keep you on your toes! It starts on July 1, when Mars enters Virgo and your twelfth house. For the next six or seven weeks, until August 19, you'll be spending a lot of time alone and probably enjoying it. This doesn't necessarily mean you'll become a hermit, Libra, but that you may need the time-out from your concerns about relationships. Think of this transit as preparation for when Mars enters your sign on August 19.

On July 2, the new moon in Cancer presents some very interesting and fresh opportunities in your career and professional life. This moon occurs only once a year, so for clues, look back to the same moon around July 6, 2007, and try to recall what kinds of professional opportunities came your way. This moon is within six degrees of Venus, indicating an element of luck and help from women.

Two weeks later, the full moon in Capricorn and your fourth house could create some tension between your professional and family responsibilities. But it's an excellent moon for setting out goals and a strategy for achieving them. Uranus forms a close angle with this moon, so whatever unfolds from this moon, it will be sudden.

In between these two moons, on July 10, Mercury enters Cancer and your tenth house, bringing the gift of gab to all of your professional activities. There's an element of intuition that rides tandem with Mercury in this sign, and until July 26 you'll be homed right in on it.

On July 12, Venus enters Leo and your eleventh house. This beautiful transit, compatible with your sun, certainly activates your social life. Suddenly, you're the light at the party and have your choice of social invitations. A romance is possible with someone you meet through a group to which you belong and whom you thought was a friend.

On July 26, Mercury enters Leo, your eleventh house, adding zest and pizzazz to your social activities with friends. It's as if everyone now gravitates toward you, particularly since Mercury is sharing this space with lovely Venus. Your sex appeal should soar!

Date to watch for: July 1, when Mars enters Virgo. You could feel a little blue today, but it will pass.

Best date: July 3, when Venus in Leo and Pluto in Sagittarius form a harmonious angle to each other and to your sun sign. You're in the driver's seat now where relationships are concerned. Don't let anyone try to tell you otherwise.

Libra—August 2008

Eclipses always make a month more challenging, and in August there are two of them. On August 1, the solar eclipse in Leo occurs in your eleventh house. You now perceive something about a friend that has eluded you before. Whatever you see should be quite positive and lead to lively discussions, thanks to Mercury's proximity to this moon. New opportunities now come to you through friends and some of those opportunities could include new friendships.

Two weeks later, on August 16, there's a lunar eclipse in Aquarius, your fifth house. Expect an emotional issue to surface related to creativity, romance, or kids. Neptune is close to this eclipse degree, so you can expect that the emotions you experience have to do with your ideals. Perhaps someone around you isn't meeting your ideals. Or maybe your creative projects don't seem to express them.

Then, on August 30, there's a second new moon, a real bonus! This new moon is in Virgo, and brings many opportunities to help others through service. You also find opportunities to enjoy your own company, in solitude, something you may need right now.

The other interesting transits this month are good for you. Mars enters your sign on August 19. This happens every two years, so look back to the fall of 2006 to get a hint about some of the things that may rush into your life. Your physical energy should be excellent, however, and if you're involved with someone right now, things should be humming right along.

Now, backing up a bit more, mark August 5, when Venus enters Virgo, your twelfth house. A secret romance or affair may be in the offing. Be sure that the heart you break isn't your own! This won't be secret for very long.

Mercury follows Venus on August 10, right into Virgo and your twelfth house. These two planets are traveling closely together all year, adding communication skills to your sex appeal. On August 28, Mercury sails into your sign and, two days later, so does Venus. Wow, this is a perfect setup for making next month utterly superb.

Dates to watch for: all of them. It's a hectic month.

Best dates: August 12–14, when Venus and Jupiter form a harmonious angle to each other, lifting your relationships out of the doldrums and into a space where you can build on what you share.

Libra—September 2008

September should be a bit calmer than August was. You can at least kick back for a while and enjoy whatever good things are unfolding in your life now, Libra. And those good things begin with Jupiter turning direct in Capricorn, your fourth house, on September 7. While this movement initially may not seem like such a big deal, you'll discover a certain smoothness to the expansion in your home and family life now. If you've been wanting to start a family, now is the time to give it a try!

The full moon in Pisces on September 15 occurs in your sixth house. Health and work, Libra. You'll have to make an attitude adjustment on or around this full moon, and it probably will be related to your daily work routine or your daily health. If you don't have a regular exercise routine already, now is the time to start one. Uranus is within three degrees of this full moon, so events happen quickly, unexpectedly, and are certain to surprise you.

Mark September 23. Venus enters Scorpio, your second house of money, and oh yes, the good times roll. Unfortunately, Mercury turns retrograde the next day, in your sign. This is a major *ouch*. Any time Mercury retrogrades in your sun sign, events disrupt your daily life at all levels. Your phones act up, your computer misbehaves, your car throws a temper tantrum, your kids act up, your partner acts strangely . . . you get the idea. Nothing is routine. Your best recourse is to revise and rethink, review and reevaluate, and try to go with the flow. By October 15, it's all over!

Now, to the new moon on September 29. It's in Libra, and does it ever promise wonderful things. This new moon happens only once a year and brings all kinds of new opportunities for you personally, in any area of your life.

Date to watch for: September 24, when Mercury turns retrograde.

Best dates: September 22–23, when Mercury and Mars are conjunct in your sign, bringing passion and zeal to your ideas and assuring that any romantic relationship that begins under this combination has a cardinal rule: *Talk to me*.

Libra—October 2008

It's a money month for you, Libra. Don't run out and splurge yet, but know that your finances are about to improve tenfold. First, let's take a look at this month's moons.

On October 14, the full moon in Aries hits your seventh house of partnerships, so romance and commitment are definitely on your mind. Pluto forms a wide trine to this moon (six degrees), indicating that you're in a powerful position personally. As long as power issues don't surface on or around this full moon, your love life should pick up considerably!

Two weeks later, on October 28, the new moon in Scorpio and your second house promises a vast improvement in your finances as new moneymaking opportunities head your way. Your values come into play during the next thirty days, too, perhaps urging you to work at something that reflects who you really are.

Besides these two moons, mark down October 3, when Mars enters Scorpio and your second house. This really starts the galvanization process for improved finances promised by the new moon. You may be working longer hours and researching ways to improve your finances. Or, you're paying off debt and working diligently to save money.

On October 15, Mercury turns direct again in your sign. This will feel as if a burden of chaos has been lifted. Then, on October 18, your ruler, Venus, enters Sagittarius, a fire sign compatible with your sun sign. This transit promises a romance or, at the very least, a flirtation with a neighbor or someone you meet through a brother or sister. If you're a writer, in the travel or communication business, Venus's transit through your third house promises an ease and smoothness to your communication skills and facilitates daily travel. You're now the darling on the block, Libra, so put this energy to good use.

Date to watch for: October 5, when Venus and Jupiter form a challenging angle to each other. But even a challenging angle with these two stars of the zodiac is not all that serious. You may just have an urge to spend more than you should today.

Best dates: October 2–3, when Mars in Libra and Pluto in Sagittarius form a nice angle to each other that empowers you.

Libra—November 2008

Mercury enters Scorpio and your second house, putting the emphasis on finances, which is right in line with last month's new moon. There's a lot of discussion about finances—perhaps setting up a budget, gauging your expenses, and balancing the books. You may be in negotiations for a raise or promotion.

Venus enters Capricorn and your fourth house on November 12, lighting up your love life at home. You and your partner are in a good place now to plan for the future and to build on the foundation you've established. Venus is now sharing your fourth house with Jupiter, so the combination of the two planets may prompt you to beautify your home in some way.

New furniture, fresh paint, more vibrant colors, even practicing some feng shui are all in order.

On November 16, Mars enters Sagittarius and your third house, heightening opportunities for travel and involvement in your neighborhood and community. The Mars transit is, in a way, a precursor to the new moon in Sagittarius on November 27, but more on that in a moment. Mars in Sagittarius is compatible with your sun sign and allows you to grasp the larger picture of a relationship with a neighbor or sibling.

The full moon on November 13 forms harmonious angles with unpredictable Uranus and with stable Saturn. Your spouse or partner may have a sudden change in income, but thanks to Saturn, other resources become available.

The new moon on November 27 should be a beauty for you. Both Mars and Mercury are close in degree to this moon, indicating lively discussions and action. You may be looking at other neighborhoods, in anticipation of a move.

Dates to watch for: November 1, when Neptune turns direct again in Aquarius, your fifth house. Now you can bring your idealism into any romantic relationship. November 26, when Pluto finally enters Capricorn again and continues its very long transit through your fourth house. Things at home may seem chaotic initially, but as this planet's transit stabilizes, a move certainly is a good possibility.

Best date: November 27, that new moon in Sagittarius.

Libra—December 2008

As you head into the last month of the year, every planet is now moving in direct motion, which means they're functioning the way they should. Good thing, because December features a number of noteworthy transits and lunations.

On December 7, Venus enters Aquarius and your fifth house, signaling one of the romantic periods for this year. Any relationship that begins under this transit will be based on solid, open communication and an almost prescient sense of recognition that the two of you have shared lives before.

Mercury enters Capricorn and your fourth house on December 12. Expect a lot of movement and activity at home between now and the end of the year. Guests arrive for the holidays, your kids are coming and going at all hours, and there's a lot of talk and discussion. Also on December 12, the full moon in Gemini heightens the discussions and illuminates differences of opinion about politics, books, spiritual issues, even foreign travel and countries. If you're a writer or work in the publishing field, this full moon brings completion to a project or issue.

Two weeks later, on December 27, the new moon in Capricorn underscores some of the Mercury themes mentioned above. You're prepared to move now and could be doing it early next year or even before the end of the year, depending on your personal situation.

On New Year's Eve, Saturn turns retrograde in Virgo, your twelfth house. This could indicate a change in your celebration plans. Or it may be that you just want to stay at home tonight, perhaps with a partner, family members, or a small group of friends.

Dates to watch for: on or around December 12. It'll be hectic.

Best date: December 25, when Venus and Neptune are conjunct in Aquarius, your fifth house, making for a romantic, inspired day!

Brainstorming

Envision yourself a year, two years, or four years from now. What is your life like? Where do you live? Is your work satisfying to you? Are you single, married, a parent? Are you happy? Do you have enough money? Is your health good? What are your spiritual beliefs? Are you a vehicle for change in your family or community? In the space below, describe the life you would like to be living a year or two or four up the line. Be as outrageous, creative, and wild as you want. After all, it's *your* life. If you can imagine it, then you can create it.

MY LIFE IN _____ (*choose a year*)

_____
_____
_____
_____
_____
_____
_____
_____
_____
_____
_____
_____

HAPPY 2009!

The Big Picture for Scorpio
in 2008

For you, 2008 is all about beginnings and endings. When you complete something—whether it's a relationship that has run its course or simply a project—the universe rushes in to fill that vacuum.

So let's start with Jupiter, the planet of luck, expansion, and success. Late last year, it entered Capricorn and your third house and it continues its journey there for all of this year. One thing that Jupiter in your third house may attract is an opportunity to move to a neighborhood or community that is larger or prettier than where you live now. It can also heal relationships with siblings and other relatives and could even bring another brother or sister into your family!

On January 25, Pluto joins Jupiter in your third house. Pluto is about profound and permanent transformation, so you can expect monumental changes in your community and neighborhood life. Pluto retrogrades back into Sagittarius and your second house of finances through the year, then finally enters Capricorn for good on November 26. This means you'll feel Pluto's impact on your finances off and on this year. But you already know what that means, since you have been living with it since 1995.

Saturn entered Virgo in the fall of 2007 and is now in your eleventh house, which governs friends and groups that support your interests and passions. You find a structure within these groups that makes you more aware of how to attain your dreams. Even though some friends may move out of your life this year, you're learning to value the friendships that you do have.

Uranus, the planet of sudden, unpredictable events, continues its transit of Pisces and your fifth house. The beneficial angle it forms to your sun indicates that your love life is going to be exciting and unusual this year. You may get involved with individuals who are experts in their fields, highly idiosyncratic, perhaps even unusually creative. Uranus will bring an inspired flavor to your creative work. An unexpected pregnancy is possible, and if this happens, the child may be exceptionally bright or creatively gifted.

Neptune is still transiting Aquarius and your fourth house, which it's been doing since 1998. Since it is the planet of higher inspiration—as well as illusion—you may not be seeing your home and family life as it really is. Or you draw a lot of inspiration from your family and your collective idealism binds you. Someone in your family—or you!—could be taking music, art, photography, or drama lessons. Nurture that creativity.

BEST TIME FOR ROMANCE

Mark the dates between September 23 and October 18, when Venus is in your sign. Your romantic quota soars. You're also more artistic and others see you in a more flattering light. You feel more confident and your sex appeal rises. Great backup dates for romance fall between March 12 and April 5, when Venus is transiting your fifth house of love and forming a beautiful angle to your sun.

Mars, as coruler of your sign, is in Scorpio between October 3 and November 16, so your libido is in high gear during this time and your physical energy is at its peak.

Other excellent dates for romance (and just about anything else) fall between May 11 and 13 and September 3 and 5, when the sun and Jupiter see eye to eye and there's a nice flow of energy between them.

BEST TIME FOR CAREER DECISIONS

Make career decisions between July 12 and August 4, when Venus is transiting your tenth house of careers. This should be quite a smooth time professionally. In fact, things may be going along so smoothly that you'll be tempted to kick back and relax. Don't. Seize the opportunity. There will be a lot of traveling, coming and going, and socializing with peers and bosses during this period. Communication will be vital.

MERCURY RETROGRADES

Every year, there are three periods when Mercury—the planet of communication and travel—turns retrograde. During these periods, it's wisest not to negotiate or sign contracts, to travel, to submit manuscripts, or to make major decisions. Granted, we can't live our lives entirely by Mercury retrogrades! If you have to travel during the periods listed below, however, then expect changes in your plans. If you have to sign a contract, expect to revise it.

It's also a good idea to back up computer files before Mercury turns retrograde. Quite often, computers and other communication devices act up. Be sure your virus software is up to date, too. Pay special attention to the house in which Mercury retrograde falls. It will tell you the area of your life most likely to be impacted. The periods to watch for in 2008 are:

January 28–February 18: retrograde in Aquarius, your fourth house. This one affects your family and home life. Computers and appliances may act up, your television or satellite could go on the fritz. Best course? Don't start anything new under this retrograde. Put home improvement projects on hold.

May 26–June 19: retrograde in Gemini, your eighth house, shared resources. Don't sign contracts or close on any loans or mortgages during this period. Your spouse or partner may be confused about your joint finances. Wills, inheritances, and tax and insurance issues could become a total puzzle.

September 24–October 15: retrograde in Libra, your

twelfth house. Good time for therapy, meditation, and dream recall.

ECLIPSES

Every year, there are four eclipses, two solar and two lunar. Solar eclipses trigger external events that allow us to see something that eluded us before. They can bring about beginnings and endings. When an eclipse hits one of your natal planets, it's especially important. Take note of the sign and house placement. Lunar eclipses bring up emotional issues related to the sign and house into which they fall.

Here are the dates to watch for:

February 6: solar eclipse at seventeen degrees Aquarius, your fourth house of family and home. You'll be able to see something about this area of your life that you haven't perceived in quite this way before. New financial opportunities open up for your partner or spouse.

February 20: lunar eclipse at ten degrees Virgo, your eleventh house. Emotions flare with a friend or group.

August 1: solar eclipse, nine degrees Leo, in your tenth house. A professional issue or relationship—with all its flaws and strengths—becomes obvious to you. New career opportunities open up.

August 16: lunar eclipse at twenty-four degrees Aquarius, your fourth house. Emotions run high at home. Go with the flow, Scorpio, and follow your hunches. You won't go wrong if you do.

LUCKIEST DAYS IN 2008

Every year, Jupiter forms a beneficial angle with the sun, usually a conjunction, when both planets are in the same sign. In 2008, the angle is a lovely trine and it occurs during two time periods: May 11–13 and September 3–5. If you're going to buy a lotto ticket, do it during these periods!

Now let's take a look at what 2008 has in store for you month by month.

Twelve Months of Predictions for Scorpio
January–December 2008

Scorpio—January 2008

The first new moon of 2008 is on January 8, in Capricorn, your third house, and sets the tone for the month. This moon, combined with expansive Jupiter in the same house, bodes well for your search for a new neighborhood or community that is more in line with what you imagine for yourself and your family. Follow your hunches on this one.

The full moon in Leo on January 22 lights up your career house, bringing professional issues and concerns right up front and personal. You deal with the challenge, whatever it is, but again, it's important to follow your instincts.

On January 7, Mercury enters Aquarius and your fourth house. There's a lot of talk at home now, possibly about a move or setting up a home office or just a lot of discussion about family issues. You may be doing more running around than usual. Then, on January 28, Mercury turns retrograde for the first time this year. Since it happens in your fourth house, be sure to back up computer files before the retrograde begins. Appliances may act up, the phones may go on the fritz, and travel plans may change. It's all over by February 18.

Venus begins the year in Sagittarius, your second house, enhancing your finances. You should have the money to pay off holiday bills, but it's just as likely that you'll be spending more money this month. On January 24, Venus enters Capricorn and your third house, signaling an excellent time to begin scouting neighborhoods and nearby communities for a place that suits you and your family.

Your coruler, Mars, starts the year in retrograde motion. There could be disagreements with in-laws or law enforcement employees. Since Mars is retrograde in your ninth house, don't speed during this retrograde period, which lasts until January 30. You could get a ticket! Mars represents our physical and sexual energy, so if you're traveling abroad during this period, you may feel overwhelmed or fatigued at times. Once Mars turns direct, things you have put on hold regarding education and advancing your business interests overseas begin to move forward again.

Dates to watch for: January 24, when Venus enters your third house, and January 25, when Pluto joins it. The Pluto transit is especially significant. Over the next several decades, this planet's transit will cause profound and permanent changes in your daily life.

Best date: January 24, when Venus and Jupiter link up in Capricorn, your third house. Plan something special with your partner. Romance is a given today.

Scorpio—February 2008

There are two eclipses this month and several other transits worth noting. Let's start with the solar eclipse in Aquarius on February 6. This one happens in your fourth house, representing family and home. Your hearth. Mercury and Neptune are close to the eclipse degree, suggesting a lot of discussion about ideals, spirituality, illusions, even your family's blind spots. Your different beliefs become apparent.

On February 20, the lunar eclipse in Virgo hits your eleventh house. A friendship or a group stirs up your emotions. Saturn is close to the degree of this lunar eclipse, a sure sign that rules and regulations, restrictions and/or delays are involved. Perhaps you're rebelling against boundaries that a group places on you.

On February 17, Venus enters Aquarius and your fourth house, lighting up your love life at home. Now is a good time to paint, redecorate, buy new furniture, and generally spruce up your house. You may want to practice feng shui, too, the Chinese art of enhancing energy through color and placement of furniture.

A day later, Mercury turns direct again, which is good news regardless of your sign. But for you, it means that things at home finally even out again. With both Mercury and Mars now moving direct, it's a good time to pitch your ideas, advance your plans for expanding your business or product overseas, and plan out your trip abroad.

Date to watch for: February 22, when Venus and Saturn form a difficult angle to each other. Your romantic relationship may feel like it's being squeezed by other obligations. Reality intervenes.

Best date: February 1, when Venus and Jupiter are conjunct in Capricorn, your third house. This beautiful configuration makes for a pleasant and romantic day; when February 22 rolls around, think back to *this* day.

Scorpio—March 2008

With several transits and two lunations this month, March is sure to keep you running. The action begins on March 7, with a new moon in Pisces, a fellow water sign, and in your fifth house. You'll love this new moon, Scorpio. It brings in new opportunities in romance and creativity. If you've been shopping a creative project, this new moon could bring a sale. If you've been hoping for a new romance, this new moon promises one. If you're already involved in a relationship, then this new moon raises the bar and may deepen the commitment.

Uranus is close to the degree of this new moon, indicating an element of surprise in whatever unfolds. Also, Jupiter forms a very close and harmonious angle to the new moon, so expansion and success are the name of the game!

Two weeks later, on March 21, the full moon in Libra takes place in your twelfth house. It's a good time to cuddle up with your honey, just the two of you—no kids, family, friends, or interruptions. This full moon also signals the culmination of a project or activity in which you've been involved. If, for instance, you've been in therapy, then you may decide you've discovered what you needed to know and move on.

In between these two moons, Venus enters Pisces and your fifth house on March 12, followed by Mercury two days later. This marks the beginning of one of your most romantic and creative times this year. Events in both areas of your life seem to unfold with immense ease and smoothness. With Mercury also in this house, you and your partner are burning the midnight oil with all your talking. If you're a writer, these two transits promise unfettered creative drive and productivity.

Uranus continues its transit through Pisces and your fifth house as well. Uranus represents sudden, unpredictable events, so combined with the other two planets and a new moon, your love life and creativity are stacked with excitement this month.

Dates to watch for: the new moon on March 7, the transits of Mercury and Venus into Pisces on March 12 and 14.

Best dates: The entire month looks good!

Scorpio—April 2008

If March had you running around like crazy, then April is sure going to make you feel as if you're living life in fast-forward. On April 2, Mercury enters Aries and your sixth house, and four days later, Venus follows. This indicates a lot of socializing and talks with coworkers and employees. There's a certain ease to your daily work routine now, but it may require some attitude adjustments on your part. If you don't already have a regular exercise routine, then start one this month. Keep it simple, make it something you enjoy, but do it.

In between the Mercury and Venus transits, on April 5 the new moon in Aries puts additional emphasis on your sixth house. This moon promises new job opportunities, if that's what you're looking for, a new chapter in your daily work routine, and a new health routine. If you want to lose weight, the next month is an excellent time for a new diet and nutritional program.

On April 17, Mercury enters Taurus, your opposite sign, and seventh house, and on April 30, Venus joins Mercury in this house. The first transit has you and your partner or spouse engaging in discussions, traveling together, perhaps even working together on a communication project. Taurus is one of the most stubborn signs in the zodiac and, like Scorpio, a fixed sign. You'll be hardheaded about things, unwilling to change your mind unless the other person has a very convincing argument, and you won't be particularly flexible. But perhaps all this is what's called for right now. When Venus joins Mercury in your seventh house, your love life should take off and a deeper commitment is possible in your closest relationship.

Before Venus enters Taurus, look to April 20 for a full moon in your sign. Wow. You'll love this one, Scorpio. Even Saturn will be cooperating with this full moon, indicating that your emotions and intuition are right on target. It's a romantic time, too. Plan something special on or around this full moon with the one you love.

Dates to watch for: The first ten days of the month feature a sextile between Jupiter and Uranus, in signs compatible with your own. Surprises that unfold happen suddenly and are intended to expand your life in some way.

Best dates: The Mercury, Venus, and Uranus conjunction in Pisces on April 1–2 should be quite exciting romantically and creatively. You have unusual creative ideas now that are begging for expression.

Scorpio—May 2008

May is hectic, too, but if you live in a northern climate, it's spring and that goes a long way toward soothing your nerves.

On May 2, Mercury enters Gemini, one of the signs that it rules, and your eighth house. Your conscious thoughts for the next few weeks—until May 26—turn to taxes, wills, legacies, inheritances, and things that go bump in the night. After May 26, when Mercury enters Cancer and your ninth house, your attention turns to loftier ideals—your worldview, for instance, your spiritual beliefs, even educational goals. What you need to remember about Mercury is that it governs the conscious mind. In Gemini, then, your focus may be on gathering information through books, the Internet, television, and radio; in Cancer, your focus will be more inward, intuitive, and nurturing. Mercury retrogrades on May 26, however, and if you can't recall what that means, read the section in the big picture on Mercury retrogrades in 2008.

The new moon on May 5 is in Taurus, your seventh house, and brings new opportunities for partnerships—both professional and personal. If you're involved in a relationship already, this new moon could indicate a deeper commitment. You and your partner move in together or even get married.

On May 9, your coruler, Mars, enters Leo and your tenth house. This powerhouse transit triggers events and activity in your profession. It's a good time to brainstorm and pitch ideas, to hobnob with peers and bosses, and to push your agenda, whatever it is. You have a window of opportunity here that lasts until July 1.

On May 19, the full moon in Scorpio should be quite intense for you. Not only is it in your sign, but in a late degree, suggesting a sense of urgency. Also, Uranus forms a wide and beneficial angle to this moon, an indication that events happen quickly, unexpectedly, and you need to be alert and on your toes to take full advantage of what happens.

Finally, on May 24, Venus joins Mercury in Gemini for a few days, in your eighth house. A seminar or workshop is likely on some type of esoteric topic, or perhaps on taxes or estate planning. The Venus transit bodes well for a romance with a foreign-born individual and facilitates the expansion of your business or product to an overseas market.

Dates to watch for: May 1–2, when Jupiter in Capricorn and Uranus in Pisces form a harmonious angle to each other, in your third and fifth houses respectively. One possible interpretation? A romantic relationship begins suddenly, perhaps with someone you meet in your own neighborhood.

Best date: the new moon on May 5.

Scorpio—June 2008

The new moon on June 3 is in Gemini, your eighth house. This moon bodes well for applying for and obtaining mortgages and loans. Also, you may get a tax refund, an insurance payment, or may teach or take a workshop in a topic that interests you.

The full moon on June 18 is in Sagittarius and Pluto is within a degree of this moon. Something related to your finances looks positive—and powerful. Whatever it is, this full moon brings it right up close and personal. Also, Mars forms a wide but beneficial angle with this moon, suggesting that you don't sit by passively, but actively and aggressively pursue what you want. Also on June 18, Venus enters Cancer and your ninth house. As soon as Mercury turns direct tomorrow, plan your overseas travel. Also, any business dealings you have with foreign countries look very good now.

Dates to watch for: June 20–26, when Mars is opposed to Neptune. This sets up a conflict between your ideals and your ability to act decisively.

Best date: June 13, when Pluto enters Capricorn once again. Your third house is about to undergo a major transformation. This could be the time to move, Scorpio.

Scorpio—July 2008

The new moon in Cancer on July 2 is in your ninth house and forms a beautiful angle to your sun. This moon may bring new opportunities related to overseas travel, expanding your business or product overseas, and in education. Venus is within six degrees of this moon, so it looks as if whatever evolves is beneficial and may concern the arts.

Two weeks later, on July 18, the full moon in Capricorn lights up your third house, and forms a very wide angle to expansive Jupiter. Whatever this full moon brings, Jupiter exaggerates it. So if you feel tension concerning a relationship with a brother or sister, things aren't as bad as they seem.

There are several transits that deserve attention this month, too. On July 1, Mars enters Virgo, an earth sign compatible with your sun sign, and your eleventh house. Suddenly, you're inundated with social invitations—friends you haven't heard from in ages stop by, call, e-mail you, and everyone wants you at the party. It's an excellent time to do publicity and advertising for your company or product, too. The public is receptive.

On July 10, Mercury enters Cancer and your ninth house, underscoring some of the new moon themes. There's a lot of talk now about overseas travel and education. If you're college bound, this certainly brings your concerns and issues about college right up close and personal. Then, on July 26, Mercury enters Leo and your tenth house, putting you in a very strong position professionally. It's a good time to pitch ideas, negotiate contracts, and brainstorm with peers and bosses about ways to improve your company's performance.

Venus enters Leo on July 12, aiding and abetting Mercury, adding flow and ease to the whole equation.

Date to watch for: On July 25, energetic Mars and karmic Saturn form a harmonious angle to each other and to your sun. You finally have a venue into which you can put your energy and ideas!

Best dates: July 25–28, when Mars and Jupiter form a harmonious angle to each other, increasing your physical energy and kicking your libido up a couple of notches.

Scorpio—August 2008

Buckle up. There are two eclipses this month, a second new moon, and five transits to pay attention to. The action begins on August 1, with the new moon solar eclipse in Leo, your tenth house of career. Since a solar eclipse is always a new moon, new professional opportunities head your way as a result of something you recognize about your career. Mercury is close to the eclipse degree, signaling a lot of discussion, and chatter ensues. If you've been wanting to change career tracks, this eclipse could bring the opportunity to do exactly that.

Two weeks later, on August 16, the lunar eclipse in

Aquarius hits your fourth house. An emotional issue concerning your home life and family surfaces. Neptune is close to this eclipse degree, so you may not have the full story or all the information you need. Step back, take a deep breath. It's not as bad as it may look.

The new moon on August 30, in Virgo and your eleventh house, is compatible with your sun sign. It promises new friendships and new opportunities with group activities. You may get involved with a political group, a theater group, or a writers' group. It all depends on your current interests and needs.

In between these moons, Mercury, Venus, and Mars all change signs. On August 10, Mercury enters Virgo and your eleventh house, offering a peek at what the new moon on August 30 promises. You socialize more with bosses, network with peers, and may be traveling for professional reasons. On August 28, Mercury enters Libra and your twelfth house, where it will turn retrograde next month. Before it retrogrades, however, you'll be trying to understand long-standing issues that surface. Therapy, meditation, even dream recall can be advantageous now.

August 5 features Venus entering Virgo and joining Mercury in your eleventh house. The combination of planets indicates that you may be traveling with friends or with a group of acquaintances. Any romance that begins under these two transits could be with a friend or someone you meet through friends and communication will be vital to its success. On August 30, Venus follows Mercury into Libra, one of the signs that it rules, and your twelfth house. A secret romance may be in the offing. If it isn't secret, then it's sure to be private. And romantic. Consider it a preparation for when Venus enters your sign on September 23.

Interestingly, Mars enters Libra on August 19, so it's the first of the three planets to enter your twelfth house this month. This energizes everything you do in seclusion, behind the scenes, by yourself. If you need to meet a deadline, Mars pushes you until you achieve it.

Date to watch for: August 16, when Mars forms a challenging angle to Pluto. Power issues surface.

Best dates: August 16–18, when Venus and retrograde Jupiter form a terrific angle to each other and to your sun. Romance. Success. Expansion.

Scorpio—September 2008

The full moon on September 15 should be a beauty for you, Scorpio. It's in Pisces, your fifth house, and forms a harmonious angle to your sign. The fifth house is all about romance and creativity, so be sure to plan something special with the one you love. If you aren't involved right now, then this full moon signals the culmination of a creative project. Uranus in Pisces is within three degrees of this moon, so whatever unfolds on or around September 15 will be unexpected, surprising.

On September 29, the new moon in Libra falls in your twelfth house and brings opportunities to work in seclusion, behind the scenes. You may be visiting people who are in hospitals, prisons, or nursing homes, perhaps through some sort of charity work or because someone you know is in one of these institutions.

Venus enters your sign on September 23, marking one of the most romantic and creative periods of this year. This transit lasts until October 18, so take advantage of it. Pitch your ideas at work, plan a getaway with your partner, get out and be seen, network with friends, or plan your wedding. You get the idea . . . this is a special time when other people embrace you and your ideas.

On September 24, Mercury turns retrograde for the last time this year, in Libra, your twelfth house. This retrograde period will coincide with the new moon in the same sign and house, indicating that old friends and lovers may be reentering your life and that you may be revising and reviewing projects and ideas. Read over the material on Mercury retrogrades in the big picture section.

Dates to watch for: On September 7, Jupiter turns direct in your third house. This planet is always about expansion, success, and luck, and once it's moving direct, it's functioning as it should. Expect more travel, more contact with siblings and other relatives, and a search for a bigger neighborhood, perhaps in anticipation of a move. Keep an eye out for the Mercury retrograde date, too, September 24.

Best dates: From September 13 to 20, Mercury, Venus, and Mars are all crowded in Libra, your twelfth house. This combination could bring romantic intrigue—and a deep need for privacy.

Scorpio—October 2008

The full moon on October 14 is in Aries, your sixth house, and Pluto forms a wide but harmonious angle to it—but not to your sun sign. Translated: there could be some tension on or around this date related to money and work. But because you're such a resilient person, you manage to go with the flow and get through this just fine.

The new moon on October 28 is the one to watch for—it's in your sign, something that happens only once a year. This moon ushers in new opportunities in your personal life. There's no predicting exactly which area will be most impacted—that depends on where you are in your life, what you desire, and how willing you are to visualize a desired outcome. Several days before this new moon, it would be a good idea to create a "manifestation list," circumstances you would like to see in your life. Meditate on them, perform a symbolic ritual of some kind.

October 3 is a very important date for you. Your

coruler, Mars, enters your sign. Between now and November 16, you have an opportunity to tackle everything with your characteristic passion and resolve. This transit boosts your physical energy, your ambition and drive, and should spice up your sex life as well!

On October 15, Mercury turns direct again. This sets the stage for the new moon on October 29 and makes it easier to manifest what you would like in your life. You get a boost on October 18, when Venus moves into Sagittarius and your second house. Not only does Venus here enhance your finances and earning capacity—through a raise or promotion, perhaps—but it also allows you to see the larger picture. Are your values in line with your life? Is your life a reflection of your values?

Date to watch for: October 15, when Mercury turns direct in Libra. Go celebrate.

Best dates: There's a lot of them! October 3, when Mars enters your sign; October 5–6, when Venus and Jupiter form a beautiful angle to each other and to your sun, enhancing your love life and your creativity; and October 19–31, when Jupiter and Saturn are sending positive energy to each other.

Scorpio—November 2008

With five transits and three planets changing direction, plus the full and new moons, November is a fireball of activity. In addition, the national election is this month. Before you cast your vote, be sure to read the introductory section about how important this election is in terms of world affairs.

On November 4, Mercury enters Scorpio, and suddenly your gift of gab exceeds your wildest expectations. Now is the time to pitch your ideas, garner support for your favorite charity, group, or political party, and to investigate and research to your heart's content.

Venus enters Capricorn and your third house on November 12, galvanizing all your associations with siblings, relatives, and neighbors. A romance or flirtation is certainly likely with someone in your neighborhood or community whom you meet through a sibling or neighbor. Your daily activities unfold more smoothly during this transit, perhaps because your conscious thoughts are more focused on the task at hand.

On November 13, the full moon in Taurus occurs in your seventh house and opposite sign. Saturn forms a harmonious angle to this full, indicating that you recognize the flaws and strengths of a particular structure in your life—a relationship, a project, a situation. Neptune, the planet of illusions and inspiration, forms a harsh angle to this moon, so you may not have all the information you need to make a decision.

On November 27, the new moon in Sagittarius promises opportunities in finances. You may pick up a part-time job, get a raise or promotion, or even find a better-paying job that is more in line with your values. Both Mercury and Mars are close to the degree of this moon, so the situations that evolve have plenty of energy and discussion behind them.

Before this new moon, however, Mars enters Sagittarius on November 16, triggering lots of activity related to finances and giving you a taste of what kinds of things the new moon may offer.

Dates to watch for: November 1, when Neptune turns direct in Aquarius, your fourth house. You can now turn your idealism into action. It involves your home and family. November 26, when your ruler, Pluto, enters Capricorn again. This significant transit is long and ushers in profound changes in your daily life, but over a long period of time. Read about the Pluto transit in the introduction. On November 27, Uranus turns direct in Pisces, your fifth house. This will feel pretty good, Scorpio. Expect pleasant surprises related to your love life and your creativity.

Best dates: November 1–2, when Mars, Jupiter, Saturn, and Uranus are all in close angles to each other and form a harmonious angle to your sun. No telling what these two days may bring—surprise, a burst of physical and sexual energy, structure, or expansion.

Scorpio—December 2008

As you enter the final month of the year, every planet is moving in direct motion—that is, they're functioning exactly as they should. This condition remains stable until New Year's Eve, when Saturn turns retrograde in Virgo, your eleventh house. But more on that in a moment.

On December 7, Venus enters Aquarius and your fourth house. This very pleasant transit should spice up your love life at home. If you aren't involved with anyone, then simply enjoy the smoothness that Venus brings to your home and family life. You may decide to set up a home office or take some time off this month from your day job to pursue what you're passionate about, to indulge your creativity.

On December 12, there are two events: a full moon in Gemini, your eighth house, and Mercury's transit into Capricorn, your third house. The Gemini full moon brings to light something about finances and resources that you share with others. There could be some tension surrounding this full moon because Saturn forms a harsh angle to it. A confrontation with authority could be possible.

Mercury's transit into Capricorn should be good for you. It forms a good angle to your sun and urges you to plan out your goals for the upcoming year. Actually, it's good for all sorts of planning and strategizing. It should make you more focused, too.

On December 27, your coruler, Mars, follows Mercury into Capricorn. And remember, Pluto and Jupiter are also there, creating a distinct emphasis on all third house activities—your brothers, sisters, and other relatives; your neighbors, daily activities and conscious thoughts; your communication abilities and travel.

Also on December 27, the new moon in Capricorn follows this lineup of planets into your third house. Pluto is within five degrees of this moon, Mars within six; expect excellent developments to result from this moon. Mars is at zero degrees of Capricorn, and any time a cardinal planet hits zero degrees, it sets off activity in the other cardinal signs. For you, this means the third house, the ninth (worldview, higher education, overseas travel), and the twelfth (what is hidden).

Dates to watch for: In addition to the dates already mentioned, Saturn turns retrograde on December 31. This may mess up your New Year's plans, since it occurs in your eleventh house of friends. Just be prepared to change your plans at the last moment!

Best dates: the last week of the month.

Brainstorming

Envision yourself a year, two years, or four years from now. What is your life like? Where do you live? Is your work satisfying to you? Are you single, married, a parent? Are you happy? Do you have enough money? Is your health good? What are your spiritual beliefs? Are you a vehicle for change in your family or community? In the space below, describe the life you would like to be living a year or two or four up the line. Be as outrageous, creative, and wild as you want. After all, it's *your* life. If you can imagine it, then you can create it.

My Life in _____ (choose a year)

HAPPY 2009!

The Big Picture for Sagittarius in 2008

For you, 2008 is all about leadership, pulling out in front of the pack, thinking outside of the box. All these clichés just happen to be true for you this year.

Pluto will finally be leaving your sign, where it has been since the mid-1990s. It moves into Capricorn and your second house of finances on January 25. Pluto here will transform your financial picture—for better or worse, it all depends on how you regard money. Over the past years, you have seen this planet change your personal life irrevocably and it will now do the same to your values and your money. It slides back into your sign for part of the year, however, and may bring some last-minute changes to your personal life when it does this, but by late November you're free and clear. Forever.

While Pluto is slipping in and out of your money house, Jupiter is also in this house and that's a wonderful thing! It hasn't happened for twelve years, and there's no doubt that your finances are going to reap the rewards of expansive Jupiter. So even though Pluto is changing your financial picture, Jupiter offers backup protection and kisses you with abundance.

Late last year, when Jupiter entered your second house, you probably were spending money like crazy—for the holidays, birthdays, perhaps on some big-ticket household item. That's often the case when Jupiter enters the financial sector of your chart. So let's start with Jupiter, the planet of luck, expansion, and success. Late last year, it entered Capricorn and your second house and it continues its journey there for all of this year. One thing that Jupiter in your second house may attract is an opportunity to move to a neighborhood or community that is larger or prettier than where you live now. It can also heal relationships with siblings and other relatives and could even bring another brother or sister into your family!

On January 25, Pluto joins Jupiter in your second house. Pluto is about profound and permanent transformation, so you can expect monumental changes in your community and neighborhood life. Pluto retrogrades back into Sagittarius through the year, then finally enters Capricorn for good on November 26. This means you'll feel Pluto's impact on your finances off and on this year. But you already know what that means, since you have been living with it since 1995.

Saturn entered Virgo in the fall of 2007 and is now in your tenth house of career. This can be a difficult transit if you're sorely in need of a reality check or structure in your professional life. But if we assume you've been working hard, doing your best, meeting your responsibilities, then Saturn's transit through your tenth solidifies your reputation. It helps to elevate your status with bosses and peers and may bring rewards and recognition that even you haven't anticipated. It could also bring challenges with a parent or with an authority figure.

Uranus, the planet of sudden, unpredictable events, continues its transit of Pisces and your fourth house. This transit brings unpredictability and abrupt events and situations concerning your family and home. Before you panic, Uranus has been in this position since the spring of 2003, so it's nothing new for you!

Neptune is still transiting Aquarius and your third house, which it's been doing since 1998. Since it is the planet of higher inspiration—as well as illusion—you may not be seeing your siblings, neighbors, or neighborhood as they actually are. Yet you draw inspiration from these facets of your life and may share some of the same ideals with these individuals.

BEST TIME FOR ROMANCE

Mark the dates between October 18 and November 11, when Venus is in your sign. Your romantic quota soars. You're also more artistic and others see you in a more flattering light. You feel more confident and your sex appeal rises. Great backup dates for romance fall between April 6 and 30, when Venus is transiting your fifth house of love and forming a beautiful angle to your sun.

Mars, symbolic of your physical and sexual energy, is in your sign between November 16 and December 26, so during these dates your libido is soaring.

Other excellent dates for romance (and just about anything else) fall between May 11 and 13 and September 3 and 5, when the sun and Jupiter see eye to eye and there's a nice flow of energy between them.

BEST TIME FOR CAREER DECISIONS

Make career decisions between August 5 and 29, when Venus is transiting your tenth house of careers. This should be quite a smooth time professionally. In fact, things may be going along so smoothly that you'll be tempted to kick back and relax. Don't. Seize the opportunity. There will be a lot of traveling, coming and going, and socializing with peers and bosses during this period. Communication will be vital.

MERCURY RETROGRADES

Every year, there are three periods when Mercury—the planet of communication and travel—turns retrograde. During these periods, it's wisest not to negotiate or sign contracts, to travel, to submit manuscripts, or to make major decisions. Granted, we can't live our lives entirely by Mercury retrogrades! If you have to travel during the periods listed below, however, then expect changes in your plans. If you have to sign a contract, expect to revise it.

It's also a good idea to back up computer files before Mercury turns retrograde. Quite often, computers and other communication devices act up. Be sure your virus software is up to date, too. Pay special attention to the house in which Mercury retrograde falls. It will tell you the area of your life most likely to be impacted. The periods to watch for in 2008 are:

January 28–February 18: retrograde in Aquarius, your third house. This one affects your daily life. Computers and appliances may act up, your television or satellite could go on the fritz. Best course? Don't start anything new under this retrograde. Put neighborhood improvement projects on hold.

May 26–June 19: retrograde in Gemini, your seventh house, partnerships. Don't sign contracts during this time. Be sure to communicate clearly with business and personal partners.

September 24–October 15: retrograde in Libra, your eleventh house. There could be some bumps and bruises with friends and groups during this period.

ECLIPSES

Every year, there are four eclipses, two solar and two lunar. Solar eclipses trigger external events that allow us to see something that eluded us before. They can bring about beginnings and endings. When an eclipse hits one of your natal planets, it's especially important. Take note of the sign and house placement. Lunar eclipses bring up emotional issues related to the sign and house into which they fall.

Here are the dates to watch for:

February 6: solar eclipse at seventeen degrees Aquarius, your third house. You'll be able to see something about siblings, relatives or neighbors—or your neighborhood—that you haven't perceived in quite this way before. This eclipse could trigger an itch to move!

February 20: lunar eclipse at ten degrees Virgo, your tenth house. Emotions surface that are related in some way to your career.

August 1: solar eclipse, nine degrees Leo, in your ninth house. Your worldview or your educational opportunities are revealed in all their strengths and flaws. Think drama with this eclipse!

August 16: lunar eclipse at twenty-four degrees Aquarius, your third house, again. Emotions run high in your neighborhood or community.

LUCKIEST DAYS IN 2008

Every year, Jupiter forms a beneficial angle with the sun, usually a conjunction, when both planets are in the same sign. In 2008, the angle is a lovely trine and it occurs during two time periods: May 11–13 and September 3–5. If you're going to buy a lotto ticket, do it during these periods!

Now let's take a look at what 2008 has in store for you month by month.

Twelve Months of Predictions
for Sagittarius
January—December 2008

Sagittarius—January 2008

The first new moon of 2008 is on January 8, in Capricorn, your second house, and sets the tone for the month. This moon, combined with expansive Jupiter in the same house, bodes well for your finances this year. Follow your hunches on investments, new money-earning opportunities, and new jobs that offer more than what you presently make. But back up your hunches with facts.

The full moon in Leo on January 22 brings to light an issue or situation related to education, publishing, or overseas travel. This moon is harmonious with your sun sign, so the events that transpire should be positive. Some possibilities: a romantic evening in a far-flung corner of the world, fresh insights into the expansion of your business or product to overseas markets, and—if you're a high school or college student—greater insight into your educational goals.

On January 7, Mercury enters Aquarius and your third house, a transit that's compatible with your sun sign. Your daily life now picks up steam. You may be running around more than usual—carpooling, doing errands—and there's more social contact with your siblings and other relatives. On January 28, Mercury retrogrades for the first time this year, in your third house, and doesn't turn direct again until February 18.

Your best way to navigate this period is to revise, review, reevaluate. Don't start anything new. Since it occurs in your third house, your daily activities are likely to be impacted. Just be sure to communicate clearly with everyone around you so you're not misunderstood.

January 24 features Venus transiting into Capricorn, your second house of finances. This transit complements the new moon themes related to money. Although you may initially spend more, there's a certain ease now to earning money. You could have your eye on a big-ticket item, but before you buy, make sure the checks have cleared, and buy before Mercury turns retrograde on January 28.

On January 30, Mars turns direct in Gemini, your seventh house. This should be good news for your partnerships, particularly if you and your partner have been at odds the last few weeks.

Dates to watch for: January 24, when Venus enters your second house, joining expansive Jupiter, and January 25, when Pluto joins it. The Pluto transit is especially significant. Over the next several decades, this planet's transit will cause profound and permanent changes in your values and your financial picture.

Best date: January 24, when Venus and Jupiter link up in Capricorn, your second house. Romance with someone who shares your values is a good possibility.

Sagittarius—February 2006

Let's start with the two eclipses this month. On February 6, the solar eclipse in Aquarius is in your third house. Both Mercury and Neptune are close to the eclipse degree, suggesting that you may not have the full information about a sibling, relative, or neighbor. Nonetheless, there is a lot of discussion about the situation. If the situation concerns your neighborhood or community, don't make any decisions until after February 18.

Two weeks later, on February 20, the lunar eclipse in Virgo hits your tenth house. Expect an emotional reaction related to your career. Saturn is within four degrees of the eclipse degree, so your emotions find a constructive outlet and you're able to weather this emotional storm, whatever it is.

On February 17, Venus enters Aquarius and your third house, highlighting some of the same themes as the solar eclipse in this house. Romance with a neighbor, Sagittarius? Or with someone you meet through a brother or sister? Both are possible. In fact, most of the emphasis this month is on your third house. Even on February 18, Mercury turns direct in Aquarius, this same house. This movement is good news, certainly, for your daily life. A relationship with a sibling or neighbor now straightens out, and previous misunderstandings are a thing of the past. If you're intent on moving soon, then now is the time to start your search for a neighborhood or community that is more to your liking.

This month, Mars is transiting Gemini, your seventh house. As the planet that represents our sexual and physical energy, Mars's transit through your house of partnerships brightens up your sex life. But it can also put you and your partner at odds with each other over silly disagreements. Patience is called for!

Dates to watch for: the eclipse dates, of course, but also February 22, when Venus and Saturn form a challenging angle to each other. Tension with authority is possible.

Best date: February 29, when the sun and Uranus form a wide angle to each other. Look for excitement and unpredictable events at home.

Sagittarius—March 2008

March is another busy month with the stars and the action starts on March 4, when Mars enters Cancer, your eighth house. This transit galvanizes resources you share with others—a spouse, a business or romantic partner, even a child. This transit should make it easier for you to obtain mortgages and loans and to make insurance claims. Check on your insurance premiums and make sure they're up to date.

On March 7, the new moon in Pisces occurs in your fourth house, promising new opportunities and events related to your home and family. This new moon could have you looking at real estate or homes in anticipation of a move. It's also possible that your family gains a new member—a baby, a relative, even a friend who moves in for a while.

Venus enters Pisces and your fourth house on March 12, so expect a repetition of some of the new moon themes. Venus brings softness, joy, and romance to your home life. It may also urge you to set up your home office and to beautify your surroundings in some way. This would be a great time to practice some feng shui—add a fountain and the color lavender to the prosperity corner of your home.

On March 14, Mercury follows Venus in Pisces and your fourth house. These two planets follow each other closely all year, always enhancing and supporting each other's energies. So if there's romance at home, there's also a lot of discussion and brainstorming going on. Mercury invariably brings lots of social activities, some of them related to young people.

On March 21, the full moon in Libra should please you. On or around that date your social life picks up and you have so many invitations to choose from that you aren't sure which to honor. The gregarious part of your personality loves such choices; the nomadic part of you yearns for the open road. Perhaps a trip with several friends is in order, Sagittarius.

This full moon receives a harsh angle from Pluto, so there could be some tensions related to money. Maybe you feel you can't afford a trip right now. If so, remember that your trip doesn't have to be to

Greece; someplace near home may satisfy your travel itch.

Date to watch for: March 21, when Mars and Uranus form a harmonious angle to each other, but not to your sun. There could be some tension or strange events related to your home life or your partner's income.

Best date: March 7, when Mercury and Venus are conjunct in Aquarius, your third house. Lots of communication with your partner today! Make good use of it.

Sagittarius—April 2008

The new moon on April 5 is in Aries, a fellow fire sign, and your fifth house. This one is going to be especially beautiful for new opportunities in romance and creativity. Whether or not you're currently involved in a relationship is irrelevant. This new moon brings new people into your life and you have your choice—something that will please your freewheeling personality. On the creative front, that manuscript or screenplay, portfolio or music CD that has been languishing in a drawer now sees the light of day. There may be interest in your creative endeavors. Since the fifth house also governs children, this new moon could portend a pregnancy or even a birth. This new moon really sets the tone for the month.

Before the new moon, though, look to April 2 for Mercury's entry into Aries and your fifth house. Here, again, you'll find repetition of the new moon themes. You and your partner may be traveling together between now and April 17, when Mercury enters Taurus. There will be lots of discussion about your relationship and the air will be perfect for romance, particularly after April 6, when Venus joins Mercury in Aries.

The full moon on April 20 is in Scorpio, your twelfth house. This moon shines a brilliant light on something in your life that is hidden. It may be a motive—yours or someone else's—or an issue that you simply have pushed away to deal with later. On or around this date, consider having a past-life regression or taking a meditation class. Be sure to work with your dreams, too, as answers and insights can come through them.

April 30 has Venus following Mercury into Taurus, your sixth house. Things in your daily work should hum along quite smoothly now, although you may have to adjust your attitude concerning an employee or coworker.

Your ruler, Jupiter, went into Capricorn late last year and is continuing its transit through your second house. Even if your initial expenditures seemed extreme, by now it should be expanding your financial base. Think of this transit as the Midas touch! In May, Jupiter turns retrograde, so complete your stock and investments plans before then.

Dates to watch for: During the first ten days of the month, Jupiter in Capricorn and Uranus in Pisces form a harmonious angle to each other—but not to your sun. Look for unexpected fluctuations in your home situation and with your finances.

Best dates: the new moon on April 5, and between April 6 and 17, when Mercury and Venus are traveling hand in hand through your fifth house.

Sagittarius—May 2008

If you live in a northern climate, then you're feeling wonderful just because spring is here. Even if you don't live in the north, you're feeling pretty good. The passage of seasons really does affect your moods, Sadge!

On May 2, Mercury enters Gemini, a planet that it rules, and your seventh house. This transit is good for contract negotiations and for discussions with any partner—professional or romantic. Your spouse, in fact, may have a lot on his or her mind, so it would be to your advantage to really listen, then mull it all over before saying your piece.

May 5 features a new moon in Taurus, your sixth house. If you've been looking for a new job, this moon may bring you the opportunity you've been hoping for. There may be a reshuffling of the workforce that benefits you in some way. There could be a promotion for you, too. Uranus makes a wide and harmonious angle to this moon, so whatever comes about will be sudden and unexpected.

Mars enters fellow fire sign Leo on May 9, a transit you're sure to like. It really triggers your nomadic tendencies, Sadge, so you may be on the computer a lot, planning a trip to some exotic locale. Just be sure that you don't travel between May 26 and June 19, when Mercury is retrograde in Gemini. Another possibility with this transit is that your business interests or your product expands to an overseas market or that you're actively pursuing your educational goals.

On May 24, Venus joins Mercury in Gemini, your seventh house. You and your partner should plan some private time together, even if it means getting out of town. Do it quickly, though, because on May 26 Mercury turns retrograde in Gemini, so after that date, you two may not be seeing eye to eye on things.

Dates to watch for: May 2, when Saturn turns direct in Virgo, your tenth house. This movement releases energy that impacts your career, insurance, and taxes, and highlights mortgages and loans in a positive way. On May 9, Jupiter turns retrograde in your second house—money. While this retrograde unfolds over a period of months—so the impact isn't as obvious—it's still a good idea to have all your financial ducks exactly where you want them before this date.

Best dates: May 29–31. Despite the Mercury retrograde, Venus in Gemini and Mars in Leo form a harmonious angle to each other, infusing your partnerships and worldview with new energy.

Sagittarius—June 2008

Summer is here and the living, at least for this month, should be pretty easy. On June 3, the new moon in Gemini brings new opportunities in partnerships, both romantic and professional. After June 19, sign any contracts that come your way.

Both Mercury and Venus are close to this new moon, indicating discussions surrounding whatever unfolds and a certain ease, almost as if the events are meant to happen.

Mark down June 18—Venus enters Cancer and your eighth house. So any problems or challenges you've been facing at work should now smooth out. Also, this transit supports a flirtation or romance with a co-worker or employee. Be careful, though, that your heart isn't broken in the course of this romance!

The full moon also falls on June 18. It's in your sign, too, Sadge, and Pluto is in a very close degree. Power issues may surface, but it looks as if you're the one in the driver's seat.

Then, June 19 brings a direct motion for Mercury. Finally. Get ready for your summer vacation, your move, whatever it is you've been delaying.

Dates to watch for: that full moon in your sign on June 18. Romance looks promising. In fact, most areas of your personal life benefit. June 13, when Pluto enters Capricorn, joining Jupiter in your second house. This transit is long—it lasts until 2024—and indicates profound changes in your financial picture and your values.

Best dates: June 4–8, when Venus and Mars form a harmonious angle to each other, promising an upswing in your love life.

Sagittarius—July 2008

If June was relatively calm, July is the opposite. Things get off to a running start with Mars entering

Virgo and your tenth house on July 1. This transit hasn't happened for two years, since late July and August of 2006. Expect an opportunity related to your career. You might find clues about this transit if you look back two years. What was going on in your life back then?

On July 10, Mercury joins Mars in Virgo and your tenth house. Your communication skills are exceptional now and anything you have to say professionally will be well received. You may be traveling for business during this period and social activities with peers and bosses are likely to be more frequent.

Venus enters Leo and your ninth house on July 12, a very nice transit for overseas travel, taking courses related to philosophy and spiritual issues, and if you're college bound in the fall, for visiting the campus of your choice. On July 20, Mercury joins Venus in Leo, creating a powerful combination for romance overseas. If you've been wanting to expand your business overseas, this combination suggests your success is just around the corner. Women and people in the arts help you to achieve your goals.

What about the moons this month? The new moon on July 2 is in Cancer, your eighth house. Expect opportunities related to mortgages, loans, taxes, and insurance. A tax refund is a possibility and so is an insurance payout of some kind. Your spouse or partner could be looking at a substantial raise or a new job opportunity.

The full moon on July 18 falls in Capricorn, your second house. Tensions surface about money. Things may look worse than they really are, so don't freak out. Delay making any decisions until later in the month.

Date to watch for: July 5, when Mars and Saturn are conjunct in Virgo, your tenth house. Mars yearns for action, Saturn advises caution. You'll feel pulled between one and the other. Just pay attention to details. You'll figure it out.

Best date: the new moon on July 2.

Sagittarius—August 2008

There are two new moons this month and one of them features a solar eclipse. August 1 sets the stage for the next six months, with a solar eclipse in Leo, your ninth house. Your worldview snaps into clarity, Sadge, and you may be doing some fine-tuning on your beliefs. It's the kind of thing you enjoy doing, though, since you forever are searching for the larger picture. Since Mercury is close to the solar eclipse degree, expect discussion and travel related to education, publishing, and perhaps an expansion of your business interests.

Two weeks later, on August 16, the lunar eclipse is in Aquarius, your third house. A situation surfaces in your neighborhood, community, or with a sibling or other relative that may get a rise out of you. Neptune is close to this eclipse degree, suggesting that you may not have all the facts. Best to keep your emotions to yourself for the time being and make sure you have the full picture before you say something you might regret later.

The second new moon, on August 30, is in Virgo, your tenth house. This one brings in new opportunities and events related to your career. Saturn is close to the eclipse degree, so the opportunities that arrive are serious and may require a greater sense of responsibility and commitment on your part.

In between these three events are several noteworthy transits. On August 5, Venus enters Virgo and your tenth house, indicating that professional matters hum along smoothly. Your biggest concern is details. This theme is enhanced when Mercury joins Venus in Virgo on August 10. Now you're in a very good position to lay out your agenda, strategy, and goals to bosses and peers. Because you've done your homework, your ideas are well received. Business travel is a possibility during the next few weeks, and so is a flirtation or romance with someone you know professionally. Tread carefully, Sadge. The adage about not mixing business with pleasure may be your best course.

Mars enters Libra, an air sign compatible with your sun sign, on August 19. This transit, which lasts until early October, triggers social activities with friends and groups. You may be gearing up for the November election by joining a political group. Or you may join a group that reflects your creative interests.

On August 28 Mercury enters Libra and Venus follows it two days later. So now all three of the inner planets are transiting your eleventh house and friends and group activities really do become your focus. Romance is possible with someone you thought was a friend. Another possibility? You and a friend work together on a creative project or to promote and advertise a product or idea. Things are hectic, but it's the kind of chaos on which you thrive.

Dates to watch for: the eclipse dates, of course, but also mark down August 16. Pluto and Mars are square to each other that day, a potentially challenging aspect related to your finances and your career.

Best dates: August 16–18, when Venus and Jupiter are very chummy and romance looks quite pleasant—despite the Pluto-Mars square mentioned above.

Sagittarius—September 2008

The biggest news bite in September is that Mercury turns retrograde for the last time in 2008. This happens on September 24, in Libra, your eleventh house. By now you should be an old hand at navigating these retrograde periods. But just to refresh your memory: revise and review rather than start something new. Friendships may suffer some bruises and misunderstandings during this retrograde. Back up your computer files. Delay advertising and promoting your product until after October 15, when Mercury turns direct again.

Before Mercury turns retrograde, however, there's a full moon in Pisces on September 15. It brings clarity to a situation involving your home life. Pluto forms a wide and inharmonious angle to this moon, and because it's transiting in your sign again, the challenge may involve power issues. Since Uranus is close to this moon, whatever unfolds does so quickly and unexpectedly.

On September 23, Venus enters secretive Scorpio, your twelfth house. If you're involved already, then this transit has you and your partner sneaking off for time alone. If you get involved under this transit, the relationship is likely to be passionate and karmic, and you keep it a secret.

The new moon on September 29 should be terrific for you. It's in Libra, your eleventh house, and brings new friends and activities into your life. It may even bring a new relationship with someone you meet through a group in which you're involved, and you and your partner keep it a secret from other members of the group. Shades of conspiracy, Sadge?

Dates to watch for: On September 7, Jupiter turns direct in Capricorn, your second house. This movement should bring about an expansion in your financial base. On September 8, Pluto turns direct again, heading for its conjunction with Capricorn in late November. The release of all this Plutonian energy, in your sign, may startle you out of complacency.

Best dates: September 22–23, when Mercury and Mars are conjunct in Libra, your eleventh house. Get together with friends, throw a party, get out and have fun!

Sagittarius—October 2008

On October 3, Mars enters Scorpio, a sign that it co-rules, and your twelfth house. This transit favors working with your own unconscious—through dream recall, meditation, even therapy. Between October 3 and November 16, you'll be doing more behind the scenes, working in solitude, and may be visiting relatives or friends who are in the hospital, nursing homes, or similar institutions. Given the passion of Scorpio, a romantic relationship now heats up sexually.

There's a full moon on October 14, in Aries, a fellow fire sign, and your fifth house. Plan something special with your partner. This should be a very romantic time. On or around the date of the full moon, your creative drive accelerates and ideas fly your way fast and furiously. Keep a notepad or recorder handy.

October 15 is a celebration day—Mercury turns direct again! If you've forgotten what this means, check out the overview section on Mercury retrogrades. Three days later, Venus enters Scorpio, joining Mars in your twelfth house. This duo really sets the stage for a secretive romance. Any creative work that you do now will come to you easily, as if you've plugged into something greater than yourself.

October 18 marks the beginning of one of your best times for romance all year—Venus enters your sign. If you're not involved now, you probably will be before this transit ends on November 12. If you are involved, things can only improve now. Because you're such a freedom-loving sign, however, be careful about committing to someone if there's any doubt that you can't keep that commitment.

October 28 marks another new moon—in Scorpio and your twelfth house. Lots of secretive, behind-the-scenes stuff going on this month, Sadge, and this new moon opens doors to more of it!

Date to watch for: October 15, when Mercury turns direct again! Pack your bags. Sign contracts. Get your life moving forward again.

Best dates: October 5–6, when Venus and Jupiter, the two best planets, are in harmonious angles to each other, and October 18, when Venus enters your sign.

Sagittarius—November 2008

Mercury moves into Scorpio on November 4, signaling the beginning of a solitary period for you. If you're a writer, this is a terrific transit for completing a project and meeting a deadline. It's also great for research and investigative work. You're preparing yourself for when Mercury moves into your sign on November 23—that's when your communication skills are about as sharp as they get.

Venus is in your sign until November 12, and while it's there your love life is doing extremely well. Artistically, Venus in your sign heightens your creative perceptions and makes it easier for you to sell your creative projects, if that's what you want to do. Once Venus enters Capricorn and your second house on November 12, your finances should perk up. After all, you'll have the two best planets in the financial sector of your chart.

On November 13, the full moon in Taurus falls in your sixth house. A challenging situation may surface at work. You'll be more stubborn than you usually are and will dig in your heels, insisting that your way is the right way. Try to see the other person's viewpoint.

Three days after the full moon, Mars enters your sign. Talk about energy, Sadge. You can accomplish just about anything now—the sky really is the limit. You really grasp the reality of that statement on or around November 27, with the new moon in your sign. This moon happens only once a year and signals the beginning of a whole new period in your life. It's wise to prepare for this new moon with a ritual, a wish list, a visualization, and meditation, so that you can attract what you need and want.

Dates to watch for: November 1, when Neptune turns direct in Aquarius, your third house. The effects of this movement are subtle, unfolding over a long period of time, but you probably will notice that it's easier now to put your ideals into motion in your daily life. On November 26, Pluto enters Capricorn, leaving your sign for good. It will transit your money house until 2024.

Best date: that new moon on November 27!

Sagittarius—December 2008

As you enter the last month of the year, every planet is in direct motion, so they're all functioning at peak efficiency. This is a good thing, Sadge, because with last month's new moon in your sign, and with both Mercury and Mars still in your sign until December 12, you've got a lot going on.

The shift begins on December 7, when Venus enters Aquarius and your third house. A flirtation with a neighbor may turn into something much more; then again, it could just be a meeting of the minds. It all depends on what you're looking for right now—fun or commitment?

On December 12, there are two events—Mercury enters Capricorn and your second house, and a full moon in Gemini. The first transit means you're going to be thinking a lot about money between now and the end of the year. How you spend it, earn it, and wish you had more of it. Love with a neighbor? Possible.

Then, on December 27, there are two more events—Mars enters Capricorn and your second house, and there's a new moon in Capricorn. So the planetary energies have shifted from you and your personal life to finances. Try not to fret about holiday spending. Be generous, but don't go overboard. The money to pay all these holidays bills is promised by the new moon on December 27!

Date to watch for: December 31, when Saturn turns retrograde in Virgo, your tenth house. Things could slow down career-wise for a while, but the more immediate impact could be on your New Year's Eve plans. Be flexible. Be willing to change your plans.

Best date: December 25, when Venus and Neptune are conjunct in Aquarius. Your idealism is at an all-time high.

Brainstorming

Envision yourself a year, two years, or four years from now. What is your life like? Where do you live? Is your work satisfying to you? Are you single, married, a parent? Are you happy? Do you have enough money? Is your health good? What are your spiritual beliefs? Are you a vehicle for change in your family or community? In the space below, describe the life you would like to be living a year or two or four up the line. Be as outrageous, creative, and wild as you want. After all, it's *your* life. If you can imagine it, then you can create it.

MY LIFE IN _____ (*choose a year*)

_____

_____

_____

_____

_____

_____

_____

_____

_____

_____

_____

_____

HAPPY 2009!

The Big Picture for Capricorn in 2008

Welcome to 2008, Capricorn! This is a year all about cooperation and change. As the changes occur, you'll discover that cooperation takes you much further than confrontation. Jupiter, the planet of expansion and success, went into your sign late last year and continues its transit through Capricorn. You can expect all kinds of positive expansion in your life now. If you want to start a family, for instance, then this is the year it could happen. Other possibilities: a move, a different career path, a better-paying job, a marriage, an expansion in your business, a promotion . . . you get the idea.

On January 25, Pluto enters your sign, a landmark transit. It's the outermost planet, the slowest moving, and its lengthy transit of your sign—until 2024—will create profound and permanent changes in your life. Over the past years, as Pluto transited Sagittarius and your twelfth house, many things that were hidden in your life surfaced. Some of the themes you experienced during those years will come up again as Pluto retrogrades back into Sagittarius throughout the year. By November 26, however, it's in your sign for good.

While Pluto is slipping in and out of your sign, Jupiter in your sign confers an element of protection and luck. Jupiter's position in your sign won't happen for another twelve years, so take advantage of it!

Saturn entered Virgo in the fall of 2007 and is now in your ninth house—your worldview, higher education, overseas travel and foreign cultures, spiritual beliefs, publishing, and the law. This transit should bring stability and structure to your life, particularly in how you view life. Your personal philosophy and how you see yourself within the context of the larger world are important themes. Your business or product may expand overseas this year or you may move overseas or do more foreign traveling than usual.

Uranus, the planet of sudden, unpredictable events, continues its transit of Pisces and your third house. This transit brings unpredictability and abrupt events and situations concerning your neighborhood, community, and relationships with siblings and relatives. Before you panic, Uranus has been in this position since the spring of 2003, so it's nothing new for you!

Neptune is still transiting Aquarius and your second house, which it's been doing since 1998. Since it is the planet of higher inspiration—as well as illusion—you may not be seeing your financial picture or your values as they actually are. Yet, you have the ability to make your living from using your ideals in some way—through fiction, photography, dance, even acting.

BEST TIME FOR ROMANCE

Mark the dates between January 24 and February 16, when Venus is in your sign. Your romantic quota soars. You're also more artistic and others see you in a more flattering light. You feel more confident and your sex appeal rises. Great backup dates for romance fall between May 24 and June 17, when Venus is transiting your fifth house of love and forming a beautiful angle to your sun.

Other excellent dates for romance (and just about anything else) fall between May 11 and 13 and September 3 and 5, when the sun and Jupiter see eye to eye and there's a nice flow of energy between them.

BEST TIME FOR CAREER DECISIONS

Make career decisions between August 30 and September 22, when Venus is transiting your tenth house of careers. This should be quite a smooth time professionally. In fact, things may be going along so smoothly that you'll be tempted to kick back and relax. Don't. Seize the opportunity. There will be a lot of traveling, coming and going, and socializing with peers and bosses during this period. Communication and networking will be vital.

MERCURY RETROGRADES

Every year, there are three periods when Mercury—the planet of communication and travel—turns retrograde. During these periods, it's wisest not to negotiate or sign contracts, to travel, to submit manuscripts, or to make major decisions. Granted, we can't live our lives entirely by Mercury retrogrades! If you have to travel during the periods listed below, however, then expect changes in your plans. If you have to sign a contract, expect to revise it.

It's also a good idea to back up computer files before Mercury turns retrograde. Quite often, computers and other communication devices act up. Be sure your virus software is up to date, too. Pay special attention to the house in which Mercury retrograde falls. It will tell you the area of your life most likely to be impacted. The periods to watch for in 2008 are:

January 28–February 18: retrograde in Aquarius, your second house. This one affects your money. Ouch. Checks you've been expecting may be delayed; be sure to check your bank statements for errors, and don't buy any big-ticket items. The list of *do not*s is large and tedious. Just remember, the key is to revise and review, not to start anything new.

May 26–June 19: retrograde in Gemini, your sixth house of daily work and health. Again, revise and review. Don't pitch new ideas during this retrograde period, don't buy office equipment, and don't hire new employees.

September 24–October 15: retrograde in Libra, your tenth house. This one impacts your career, so tread carefully. If you have to travel for business under this retrograde, your schedule may change abruptly. Go with the flow.

ECLIPSES

Every year, there are four eclipses, two solar and two lunar. Solar eclipses trigger external events that allow us to see something that eluded us before. They can bring about beginnings and endings. When an eclipse hits one of your natal planets, it's especially important. Take note of the sign and house placement. Lunar eclipses bring up emotional issues related to the sign and house into which they fall.

Here are the dates to watch for:

February 6: solar eclipse at seventeen degrees Aquarius, your second house. You'll be able to see something about your financial picture that eluded you before. Since solar eclipses involve a new moon, there may be new financial opportunities coming your way.

February 20: lunar eclipse at ten degrees Virgo, your ninth house. Emotions surface that are related in some way to your beliefs, educational goals, or to overseas business interests.

August 1: solar eclipse, nine degrees Leo, in your eighth house. The resources you share with others—a spouse or partner, a parent, even a child—are revealed in all their strengths and flaws. Think drama with this eclipse!

August 16: lunar eclipse at twenty-four degrees Aquarius, your second house, again. Emotions run high around money and finances.

LUCKIEST DAYS IN 2008

Every year, Jupiter forms a beneficial angle with the sun, usually a conjunction, when both planets are in the same sign. In 2008, the angle is a lovely trine and it occurs during two time periods: May 11–13 and September 3–5. If you're going to buy a lotto ticket, do it during these periods!

Now let's take a look at what 2008 has in store for you month by month.

Twelve Months of Predictions
for Capricorn
January–December 2008

Capricorn—January 2008

The first new moon of 2008 is on January 8, in Capricorn, your first house, and sets the tone for the month. This moon, combined with expansive Jupiter in your sign, bodes well for your personal life this year. Follow your hunches on everything. Uranus forms a close and positive angle to this moon, so whatever events unfold will do so suddenly and unexpectedly. Remain alert and ready to seize advantage when you see it.

The full moon in Leo on January 22 brings to light an issue or situation related to the resources you share with others. Something culminates with your spouse or partner—he or she gets a raise or a promotion, for instance, at the end of a project. If your natal moon or rising is in Leo, this full moon should be romantic and enjoyable.

On January 7, Mercury enters Aquarius and your second house. Discussion and communication proliferate about money—what you earn, spend, and how you might be able to work at something that reflects your true values. You may be brainstorming with friends or coworkers about cutting-edge financial ideas.

On January 28, Mercury retrogrades for the first time this year and doesn't turn direct again until February 18. Your best way to navigate this period is to revise, review, and reevaluate. Don't start anything new.

January 24 features Venus transiting into Capricorn. This marks the beginning of a romantic period for you. If you aren't involved when it starts, you probably will be before this transit ends on February 17. If you're involved in a relationship already, then things may develop to a point of deeper commitment. You could move in together or even tie the knot.

On January 30, Mars turns direct in Gemini, your sixth house. This should be good news for your daily work. Mars now heads toward its conjunction with Cancer on March 4.

Dates to watch for: January 24, when Venus enters your sign, joining Jupiter and, on January 25, Pluto. The Pluto transit is especially significant. Over the next several decades, this planet's transit will cause profound and permanent changes in your life. Also be prepared for the Mercury retrograde on January 28.

Best date: January 24, when Venus and Jupiter link up in Capricorn. A beautiful recipe for romance.

Capricorn—February 2008

With two eclipses and several transits this month, February promises to keep you running! The solar eclipse on February 6 is in Aquarius, your money house. Mercury and Neptune are close to the degree of the eclipse, indicating there's a lot of discussion around this eclipse about your finances. You may not have all the information you need to make a decision, so wait until later in the month. But keep talking and brainstorming. Ideas will come to you that will help you make the choices that are right for you.

The lunar eclipse on February 20 is in Virgo, your ninth house. Expect emotional issues to surface regarding your worldview or educational goals. This eclipse, however, is harmonious with your sun sign, so it's likely that you'll experience positive emotions around this date. Saturn is close to the degree of this moon, suggesting that your emotions find a constructive outlet.

In addition to the eclipses, look to February 17, when Venus enters Aquarius and your second house. This should be great for your financial picture. Even if you tend to spend more during this transit, you have more coming in. Any check you've been expecting should arrive after Mercury turns direct on February 18.

Your ruler, Saturn, is currently moving retrograde through Virgo, your ninth house. It urges you to review your spiritual beliefs and how they fit (or not) into the rest of your life. It isn't a great transit for overseas travel, but if you need to travel internationally between now and May 2, when it turns direct again, your trip may end up being a spiritual quest of some kind.

Dates to watch for: the eclipse dates, of course, but also watch for February 6–7, when something just beneath the surface emerges. Also, February 22 could bring about a minor challenge in a romantic relationship.

Best dates: February 23–26, an exciting time, with unexpected events and surprises.

Capricorn—March 2008

With two moons and three transits this month, March is going to keep you plenty busy. The action starts on March 4, when Mars enters Cancer, your opposite sign, and your seventh house. This transit can work in several ways—it can create tension between you and your partner or set off fireworks in your sex life. You may feel more pressured for time (that you don't have enough of it) and this can cause you to move too quickly. Don't break the speed limit under this transit, unless you don't mind sitting in traffic court paying a hefty fine.

On March 7, the new moon in Pisces should be quite pleasant and surprising for you. New relationships are forged with neighbors, relationships with siblings are healed, and you have new opportunities for travel. The Pisces moon boosts your imagination and intuition, too.

Venus comes along and boosts the new moon energy on March 12, when it enters Pisces and your third house. This transit can bring about a romance with a neighbor or someone your meet through a brother, sister, or other relative. You also could get involved in some sort of neighborhood or community beautification project. On March 14, Mercury joins Venus in your third house, so now there's a lot of talk in your neighborhood about how you can all pull together and get a beautification project moving. You'll have more contact than usual with relatives, too.

The full moon on March 21 is in Libra, your tenth house. This moon should mark the culmination of a project or career concern that you have. Pluto forms a harsh angle to this moon, however, so personal power issues may surface. One possibility is that a new job offer conflicts with your personal responsibilities.

Date to watch for: the full moon on March 21.

Best date: March 21, when Mars and Uranus are trine to each other. Expect the unexpected.

Capricorn—April 2008

This month is one of your busiest and the action kicks off on April 2, when Mercury enters Aries and your fourth house. Suddenly, your home and personal environment are hotbeds of frantic activity. Everyone seems to be gathering at your place, including friends of friends of your kids. Then on April 6, Venus follows Mercury into your fourth house, adding beauty and love to the equation. Even if you're not involved with anyone when this Venus transit starts, romance may be closer than you think—like in your backyard. One thing you may do during the Venus transit is beautify your home in some way—painting rooms, rearranging furniture, practicing feng shui, even adding an addition to your house.

In between these transits, on April 5, the new moon in Aries ushers in opportunities related to your family and home life. Someone could move in (or out), your house could go on the market (or sell), a baby could be born or a marriage announced. New events and situations, Capricorn.

On April 17, Mercury enters Taurus, a fellow earth sign, and your fifth house. You're gearing up for romance and fun now, Capricorn, and in a major way. Any relationship that begins under this Mercury transit will require both of you to be communicative and honest about your feelings. This becomes especially true after April 30, when Venus joins Mercury in your fifth house. This transit, by the way, sets up May as one of the most romantic and creative periods for you this year!

Dates to watch for: The first ten days of the month are sure to be interesting, while Jupiter in your sign and Uranus in Pisces travel closely in harmonious signs. Expect a sudden expansion in opportunities.

Best dates: April 1–2, when Mercury and Venus are conjunct in imaginative Pisces, your third house. If you're a writer or in the communication or travel business, this transit certainly boosts business!

Capricorn—May 2008

May features four transits, two moons, and a change in movement for Saturn and for Neptune. Translated: busy, busy. On May 1, take a deep breath and try to figure out your agenda for the month. Set priorities and make lists so that you use your time wisely.

On May 2, Mercury enters Gemini, your sixth house. This transit, which lasts until May 26, spurs social activities with coworkers and employees. There are discussions and talks now among your coworkers, perhaps about procedures or gripes about the job in general. There could be a few rumors floating around as well.

The new moon in Taurus on May 5 should be a beauty for your love life, Capricorn. If you're not involved with anyone special now, this new moon brings opportunities for a new relationship. It also attracts new creative opportunities. Don't turn down something just because you think it's "too small" or doesn't pay enough. It may be the stepping-stone to something better.

Mars enters Leo, your eighth house, on May 9. Suddenly there seems to be a lot of activity related to insurance, taxes, inheritances, or wills. You may attend a seminar on one of the above subjects or a workshop on the more esoteric side of the eighth house—reincarnation, mediumship, or communication between the living and the dead. Be sure your insurance and tax payments are up to date! Another possibility with this transit is that your partner, spouse, or someone else with whom you share resources is spending a lot of time working.

May 19 features a full moon in Scorpio, your eleventh house. This should bring about some fun-filled days with friends or days in which you're researching and investigating something. A project or concern reaches a culmination, a harvest. One thing ends, something else begins. You may find that a friendship or a group to which you belong is more stressful than it's worth.

May 24 brings Venus into Gemini, following Mercury into your sixth house. A work flirtation may become something more or a romance with an employee really takes off. Tread carefully here, Capricorn. There's truth in the adage that you shouldn't mix business with pleasure! That said, this should be a smooth time at work, particularly if you're in a creative field.

Mercury turns retrograde for the second time this year on May 26, in Gemini. There's that work house again! Don't hire or fire employees between now and June 19, when Mercury turns direct again. Try not to start anything new, either. Clear your desk of current projects, make way for the new. And be sure to back up computer files!

Dates to watch for: May 2, when Saturn turns direct in Virgo, your ninth house. The impact will be subtle, but the direct movement provides the opportunity to use your personal philosophy in a constructive way. On May 26, Neptune turns retrograde in your second house of finances. Since this planet moves so slowly, the effects will be subtle. That said, you'll be spending the next several months examining your values, trying to figure out if you're walking the talk.

Best dates: May 1–2 should be exciting. Mars—action—and Uranus—unpredictability—form a harmonious angle to each other.

Capricorn—June 2008

June 3 features a new moon in Gemini, your sixth house. Venus is within two degrees of this moon, and Mercury within five degrees. So what can you expect? New employees may be coming on board in your office or you may become a new employee at a better-paying job. This may not happen until after June 19, however, when Mercury turns direct again. Other possibilities include an office flirtation or romance, lots of discussion about looking for a new job or improving the one you have now, or a new health regimen that's interesting enough for you to follow on a regular basis. If you want to lose weight, this new moon brings opportunities for a new diet and new nutritional awareness.

On June 18, there are two events of note—a full moon in Sagittarius and Venus's transit into Cancer, your seventh house. The first event, the full moon, occurs in your twelfth house, and Pluto is within one degree of the moon. This suggests that you're now in a powerful position to ferret out your motives or those of someone close to you. Your emotions will be very strong around this full moon, so it would behoove you to find an outlet—the gym, yoga, tai chi, bicycling, or swimming.

Venus's transit into your seventh house indicates a romantic time with your partner. If you're not involved with anyone, then get out and be seen. Accept invitations. Don't be a hermit! This transit lasts through July 11.

On June 19, Mercury turns direct again, so get out and celebrate. Plan your vacation. Sign your contracts!

Dates to watch for: June 20–26, when Mars and Neptune are opposed to each other. This can create conflict concerning your ideals and your sexuality. Pluto enters your sign again on June 13, so you may experience some of the same feelings and situations that you did around January 25.

Best dates: June 4–8, when Venus and Mars form a harmonious angle to each other. Great for romance!

Capricorn—July 2008

The new moon on July 2 sets the tone for the July Fourth weekend and for the rest of the month. It's in Cancer, your seventh house, and Venus is within six degrees of it, promising romance and heightened creativity. You and your partner should get away on or around this date, perhaps in advance of the long weekend. If the kids go along, be sure they've got separate rooms!

Before this new moon, however, Mars enters Virgo and your ninth house on July 1. This certainly sets the stage for a major travel itch, Capricorn. Also, it stimulates education, publishing, and your worldview. If you're a writer in search of a publisher, this transit helps you find the right agent or editor for your work. If you're headed off to college in the fall, this transit helps you prepare yourself for the transition from home to college life.

On July 10, Mercury enters Cancer and your seventh house, heightening the themes of the new moon and of the Mars transit. Mercury here opens up discussions between you and your partner, where you can air your gripes—and your praises for each other! Any relationship that begins under these two transits will have to begin with a meeting of the minds. Ideas will be as important to you as physical attraction.

Venus enters Leo and your eighth house on July 12. This transit facilitates and eases the way for anything related to taxes, insurance, wills, and estates. You may also take a workshop in an esoteric subject—reincarnation, communication with the dead, or the development of psychic ability. Romance is possible with someone you meet through one of these venues.

Date to watch for: July 25, when Venus and Jupiter knock heads. Minor challenges in a relationship are possible.

Best date: July 5, when Mars and Saturn link up in Virgo. Your physical energy finds the proper structure for its expression. Sounds like an exercise program—or a sexual relationship. Or both!

Capricorn—August 2008

Two eclipses, plus a second new moon, and five transits make August one of the busiest and most hectic months of the year. And it all starts on August 1, with a solar eclipse in Leo, your eighth house. New opportunities in loans, mortgages, taxes, and insurance may come about as a result of this eclipse. You also see something in these areas that you missed before. Mercury is within three degrees of this eclipse, suggesting that there's a lot of talk and discussion around you concerning these topics. So what kind of specific issues could come up?

Wills. If you don't already have one, then get one drawn up. If your state allows you to have a living will, then be sure yours is in order. Be sure that you and everyone around you has a health surrogate, who can make decisions about your health if you're unable to. For example, do you want life support if you're unable to breathe on your own? The Terri Schiavo case is probably the best recent example of what can happen if you haven't spelled out what you desire about the end of your life. And don't wait until you're eighty to do this. Schiavo was a young woman when tragedy struck her.

The lunar eclipse in Aquarius on August 16 happens in your second house of money. An emotional situation surfaces concerning finances. Neptune is close to this eclipse degree, so you may not have all the facts yet. Don't make any decision about your finances until next month.

On August 30, the new moon in Virgo is in your ninth house. This one should be excellent for you. It's compatible with your sun and Saturn is within three degrees of the moon. It's possible that opportunities for overseas travel come up and it looks like the trips are related to business. Your company may be expanding overseas or you have opportunities to sell your own product to a foreign market.

Scattered among these eclipses and moons are some important transits. On August 5, Venus enters Virgo, accenting some of the themes of the new moon on August 30. This transit certainly bodes well for a romance while traveling overseas or for success in expanding your business to foreign markets or for achieving your educational and publishing goals.

Then, on August 10, Mercury joins Venus in your ninth house, and for the next nine days Mars is there as well. All this emphasis on Virgo and the ninth house brings your philosophy, spiritual beliefs, foreign interests, and even your health into your focused awareness.

On August 19, Mars enters Libra and your tenth house, an excellent transit for your career. This happens only once every two years, so take full advantage of it. Pitch your ideas, brainstorm with peers, attend professional conferences, and get out there and be seen. Your hard work pays off. Bosses notice your diligence.

Mercury and Venus join Mars in Libra on August 28 and 30 respectively, so now all the focus shifts to your career. You're in a better position for this combination of transits now because you know what you believe and have clearer ideas about how to implement what you want.

Dates to watch for: the two eclipses, of course, and the new moon in Virgo.

Best dates: August 12–18, when Venus and Jupiter are moving in a harmonious angle to each other, lifting your love life.

Capricorn—September 2008

Except for the fact that Mercury turns retrograde this month, September should be somewhat less hectic than August. The full moon on September 15 is in Pisces, a sign compatible with yours, and occurs in your third house. You finish a community or neighborhood project, a situation with a sibling or relatives culminates, or you find the neighborhood that suits you. Uranus is within three degrees of this moon, indicating that the events on or around this date happen suddenly, without warning. Also, Pluto forms a wide and challenging angle to this moon, so power issues will surface.

September 29 features a new moon in Libra, your tenth house, and should bring new opportunities, events, and situations related to your career. You may decide that what you've been doing isn't really what you love and take steps to change it. Don't dismiss opportunities to try something new just because the pay is low or the commute is long. You never know where it might lead. Try whatever comes your way for the next thirty days. There could be more business travel around the time of this new moon, more meetings, and more activity. If you're looking for a new job or career path, then several days before this new moon write out your ideal job description. Imagine yourself in this job. Back the visualization with emotion.

In between these moons, on September 23, Venus enters Scorpio and your eleventh house. A friendship blossoms into something much more, taking you and the other person by surprise. Scorpio is a passionate, secretive sign, so there will be plenty of chemistry in this relationship. If you're already involved, then this transit has you and your partner getting involved in groups—political groups, theater groups, writers' groups, or any other kind of group that supports your passions and interests. This transit also favors artistic projects, perhaps with a group of friends. You end up being the organizer, the galvanizing force.

Mercury turns retrograde for the last time this year on September 24, in Libra, your tenth house. The professional strides you made earlier this month now slow down. There could be delays and unexpected changes in your schedule and plans. Miscommunication with bosses and peers is likely. Stick to the retrograde rule: review, revise, and reevaluate. Mercury turns direct again on October 15.

Date to watch for: the Mercury retrograde on September 24.

Best dates: September 13–20, when Mercury, Venus,

and Mars are all in Libra, creating activity and opportunities in your career. Also mark September 7 on your calendar, when Jupiter turns direct again in your sign. Now you will reap the full benefits of this planet's expansive energy.

Capricorn—October 2008

On October 3, Mars enters Scorpio, your eleventh house. This transit definitely triggers a lot of activities with friends, groups, and in terms of your personal wishes and dreams. You join groups that support your interests and passions or may get involved in group activities—a political group, for instance, that supports your presidential or senatorial preferences. This transit lasts until November 23. The consequences of the choices you make under this transit come home to roost after December 12, when Mars enters your sign.

The full moon on October 14 is in Aries, your fourth house. This moon brings a home project or concern to a culmination. Pluto forms a wide, harmonious angle to the degree of this moon, so it could shape up to be a raucous and fun time with your family. Any tensions that surface may involve a tug-of-war between your responsibilities to your family and to your professional concerns.

A day later, on October 15, Mercury turns direct again, in Libra—cause to celebrate! Read over the Mercury retrograde sections in the big-picture overview. This change in direction for Mercury releases some of the tension caused by the full moon.

Venus enters Sagittarius and your twelfth house on October 18. This transit sometimes foreshadows a secret love affair, or, if not secret, then a relationship that is very private. There could be a sense of destiny involved in the relationship, perhaps a past-life connection.

The Venus transit also favors any creative projects

237

that you do in private, in seclusion. If you're struggling to meet a deadline, this transit helps you to meet it and to be acknowledged for your talent. You're getting ready for Venus moving into your sign on November 12, which will mark the beginning of one of the most romantic and creative periods for you this year.

October 28 marks a new moon in Scorpio, your eleventh house. This moon is compatible with your sun sign and should bring about new opportunities for friendships, involvement in groups, and even new opportunities to realize a wish or dream that you have. This moon, combined with Jupiter now moving direct in your sign, indicates opportunities for personal and professional growth.

Date to watch for: October 14 and that full moon in Aries. It could present challenges.

Best dates: October 5–6, when Venus and Jupiter are in complete agreement. This combination boosts your self-confidence and brings about a smooth period in a romantic relationship, bolsters your creativity, and may bring about synchronistic experiences.

Capricorn—November 2008

Two moons, five transits, two planets changing direction, and the Thanksgiving holiday: take a deep breath, Capricorn, because November is a whirlwind.

The action starts on November 4, when Mercury enters Sagittarius and joins Venus in your twelfth house. The combination of these two planets indicates there's a lot of discussion with your partner—about the relationship, a creative project, or even about a friend or relative who may be in the hospital, a nursing home, or a similar facility. If you're a writer, the combination of these two planets indicates that you'll meet your deadline and will have plenty of solitude to do it. Then there's romance. You and your partner are spending a lot of time alone and may even get away together for a long weekend. Enjoy it while it lasts because by November 12, when Venus moves into your sign, your social life picks up.

On November 12, Venus enters your sign and doesn't leave it until December 7. This three-week period marks one of the most romantic and creative for the year. If you're not involved when the transit begins, you probably will be before it ends. And if you're not, it won't matter because you'll be enjoying yourself so much.

The full moon in Taurus on November 13 should be very nice for you. It's in your fifth house of romance and creativity and Uranus forms a harmonious angle to it. Expect the unexpected in romance and creative ventures. If you have a partner, plan something special for this full moon—a gourmet meal, for instance, or a trip to some romantic locale. Coupled with Venus in your sign, this full moon should be a date to remember!

Mars enters Sagittarius and your twelfth house on November 16 and doesn't leave until late December. This transit encourages you to clean up unresolved issues in your life. You're preparing for what happens in December, when four out of ten planets will be in your sign, tipping the odds in your favor in many areas of your life. There are a number of methods you might use to get to these issues—therapy, meditation, and actively working with your dreams.

On November 23, Mercury joins Mars in Sagittarius and your twelfth house. This is a quiet spot for Mercury and encourages you to dialogue with your own unconscious, or with a trusted friend or family member. It's an excellent opportunity to communicate with your e-mail group and touch base with clients by phone or e-mail. You're clearing the decks, Capricorn, for when Mercury enters your sign on December

The new moon in Sagittarius on November derscores the twelfth house themes mention New opportunities arrive for working scenes in some way. It may be that th need is introduced to you through a friend or family member, through an informal setting. Another possibility is that your spiritual quest finds the right mentor or direction.

Dates to watch for: November 1, when Neptune turns direct in your second house. Good news for your finances. You can now integrate your ideals into how you earn your living. November 26, when Pluto enters your sign for good. Read the overview section again on what this transit will mean for you. On November 27, Uranus also turns direct in Pisces, your third house.

Best date: November 20, when Mars, Jupiter, Saturn, and Uranus form harmonious angles to each other and to your sun. Wow. Excitement, expansion, action, and it all comes together into the proper venue or structure.

Capricorn—December 2008

As you enter the last month of the year, every planet is moving in direct motion—that is, functioning as it should be. The first transit of note is on December 7, when Venus enters Aquarius and your second house. This transit bodes well for holiday gift buying; you should have the money, within reason, to buy for everyone on your list. This transit could also mean that you sell one of your creative projects—money from the arts—or that you meet someone in the arts with whom you share certain values.

On December 12, there are two events to mark on your calendar—a full moon in Gemini and Mercury's transit into your sign. The full moon occurs in your sixth house, so there may be some unexpected events concerning work on or around that date. Employees or coworkers, for instance, could call in sick, leaving you shorthanded. Or there's an unexpected event in your neighborhood that draws you away from work.

Information, the Internet, books and authors, and travel also play a part in this full moon.

Mercury's transit into your sign, where it will be for the rest of the year, is ideal. You're now able to consciously implement plans and strategies to achieve your goals. Your daily life runs more smoothly now, more in line with who you are. There won't be any conflict between your head and your ego.

Then, on December 27, Mars joins Mercury in your sign, a transit that happens only once every two years, and you're really revved up and ready to go for the New Year. You may start a new exercise routine, go on a diet, or find a nutritional program that suits you. And, because Mars also represents our sexual energy, your libido slams into high gear. Also on December 27, there's a new moon in your sign. New opportunities flow into every corner of your life and continue to do so into the New Year.

So let's take stock: Mercury, Mars, Jupiter, and Pluto are all in your sign right now, and then the new moon in your sign tops it off. You're going to be in very good shape for 2009!

Date to watch for: December 31, when Saturn turns retrograde in Virgo, your ninth house. The effects will be subtle, but initially it may mess up your New Year's Eve plans, particularly if you're traveling overseas now.

Best dates: The entire month looks extraordinary.

Brainstorming

Envision yourself a year, two years, or four years from now. What is your life like? Where do you live? Is your work satisfying to you? Are you single, married, a parent? Are you happy? Do you have enough money? Is your health good? What are your spiritual beliefs? Are you a vehicle for change in your family or community? In the space below, describe the life you would like to be living a year or two or four up the line. Be as outrageous, creative, and wild as you want. After all, it's *your* life. If you can imagine it, then you can create it.

MY LIFE IN _____ (*choose a year*)

_____

_____

_____

_____

_____

_____

_____

_____

_____

_____

_____

_____

HAPPY 2009!

The Big Picture for Aquarius
in 2008

Welcome to 2008, Aquarius! This is a year for innovation, information, and harmony. There are changes, yes, but most of them are positive.

Jupiter, the planet of expansion, went into Capricorn last year and continues its journey through your twelfth house for all of this year. It's a wonderful time to delve into yourself—your own motives and psyche, your past lives, any long-standing issues. You excel at dream recall this year and would benefit from therapy, meditation, or workshops on the mind-body link. Your spiritual beliefs and practices are especially important. They ground you. Jupiter in your twelfth house also suggests contact with institutions—nursing homes, hospitals, or assisted-living facilities. You may be visiting friends or relatives who are in these kinds of facilities.

On January 25, Pluto enters Capricorn and your twelfth house, joining Jupiter there. It is the outermost planet, the slowest moving, and its lengthy transit of this sign—until 2024—will create profound and permanent changes in your life. Over the past years, as Pluto transited Sagittarius and your eleventh house, your friendships, wishes and dreams underwent a subtle and profound change. Some of the themes you experienced during those years will come up again as Pluto retrogrades back into Sagittarius throughout the year. By November 26, however, it's in Capricorn for good.

Saturn entered Virgo in September of last year, and continues its journey through your eighth house this year. As the planet that governs the rules of physical existence, it's urging you to find the proper structure for your joint investments. Your partner or spouse's income may not be as readily available to you now, so you'll have to watch your finances carefully.

Uranus, the planet of sudden, unpredictable events, continues its transit of Pisces and your second house, finances. This creates sudden, unexpected events concerning finances. Your financial situation could plunge—or it could soar. Depend on your hunches where this is concerned and back them up with facts. You have opportunities during this transit to find a gap in the market and fill it. Before you panic, Uranus has been in this position since the spring of 2003, so it's nothing new for you!

Neptune is still transiting Aquarius and your first house, which it's been doing since 1998. Since it is the planet of higher inspiration—as well as illusion—you may not be seeing yourself as you really are. Your talents are strong, your imagination and vision sharply honed. Use them!

BEST TIME FOR ROMANCE

Mark the dates between February 17 and March 11, when Venus is in your sign. Your romantic quota soars. You're also more artistic and others see you in a more flattering light. You feel more confident, sexier, and that in turn influences how other people treat you. Good backup dates for romance fall between May 24 and June 17, when Venus is transiting your fifth house of love and forming a beautiful angle to your sun.

Other excellent dates for romance (and just about anything else) fall between May 11 and 13 and September 3 and 5, when the sun and Jupiter see eye to eye and there's a nice flow of energy between them.

BEST TIME FOR CAREER DECISIONS

Make career decisions between September 23 and October 17, when Venus transits your tenth house of careers. This should be quite a smooth time professionally. In fact, things may be going along so smoothly that you'll be tempted to kick back and relax. Don't. Seize the opportunity. There will be a lot of traveling, coming and going, and socializing with peers and bosses during this period. Communications and networking will be vital.

MERCURY RETROGRADES

Every year, there are three periods when Mercury—the planet of communication and travel—turns retrograde. During these periods, it's wisest not to negotiate or sign contracts, to travel, to submit manuscripts, or to make major decisions. Granted, we can't live our lives entirely by Mercury retrogrades! If you have to travel during the periods listed below, however, then expect changes in your plans. If you have to sign a contract, expect to revise it.

It's also a good idea to back up computer files before Mercury turns retrograde. Quite often, computers and other communication devices act up. Be sure your virus software is up to date, too. Pay special attention to the house in which Mercury retrograde falls. It will tell you the area of your life most likely to be impacted. The periods to watch for in 2008 are:

January 28–February 18: retrograde in your sign. Whenever Mercury turns retrograde in a person's sun sign, you tend to feel the retrograde more strongly. There could be some personal delays or setbacks, communications with people around you get messed up, and checks could be delayed.

May 26–June 19: retrograde in Gemini, your fifth house of romance. Don't get involved in a new relationship under this retrograde; try to keep your current relationship clear and focused.

September 24–October 15: retrograde in Libra, your ninth house. This one impacts overseas travel, publishing, education, and your worldview. Don't expand your business overseas during this period.

ECLIPSES

Every year, there are four eclipses, two solar and two lunar. Solar eclipses trigger external events that allow us to see something that eluded us before. They can bring about beginnings and endings. When an eclipse hits one of your natal planets, it's especially important. Take note of the sign and house placement. Lunar eclipses bring up emotional issues related to the sign and house into which they fall.

Here are the dates to watch for:

February 6: solar eclipse at seventeen degrees Aquarius. A personal revelation could come about with this eclipse. Since solar eclipses involve a new moon, there may be new personal opportunities coming your way.

February 20: lunar eclipse at ten degrees Virgo, your eighth house. Emotions surface that are related in some way to resources you share with others.

August 1: solar eclipse, nine degrees Leo, in your seventh house. Something about a partnership comes to light. Think drama!

August 16: lunar eclipse at twenty-four degrees Aquarius. Your emotions run high around a personal issue or concern.

LUCKIEST DAYS IN 2008

Every year, Jupiter forms a beneficial angle with the sun, usually a conjunction, when both planets are in the same sign. In 2008, the angle is a lovely trine and it occurs during two time periods: May 11–13 and September 3–5. If you're going to buy a lotto ticket, do it during these periods!

Now let's take a look at what 2008 has in store for you month by month.

Twelve Months of Predictions
for Aquarius
January–December 2008

Aquarius—January 2008

The first new moon of 2008 is on January 8, in Capricorn, your twelfth house, and sets the tone for the month. This moon, combined with expansive Jupiter in the same sign, suggests that new, expansive opportunities come your way for work in solitude, behind the scenes, or dealing with institutions such as hospitals and nursing homes. Follow your hunches on everything. Uranus forms a close and positive angle to this moon, so whatever events unfold will do so suddenly and unexpectedly. Remain alert and ready to seize advantage when you see it.

The full moon in Leo on January 22 brings to light an issue or situation related to your personal and business partnerships. Something culminates with your spouse or partner. If your natal moon or rising is in Leo, this full moon should be romantic and enjoyable.

On January 7, Mercury enters Aquarius. This transit is terrific if you're a writer or work in any facet of the communication or travel business. Discussion and communication surrounds your cutting-edge ideas. You may be brainstorming with a friend or family member about these ideas. On January 28, Mercury retrogrades for the first time this year, in your sign, and doesn't turn direct again until February 18. Your best way to navigate this period is to revise, review, and reevaluate. Don't start anything new.

January 24 features Venus transiting into Capricorn, joining Jupiter in your twelfth house. Secret love affair? It's possible with this transit. And if it's not secret, it's very private. The secrecy lasts only until Venus enters your sign on February 17.

On January 30, Mars turns direct in Gemini, your fifth house. This should be good news for your love life. If you and your partner have been at odds, things now smooth over on their own.

Dates to watch for: January 25, when Pluto enters Capricorn and your twelfth house. The Pluto transit is especially significant. Over the next several decades, this planet's transit will cause profound and permanent changes within your own unconscious. Also be prepared for the Mercury retrograde on January 28.

Best date: January 24, when Venus and Jupiter link up in Capricorn. A beautiful recipe for a secret and romantic love affair.

Aquarius—February 2008

There are two eclipses this month and it all begins on February 6, with a solar eclipse in your sign. This eclipse highlights personal issues and concerns that you now see in a way you haven't before. Mercury is within a degree of this moon, and Neptune within four degrees. This indicates there will be a lot of discussion and debate about the issues that concern you and that you may not have all the information you need. Don't jump to conclusions. Gather your information.

The lunar eclipse on February 20 is in Virgo, your eighth house. Saturn is within four degrees of this moon. The eclipse brings up emotional issues related to resources you share with a partner or someone else and Saturn provides a constructive outlet for those emotions. Pluto also forms a close and beneficial angle to this moon, so the emotions you experience are apt to be powerful and positive.

Venus enters your sign on February 17, marking one of the most romantic—and creative—periods for you this year. If you're not involved with anyone when the transit starts, you probably will be before it ends on March 12. And if you're not, you'll be having such a grand time that you don't care. Your muse is in full attendance during this period, so perhaps it's time to dust off that manuscript, screenplay, or portfolio and get busy!

Mercury turns direct on February 18, in your sign. Time to celebrate. Why not book a cruise or hop in the car with your favorite friends or a partner and go somewhere that intrigues you? You've earned an adventure!

Your ruler, Uranus, is in Pisces, of course, where it will be all year. It's also moving in direct motion, through your second house of money. Make investments and changes in finances before June 26, when Uranus turns retrograde!

Dates to watch for: February 18, when Mercury turns direct, and February 17, when Venus enters your sign.

Best dates: February 6, the solar eclipse in your sign, and February 23–26, when Jupiter and Uranus form harmonious angles to each other. Their combination might read: expansion or success through sudden, unexpected events.

Aquarius—March 2008

The astrological weather in March is rather like March weather here on Earth—unpredictable, but with the promise of better days ahead. On March 4, Mars enters Cancer and your sixth house. Planets in water signs don't particularly agree with you—too much emotional stuff involved. But this transit really sets things on fire in your daily work. You're suddenly a powerhouse of activity and energy. Since it's in intuitive Cancer, be sure to listen to *your* intuition during this period, which lasts through May 8.

The new moon in Pisces on March 7 is in your second house. This moon should be quite good for your finances. New moneymaking opportunities come your way, and since Uranus is within a degree of this moon, whatever happens comes out of the blue. It may catch you off guard, though, if you aren't on your toes!

On March 21, the full moon falls in Libra, your ninth house, and should be quite pleasant for you, since Libra is an air sign compatible with your sun. Your travel plans culminate and it looks as if your trip overseas will happen. Or, if you're hunting for colleges or waiting to hear whether you were accepted, the news looks very positive. This moon receives a harsh angle from Pluto, however, so power issues may surface. These issues could be related to something you discover about your own motives or the motives of someone close to you.

On March 12, Venus enters Pisces and your second house. This transit helps bring about some of the situations and events related to the new moon—opportunities with money. Women are helpful and the arts may somehow play a role in this bigger picture. It's possible, too, that you sell one of your creative projects.

Two days later, Mercury follows Venus into Pisces and your second house. This interesting lineup brings about discussions and activities about money—what you earn, spend, and what you would like to earn. Your values come into play. Are you walking your talk? Is your work in line with what you value? It's possible now for you to earn money through writing or in a communications industry, through travel, or even through something you create with your hands—sculptures, for instance. Your mind is intuitively receptive during this transit.

Dates to watch for: March 1–11, when both Venus

and Mercury are in your sign. Nice combination for you personally, Aquarius. Good for your love life!

Best dates: This depends on your focus. If your focus this month is money, which it probably is, given all the astrological data, then from March 12 to the end of the month you gain a deeper understanding about what you want and need financially.

Aquarius—April 2008

There are no two ways about it: the astrological transits this month light a fire in your life. Let's take a closer look. On April 2, Mercury enters Aries and your third house. Suddenly you're hustling around on a daily basis, running errands, trying to do everything at once. If you're a writer, this transit favors a rushing flood of excellent ideas and all the mental energy you need to get them down on paper. You may be traveling more than usual—short day trips, as opposed to overseas—and find yourself in the car for more time than you would like.

The new moon in Aries on April 5 heightens the Mercury themes. But it also adds something—new opportunities open up in communication. You may land a job in public relations, for instance, or start your own business as a Web designer. It's a good idea to touch base with your clients; e-mail would do the trick. Something new may come to you through siblings and other relatives, too. If you're entertaining the idea of a move this year, this new moon combined with Mercury gets you out and about, scoping out different neighborhoods.

Venus follows Mercury into Aries on April 6, promising romance, or, at the very least, a flirtation with a neighbor or someone you meet through a brother or sister. There's also a nice creative component with this Venus transit. So be prepared to take advantage of it.

Mercury changes signs again on April 17, entering

Taurus and your fourth house. The energy is markedly different now. You may be more stubborn, particularly about elements of your home and family life. You may get involved in some sort of beautification project—painting your office, for instance—or could be buying more books than usual. Discussions with friends and family members are also part of the bigger picture.

The full moon in Scorpio on April 20 occurs in your eighth house. Saturn forms an exact, beneficial angle to this moon, so whatever is revealed concerning the resources—financial and otherwise—that you share with others should be positive. The Scorpio moon is passionate, secretive, and deeply intuitive, so all of these qualities may ride tandem with this full moon.

Venus follows Mercury into Taurus and your fourth house on April 30, setting the stage for next month. Your love life at home is about to take off big time and so is your creativity. This transit favors a move, too.

Date to watch for: the Aries new moon on April 5.

Best dates: April 1–2, when Mercury and Venus are holding hands in your second house. This could bring in delayed checks, result in a new moneymaking opportunity or investment, or bring you love with someone who shares your values.

Aquarius—May 2008

Four transits, two moons, and two planets changing directions: that means buckle up and get ready for a wild ride.

On May 2, Mercury enters Gemini, a sign that it rules and a fellow air sign, in your fifth house. Any relationship that starts under this transit will have to be a meeting of the minds, filled with political discussions, book discussions, more and more discussions.

Information will be the focus. When Venus follows Mercury into Gemini on May 24, it marks the beginning of one of the most romantic and creative times for you this year. And now, for sure, before any romantic relationship begins, you have to be seduced intellectually. Aquarius is a mental sign, anyway, and when two other planets are in communicative Gemini, all that need for intellectual stimulation is simply more pronounced.

The new moon in Taurus on May 5 brings fresh opportunities to your home and family life. A child may be born, or someone at home is pregnant. Someone may move in or out of your home or you have an opportunity to set up a home office. The Taurus moon is sensuous, sometimes mystical, stubborn emotionally, and exceptionally intuitive. All of these qualities may be part and parcel of this new moon.

May 9 finds Mars entering Leo, your opposite sign. This can be either positive or challenging, depending on how you handle relationships. It can be contentious if you let it get that way, or stimulating. Sign contracts before May 26.

On May 26, Mercury turns retrograde in Gemini, your fifth house. This one can really mess up your communication with a romantic partner or with those involved in a creative project on which you're working. The best rule of thumb is to review and revise and not start anything new. Sometimes under a Mercury retrograde, however, old friends and lovers reappear in your life. In this case, it would be a lover. There could be some interesting developments. The retrograde doesn't end until June 19.

Dates to watch for: the Mercury retrograde on May 26. On May 2, Saturn turns direct in Virgo, your eighth house, facilitating things like mortgages, insurance, and taxes. On May 9, Jupiter turns retrograde in your twelfth house. You'll spend the next several months scrutinizing your spiritual beliefs and exploring past lives.

Best dates: May 29–31, when Venus and Mars form

a harmonious angle to each other and to your sun. A nice recipe for romance and sensuality.

Aquarius—June 2008

June is a calmer month astrologically. And it begins on June 3, with a new moon in Gemini, your fifth house. You'll love this one, Aquarius. It brings you new opportunities in romance, creativity, and with your kids, if you have them. It's almost as if you're consistently in the right place at the right time, particularly after June 18, when Mercury turns direct in this house. Sometimes a new moon in this house results in a pregnancy, so if you've been talking about starting a family, this is a good month to make it a reality!

On June 18, Venus enters Cancer and your sixth house, smoothing over things at work. An office flirtation or romance is possible. You may find more creative solutions and approaches to common daily challenges and spend more time socializing with coworkers and employees.

Also on June 18, there's a full moon in Sagittarius, your eleventh house. This full moon is compatible with your sun, so it should be a good one. Get together with friends. Advertise and promote your product or your company, but start that on June 20, when Mercury will be direct. With this moon, you grasp the larger picture of what you want from your life.

On June 19, Mercury turns direct in Gemini, your fifth house. You and your partner should get out and celebrate this one. It's now safe to plan your summer vacation. Mercury doesn't turn retrograde again until late September.

Dates to watch for: June 18 is a big day, with two events to take into account. June 13, when Pluto enters Capricorn and your twelfth house again. Hop into your own psyche!

Best dates: June 4–8, when Venus and Mars form a

terrific angle to each other. Good for romance and creative endeavors.

Aquarius—July 2008

Here's another one of those busy months—two moons and four transits. The new moon on July 2 is in Cancer, your sixth house. Yes, we know you're not crazy about these water sign moons. But this one brings new opportunities with work—a promotion, a job change, new employees, or fresh blood in your business. This moon sets the tone for the month.

Before it rolls around, however, Mars enters Virgo and your eighth house on July 1. This transit stimulates your joint resources—your spouse's or partner's finances, for example. He or she may be working longer hours, but the payoff could be significant—a sharp spike in pay, a promotion. The eighth house also concerns taxes and insurance, wills and inheritances, so there may be activities in these areas, too.

Mercury enters Cancer on July 10, emphasizing some of the new moon themes concerning your daily work. You have more contact now with employees and coworkers. There's a lot of discussion about a project and some brainstorming ensues about new projects or products. If you're self-employed, this transit has you doing a lot of driving around, contacting clients, and generally engaged in the running of your business.

July 12 brings Venus's transit into Leo and your seventh house. Your love life picks up, but you may also get involved in a creative project with someone else. You and your partner could be brainstorming for ways to get out of your day jobs and into something that you're both passionate about.

On July 18, the full moon in Capricorn highlights your twelfth house and highlights something that has been hidden in your life. It's a nice moon, though, for planning long-range goals and for spending time with the one you love.

Finally, on July 26, Mercury joins Venus in Leo, your seventh house. So now, in the heated moments of romance, you and your partner open up to each other. And since Mercury isn't retrograde, there's no misunderstanding, nothing ambiguous about the discussions. If you're not living together or married, then the relationship may be headed in those directions.

Dates to watch for: the new moon on July 2, and Venus's transit into your seventh house of partnerships on July 12.

Best dates: Tough call. Even though there are dates when the transiting planets form great angles to each other, the angles they form to your sun are challenging. On July 14, for instance, Mercury and Saturn form a nice angle to each other, strengthening communication, but the angles they form to your sun are challenging. Just the same, look for activity with shared resources and your work routine.

Aquarius—August 2008

Without a doubt, August is the busiest month of the year. Take a look at the lineup: five transits, two eclipses, and a second new moon. If you're primed for action, though, then this is your month.

On August 1, the solar eclipse in Leo hits your seventh house. Mercury is within two degrees of the eclipse degree, indicating there's discussion between you and your partner about your relationship. As a result of this eclipse, you may need to compromise or be more cooperative for this relationship to work—and as a fixed sign, Aquarius, compromise isn't your strength. Everything depends on how badly you want this relationship to work.

August 5 brings Venus into Virgo, your eighth house. This is an excellent time to delve into esoteric areas—reincarnation, communication with the dead—and it's possible that you meet a romantic interest during your exploration. This transit also urges you to pay attention to details in areas like insurance and taxes.

Mercury follows Venus into Virgo on August 10, indicating discussion concerning wills, inheritance, taxes, or insurance. If you don't have a living will, be sure to have one drawn up during this transit, which ends on August 28. A parent or relative may need help on taxes and insurance matters. This is a service-oriented sign, so you're going to be doing things for other people without any thought of compensation. And you do it gladly.

Mark down August 16 for a lunar eclipse in your sign. Neptune is within two degrees of this moon, indicating that your ideals somehow play a part in whatever it is that riles your emotions. But Neptune also could mean that you don't have the full picture, that you lack information. So before you blow up at someone, Aquarius, gather more information. Then and only then will this eclipse be good for you.

Mars is marching right along this year, with only a brief retrograde period at the beginning. And on August 19, it enters Libra, your ninth house. This transit lasts until early October and really galvanizes issues revolving around publishing, education, and overseas travel. You may decide to expand your business interests overseas, you could find the right agent or editor for your manuscript, or you sell your screenplay . . . you get the idea here, Aquarius. Mars is about action. Action brings results. Go after your dream.

On August 28, Mercury follows Mars into Libra and your ninth house, and on August 30 Venus follows. So by August 30, the three inner planets are in Libra, your ninth house. This places a lot of weight on all ninth house issues (look through the introductory chapter on what the ninth house encompasses). Even though you will be attempting to balance various responsibilities now, use this portal to create what you need and want. Meditation, visualization, conscious creation: find the technique that works best for you.

August 30 also features a second new moon, in Virgo, your eighth house. Saturn is within three degrees of this moon, indicating that all the opportunities that come to you now find their proper place, their proper structure, in your life. You may, for instance, get a substantial tax refund, a break on your insurance rates, or inherit money from a relative. You also have opportunities related to the big cosmic question in life and may have some fascinating psychic experiences that break open any rigid concepts that you currently hold.

Dates to watch for: the eclipse dates, but also August 30, when three planets are transiting your eighth house. August 16 could be a bit problematic. Pluto in Sagittarius and Mars in Virgo are square to each other: power plays.

Best date: August 16, the lunar eclipse in your sign.

Aquarius—September 2008

Yes, you're coming off some frantic, hectic months, and September fits the bill for being laid-back. Well, almost laid-back. On September 15, there's a full moon in Pisces, your second house. This one illuminates a concern you have about a brother, sister, or other relative. There may be something going on in your neighborhood or community—political rallies, for instance—that you become involved in. Uranus is within three degrees of this moon, so whatever unfolds here will be abrupt and unexpected.

On September 23, Venus enters Scorpio and your tenth house. You had better be ready for this one. It's definitely an opportunity to move ahead professionally. Unfortunately, Mercury turns retrograde a day later, in Libra, your ninth house, so you may be stymied in terms of beginning anything new. Given the nature of Venus in Scorpio, however, you can move ahead in subtle ways, by keeping your agenda to yourself and working on your own or with a few peers whom you trust. With Venus here, there's a possibility of a romance with a peer or a boss. Tread carefully. There's wisdom in the adage about not mixing business with pleasure.

The Mercury retrograde on September 24 discourages overseas travel, advancing your educational goals, or submitting to publishers. Revise, review, and re-evaluate. The three Rs. That's the ticket.

On September 29, the new moon in Libra brings a breath of fresh air. Even though Mercury won't go direct until October 15, this new moon promises that romance is possible with someone whose eccentric worldview matches your own.

Date to watch for: September 24, when Mercury turns retrograde.

Best dates: September 13–20, when Mercury, Venus, and Mars are in Libra, your ninth house, urging you to travel before Mercury turns retrograde on September 24.

Aquarius—October 2008

On October 3, Mars begins its transit of Scorpio, your tenth house, triggering all kinds of activity in your career. Some possibilities: a promotion, a new career opportunity with another company, and recognition by peers and bosses for the work you are doing. You're energized. This transit also favors investigation, research, and an exploration of consciousness. Another thing about the Mars transit—a sexual relationship with a peer or boss is possible.

On October 14, the full moon in Aries lights up your third house. This moon, compatible with your sun sign, should be very enjoyable for you. It brings about a culmination in events involving your neighborhood or community or with a sibling or other relative.

Pluto forms a wide, harmonious angle with this moon, suggesting that the events unfolding make you aware of your own power.

Mercury turns direct again on October 15, in Libra, your ninth house. If ever there's a signal from the universe to pack your bags and head out of town, this is it. The farther you go, the better, and the more free you'll feel. One possible result of Mercury's change in direction: news finally arrives about your college or graduate school applications.

October 18 brings Venus into Sagittarius, a fire sign compatible with your sun, and into your eleventh house. This lovely transit indicates social activities with friends and large groups of people. It's a great time to advertise and promote your product or your company's. If you're self-employed, put some money into advertising during this transit, which lasts until November 12. It will be money well spent and should increase your business.

The new moon in Scorpio on October 28 falls in your tenth house. This one should be terrific for your career. New opportunities for advancement, a possible raise or promotion, or even a new career path are possible. Another possibility? You get a job offer you can't refuse. Synchronicities and psychic experiences are likely around the time of this new moon.

Date to watch for: October 26, when Mars and Jupiter form harmonious angles to each other, but not to your sun. It's not such a serious thing, but you may want to be careful on this date that you don't speed while driving.

Best dates: October 2–3, when Mars and Pluto form a good angle to each other and to your sun. You're in the power seat these two days.

Aquarius—November 2008

Two moons, four transits, and three planets changing direction: are you ready for all this? Read on.

Mercury enters Scorpio on November 4, joining Mars in your tenth house. This dynamic combo really gets things moving professionally. It's the perfect time to pitch ideas, to push your agenda, and to make changes. All your actions should prove to be positive for you and will be well received by bosses and peers.

Venus enters Capricorn, joining Jupiter in your twelfth house, on November 12. Anything you do in solitude or behind the scenes now will be very beneficial for you. When the two best planets are together like this, their energies mesh, so you may be involved in a romance that is private or secretive and that expands your inner world tremendously. The very next day, the full moon in Taurus brings completion or culmination to a situation with your family or at home. Both Saturn and Uranus form harmonious angles to this moon, indicating that events unfold suddenly, but your emotions find a constructive outlet. One or both of your parents may figure into the situation that evolves.

On November 16, Mars transits into Sagittarius, your eleventh house. This transit will coincide nicely with the transit of Mercury into Sagittarius on November 23, and a new moon in Sagittarius on November 27. The combination is sure to bring new friendships and involvement in groups that support your interests and passions. Expect opportunities that somehow support your wishes and dreams, too. Both Mercury and Mars are close to the degree of this moon, suggesting discussions and debates with friends, as well as a lot of social activities, right in time for the Thanksgiving holiday.

Dates to watch for: November 19, when four planets line up and form harmonious angles to each other but not to your sun. The planets are Mars, Jupiter, Saturn, and Uranus. There's no telling how this day will unfold for you—keep notes! Be attentive. November 26 is a landmark day: Pluto enters Capricorn again and begins its long, slow transit through your twelfth house.

Best dates: November 27, the new moon in Sagittarius. Keep an eye out for November 1, however, when Neptune turns direct in your sign, and for November 27, when Uranus turns direct in Pisces, your second house of finances.

Aquarius—December 2008

The last month of the year has every planet moving in direct motion, which means they're all functioning at maximum capacity. On December 7, Venus enters your sign, marking the beginning of another romantic and creative period. Things come your way without much effort on your part between now and the end of the year. Whether it's money, love, creative breaks, or simply a revival of your social life, enjoy this period. Take advantage of it.

On December 12, there are two events to watch for. The first involves Mercury's transit into Capricorn and your twelfth house, and the second is a full moon in Gemini. Mercury's transit is great for discussions with a trusted friend or family member or even a therapist about hidden issues in your life. It's also good if you're a writer because you'll have all the time you need now to work on a project and perhaps even complete it before the end of the year.

The full moon in Gemini should be a good one for you, highlighting your fifth house of romance and creativity. Plan something special with the one you love—a trip out of town, perhaps—or a special dinner or night out. If you're not involved at this time, then get out and be seen. Keep your options open. Don't become a hermit.

On December 27, there are also two events: Mars's transit into Capricorn and your twelfth house, and the new moon in Capricorn. So let's pause a moment and take stock here. Right now, Mercury, Mars, Jupiter, and Pluto are all in your twelfth house. This is a lot of weight for a house that involves introspection, karma, hidden issues, institutions, and power you have disowned. You're being called upon to go within, to clear up any long-standing issues so that you can begin the New Year with a fresh slate.

The new moon in Capricorn is close to both Pluto and Mars, with Mars at zero degrees Capricorn, a cardinal sign. Mars will stimulate the other cardinal points in your chart, so be prepared for more activity in your daily work routine and in contact with foreign cultures and individuals.

On New Year's Eve, Saturn turns retrograde in Virgo, your eighth house. Your partner may get delayed for some reason for the New Year's festivities, but don't despair. There's so much else going on that the delay isn't all that significant.

Date to watch for: the full moon in Gemini on December 12.

Best date: December 25, when Venus and Neptune are both in your sign, adding inspiration and idealism to your romantic relationships. This is also an excellent combination for all types of creative endeavors.

Brainstorming

Envision yourself a year, two years, or four years from now. What is your life like? Where do you live? Is your work satisfying to you? Are you single, married, a parent? Are you happy? Do you have enough money? Is your health good? What are your spiritual beliefs? Are you a vehicle for change in your family or community? In the space below, describe the life you would like to be living a year or two or four up the line. Be as outrageous, creative, and wild as you want. After all, it's *your* life. If you can imagine it, then you can create it.

My Life in _____ (*choose a year*)

_____
_____
_____
_____
_____
_____
_____
_____
_____
_____
_____
_____
_____
_____
_____

HAPPY 2009!

The Big Picture for Pisces
in 2008

Welcome to 2008, Pisces! This is your year for setting down foundations on which you'll be building throughout 2008. Jupiter, the planet of expansion, went into Capricorn and your eleventh house late last year and continues its transit through your eleventh house. This transit broadens your base of friendships, your involvement in groups, and even your wishes and dreams.

On January 25, Pluto joins Jupiter in your eleventh house. As the outermost and slowest-moving planet, its lengthy transit—until 2024—will create profound and permanent changes in your life. Over the past years, as Pluto transited Sagittarius and your tenth house, your career underwent a subtle and permanent change. Some of the themes you experienced during those years will come up again as Pluto retrogrades back into Sagittarius throughout the year. By November 26, however, it's in Capricorn for good.

Saturn entered Virgo, your opposite sign, in September of last year, and continues its journey through your seventh house this year. As the planet that governs the rules of physical existence, a personal relationship may end or be taken to the next level. It all depends on whether this relationship is answering your needs. In terms of contracts and other legal documents, Saturn in your seventh house indicates that you should always read the fine print before signing anything.

Uranus, the planet of sudden, unpredictable events, continues its transit through your sign. It's been here since 2003, so you're accustomed to its energy. One or several areas of your life have been, are, or will be going through sudden, unexpected change. Uranus's job is to shake up the status quo, to shove you out of your comfortable routine so you can grow and evolve creatively, spiritually, personally.

Neptune is still transiting Aquarius and your twelfth house, which it's been doing since 1998. Since it is the planet of higher inspiration—as well as illusion—you may not perceive your real motives or those of the people around you. But this transit really favors the development of psychic abilities, spontaneous past-life recall, and dream recall.

BEST TIME FOR ROMANCE

Mark the dates between March 12 and April 5, when Venus is in your sign. Your romantic quota soars. You're also more artistic and others see you in a more flattering light. You feel more confident, sexier, and that in turn influences how other people treat you. Good backup dates for romance fall between June 18 and July 11, when Venus is transiting your fifth house of love and forming a beautiful angle to your sun.

Other excellent dates for romance (and just about anything else) fall between May 11 and 13 and September 3 and 5, when the sun and Jupiter see eye to eye and there's a nice flow of energy between them.

BEST TIME FOR CAREER DECISIONS

Make career decisions between October 18 and November 11, when Venus transits your tenth house of careers. This should be quite a smooth time professionally. In fact, things may be going along so smoothly that you'll be tempted to kick back and relax. Don't. Seize the opportunity. There will be a lot of traveling, coming and going, and socializing with peers and bosses during this period. Communication and networking will be vital.

MERCURY RETROGRADES

Every year, there are three periods when Mercury—the planet of communication and travel—turns retrograde. During these periods, it's wisest not to negotiate or sign contracts, to travel, to submit manuscripts, or to make major decisions. Granted, we can't live our lives entirely by Mercury retrogrades! If you have to travel during the periods listed below, however, then expect changes in your plans. If you have to sign a contract, expect to revise it.

It's also a good idea to back up computer files before Mercury turns retrograde. Quite often, computers and other communication devices act up. Be sure your virus software is up to date, too. Pay special attention to the house in which Mercury retrograde falls. It will tell you the area of your life most likely to be impacted. The periods to watch for in 2008 are:

January 28–February 18: retrograde in Aquarius, your twelfth house. This retrograde indicates that you may be rehashing long-standing issues and concerns.

May 26–June 19: retrograde in Gemini, your fourth house. Things at home seem confused, perhaps even chaotic. Be sure to back up all computer files.

September 24–October 15: retrograde in Libra, your eighth house. Don't apply for mortgages or loans under this retrograde. Tax or insurance issues may need to be addressed.

ECLIPSES

Every year, there are four eclipses, two solar and two lunar. Solar eclipses trigger external events that allow us to see something that eluded us before. They can bring about beginnings and endings. When an eclipse hits one of your natal planets, it's especially important. Take note of the sign and house placement. Lunar eclipses bring up emotional issues related to the sign and house into which they fall.

Here the dates to watch for:

February 6: solar eclipse at seventeen degrees Aquarius. You perceive your own motives—or those of someone close to you—in a completely new way. New opportunities surface for working in solitude or behind the scenes.

February 20: lunar eclipse at ten degrees Virgo, your seventh house. Emotions surface with a partner—professional or romantic.

August 1: solar eclipse, nine degrees Leo, in your sixth house. Your daily work is impacted with this eclipse. New employees or coworkers are the focus. Also, something about your health maintenance program may come up.

August 16: lunar eclipse at twenty-four degrees Aquarius. Whatever you discovered about yourself during the solar eclipse in February may now come back to haunt you!

LUCKIEST DAYS IN 2008

Every year, Jupiter forms a beneficial angle with the sun, usually a conjunction, when both planets are in the same sign. In 2008, the angle is a lovely trine and it occurs during two time periods: May 11–13 and September 3–5. If you're going to buy a lotto ticket, do it during these periods!

Now let's take a look at what 2008 has in store for you month by month.

Twelve Months of Predictions
for Pisces
January–December 2008

Pisces—January 2008

The first new moon of 2008 is on January 8, in Capricorn, your eleventh house, and sets the tone for the month. This moon, combined with expansive Jupiter in the same sign, suggests that new opportunities come through your friends, with friends, or with involvement in groups that support your interests and passions. Uranus forms a harmonious angle to this moon, so whatever comes about will happen suddenly, unexpectedly.

The full moon in Leo on January 22 brings to light an issue or situation related to your daily work and health routine. It's a good time to start a regular exercise routine if you don't have one already. You may also be concerned with your physical appearance and decide to buy some new clothes and get a new hairstyle.

On January 7, Mercury enters Aquarius and your twelfth house. This transit is terrific if you're a writer; you suddenly have all the time you need to complete a project. You may be discussing certain elements of a creative project with a partner or trusted friend.

On January 28, Mercury retrogrades for the first time this year, in your twelfth house. You'll be revisiting issues you thought were solved and someone from your past may reenter your life again. Your best way to navigate this period is to revise, review, and reevaluate. Don't start anything new.

January 24 brings Venus transiting into Capricorn, joining Jupiter in your eleventh house. Romance with someone you thought was a friend or with someone you meet through friends is possible. This transit should be socially active, with more participation in groups.

Dates to watch for: January 25, when Pluto enters Capricorn and your eleventh house. The Pluto transit is especially significant. Over the next several decades, this planet's transit will cause profound and permanent changes within your own unconscious. Also be prepared for the Mercury retrograde on January 28.

Best date: January 24, when Venus and Jupiter link up in Capricorn. A beautiful recipe for romance.

Pisces—February 2008

There are two eclipses this month and it all begins on February 6, with a solar eclipse in your twelfth house. This eclipse highlights issues you haven't wanted to deal with and have pushed underground. Mercury is within a degree of the eclipse, indicating that a lot of discussion ensues, perhaps with a therapist or close friend. Neptune is within four degrees, so you may not have all the information you need. Don't jump to conclusions. Gather your information.

The lunar eclipse on February 20 is in Virgo, your seventh house. Saturn is within four degrees of this moon. This eclipse brings up emotional issues related to partnerships—either romantic or professional. Saturn provides a constructive outlet for those emotions. Pluto also forms a close and beneficial angle to this moon, so the emotions you experience are apt to be powerful and positive.

Venus enters Aquarius on February 17, a perfect recipe for a secret or very private romance. If you're not involved with anyone when the transit starts, the planet's energy could manifest itself through focused work on a creative project. Mercury turns direct on February 18, in Aquarius. Time to celebrate. Why not book a cruise or hop in the car with your favorite friends or a partner and go somewhere that intrigues you? You've earned an adventure!

With Jupiter in Capricorn and your eleventh house all year, new people are entering your life daily. Some of them hold the same spiritual beliefs that you do and those beliefs may be a focus throughout the year.

Dates to watch for: February 18, when Mercury turns direct, and February 17, when Venus enters your twelfth house.

Best dates: February 6, the solar eclipse in Aquarius, and February 23–26, when Jupiter and Uranus form harmonious angles to each other. Their combination might read: personal expansion or success through sudden, unexpected events.

Pisces—March 2008

The astrological weather this month is unpredictable and often tumultuous. But there's also great promise. On March 4, Mars enters Cancer and your fifth house, so your libido really heats up. Creatively, you've got all the energy you need to complete projects and meet deadlines. It's time to dust off your manuscripts, screenplays, portfolios, and invest in your creative potential. With Mars in intuitive Cancer, a fellow water sign, be sure to listen to your intuition during this period, which lasts through May 8.

The new moon in Pisces on March 7 should be glorious for you. This moon comes along only once a year and ushers all sorts of new opportunities into your life. Whether you're looking for romance, a new job, a better-paying job, or more travel, or even if you're on a spiritual quest, this new moon can help.

On March 21, the full moon falls in Libra, your eighth house. Something concerning joint finances, taxes, insurance, wills, or inheritances becomes clearer to you. It could be that you're preparing your taxes and find that you owe more or less than you thought. Be sure that your insurance payments are up to date. Another possibility is that you have odd, perhaps psychic experiences around this full moon. This moon receives a harsh angle from Pluto, however, so power issues may surface.

On March 12, Venus enters your sign, signaling the start of one of the most romantic periods for you this year. Then, two days later, Mercury follows Venus into Pisces. This interesting lineup means that if you get involved in a relationship now, it will have to be one in which you can communicate freely and honestly. You won't be in the mood to play games. Your mind will be intuitively receptive now and it's possible that you'll meet someone with whom you have shared other lives.

Dates to watch for: March 18–19, when both Venus and Mercury are in your sign. This combination is conducive to a great love life.

Best date: March 21, when Mars and Uranus form a good angle to each other and to your sun. Expect sudden and positive changes in romance and creative endeavors.

Pisces—April 2008

Money and finances will be your focus this month and it begins on April 2, when Mercury enters Aries and your second house. You're on the lookout for different kinds of investments—the offbeat, the unusual. You may be writing about money and finances, either privately, like in e-mails, or for the public. Any travel you do under this transit could be related to money or to your values. An example would be a trip to a place that holds sacred meaning for you.

Then, on April 5, along comes a new moon in—you guessed it—Aries. So now you've got opportunities for new moneymaking ventures. You may be taking a closer look at your budget, your expenditures, taxes, the whole picture. And of course you're probably getting ready to send off your income tax return, or have just done it.

Venus follows Mercury into Aries on April 6, promising that your financial concerns now go smoothly. Even if you seem to be spending more, there's more coming in, too. The Venus transit can also bring romance with someone who shares your values.

Mercury changes signs again on April 17, entering Taurus and your third house. You'll like this transit; Taurus's earth energy grounds you and you have an easier time making decisions. The energy is markedly different now. You may be more stubborn, particularly with siblings and relatives.

The full moon in Scorpio on April 20 occurs in your ninth house. Saturn forms an exact, beneficial angle to this moon, so whatever is revealed concerning education, publishing, and overseas ventures should be positive. The Scorpio moon is passionate, secretive, and deeply intuitive, so all of these qualities may ride tandem with this full moon.

Venus follows Mercury into Taurus and your third house on April 30, setting the stage for next month. Your love life—right in your backyard—is about to take off big time and so is your creativity. This transit favors a move, too.

Date to watch for: the Aries new moon on April 5.

Best dates: April 1–2, when Mercury and Venus are holding hands in your sign.

Pisces—May 2008

Four transits, two moons, and two planets changing directions: that means buckle up and get ready for a wild ride.

On May 2, Mercury enters Gemini, a sign that it rules, and your fourth house. This transit promises discussions and even debates at the dinner table, and any topic is fair game—politics, religion, books, movies, even your neighbor's sex life. If you're a writer, then this transit is terrific for getting your work done, in your home office. You may be doing more than your share of running around, too, between now and May 26, when Mercury turns retrograde.

In fact, this retrograde asks that you please back up computer files the day before the retrograde begins. Also, if you have a second computer, put your files on there. There's no such thing as too much redundancy. The best rule of thumb is to review and revise and not start anything new. Sometimes under a Mercury retrograde, however, old friends and lovers reappear in your life.

When Venus follows Mercury into Gemini on May 24, it marks the beginning of a romantic time at home. If you're not involved, romance somehow finds its way to your doorstep. Things at home and within your family run smoothly under this transit, except for that little glitch called Mercury retrograde, which won't end until June 19.

The new moon in Taurus on May 5 could mark a period when you're actively searching for the right neighborhood, in anticipation of a move. This moon may bring about more contact with siblings and other relatives or with neighbors. You have new opportunities for short travel, too—weekend getaways, for instance, or even a trip across the country. New avenues of information open up to you.

May 9 finds Mars entering Leo, your sixth house.

Expect a lot of activity and perhaps socializing with coworkers and employees. You may initiate changes that are controversial or your boss may initiate policies or changes that mean longer hours. Drama is the keynote.

Dates to watch for: the Mercury retrograde on May 26. On May 2, Saturn turns direct in Virgo, your seventh house, bringing a sounder structure to your partnerships. You and your romantic partner, for instance, may decide to go into business together. On May 9, Jupiter turns retrograde in your eleventh house. This brings some internal searching about your spiritual beliefs and how those beliefs connect (or don't) to your friends.

Best dates: May 1–5, when Mars and Uranus form a terrific angle to each other and to your sun. Expect the unexpected in a sexual relationship.

Pisces—June 2008

June is a calmer month, with both challenges and triumphs. On June 3, the new moon in Gemini happens in your fourth house, ushering in new opportunities in your home and family life. Someone may move in—or out. A pregnancy is announced, a birth occurs, or you move. One of your parents has new plans that impact you.

On June 18, Venus enters Cancer and your fifth house, beginning one of the most romantic times for you this year. It's also one of your most creative times, when you're in the right place, meet the right people, open the right doors. You may start or complete a manuscript, land a part for which you've auditioned, or sell your photos or paintings.

Also on June 18, there's a full moon in Sagittarius, your tenth house. This marks a culmination concerning your career. You land the job you wanted, get the raise you asked for, win a promotion, or are recognized for your work. With this moon, you grasp the larger emotional picture concerning your career choices.

On June 19, Mercury turns direct in Gemini, your fourth house. Pack your bags, sign contracts, move, buy that new computer or cell phone. You're in the clear now. It's now safe to plan your summer vacation. Mercury doesn't turn retrograde again until late September.

Dates to watch for: June 18 is a big day, with two events to take into account. On June 13, Pluto enters Capricorn and your eleventh house again.

Best dates: June 19–20, when Venus and Saturn form harmonious angles to each other. The commitment level in a romance deepens.

Pisces—July 2008

Here's another one of those busy months—two moons and four transits. The new moon on July 2 is in Cancer, your fifth house. This moon happens only once a year and promises new opportunities in romance, creativity, and for doing whatever brings you the greatest pleasure. It sets the tone for the month.

Before it rolls around, however, Mars enters Virgo and your seventh house on July 1. This transit stimulates your partnerships—both romantic and professional. You and your romantic partner may become involved in a business partnership or another kind of cooperative venture. Sometimes, Mars in the seventh creates conflict, but it doesn't have to. You can use this energy to stimulate the relationship. Your sex life will certainly heat up under this transit, which is a much better use of this energy than conflict.

Mercury enters Cancer on July 10, emphasizing

some of the new moon themes concerning your love life and creative projects. This transit also brings a lot of talk and chatter with your kids, if you have children, and can indicate short trips that are purely for pleasure and fun.

July 12 brings Venus's transit into Leo and your sixth house. An office flirtation or a full-blown romance at work is possible. This could be a relationship with a coworker or an employee, if you're the boss. Other possibilities? You meet someone at the gym, in a yoga class, or while running . . . in other words, you're exercising and you meet this individual. You may decide to start a different kind of exercise routine or even follow a new diet or nutritional program.

On July 18, the full moon in Capricorn highlights your eleventh house. It's a good time to get out and about with friends. If you're involved in a group activity—political, artistic, spiritual—then now is the time to commit to even more involvement. But deeper involvement could take away time you may want to spend with your kids or working on your own creative projects. Think about it before you commit.

Finally, on July 26, Mercury joins Venus in Leo, your sixth house. That office flirtation suddenly takes on new meaning. You open up to each other, you and your water fountain buddy, and find there's a lot more between you than you thought. Another possibility is that you get more creative at work, seek cutting-edge solutions, and rely more on your intuition and imagination to find solutions or new ways of doing things.

Date to watch for: the new moon on July 2.

Best date: July 14, when Mercury and Saturn form a nice angle to each other and to your sun. This configuration strengthens your communication skills.

Without a doubt, August is the busiest month of the year. Take a look at the lineup: five transits, two eclipses, and a second new moon. If you're primed for action, though, then this is your month.

On August 1, the solar eclipse in Leo hits your sixth house. Mercury is within two degrees of the eclipse degree, indicating there's discussion between you and your coworkers or employees about the routine at work. As a result of this eclipse, you may need to compromise or be more cooperative at work.

August 5 brings Venus into Virgo, your seventh house. This transit may result in a deeper commitment between you and your partner, romantic or professional. If you're married, it helps bring the two of you closer together. This transit also favors contract negotiations. Don't hesitate to ask for what you believe is fair. All too often, you underestimate yourself and the value you put on your services and talents.

Mercury follows Venus into Virgo on August 10, indicating discussion with your partner, perhaps about a new business plan or goals for your joint venture. You and your romantic partner may be doing a lot of talking, too, perhaps ironing out differences or trying to find a division of domestic chores that is fair and equitable and acceptable to both of you.

Mark down August 16 for a lunar eclipse in Aquarius, your twelfth house. Neptune is within two degrees of this moon, indicating that your ideals somehow play a part in whatever is it that riles your emotions. But Neptune also could mean that you don't have the full picture, that you lack information. So before you make any decisions, gather more information.

Mars is marching right along this year, with only a brief retrograde period at the beginning. And on August 19, it enters Libra, your eighth house. This transit lasts until early October and really galvanizes issues revolving around shared resources. Your spouse or partner could get a significant raise, or you could get a break in your taxes or insurance rates. Action brings results. Mars urges you to stay on top of things.

On August 28, Mercury follows Mars into Libra and your eighth house, and on August 30 Venus follows. So by August 30 the three inner planets are in Libra. This places a lot of weight on all eighth house issues (look through the introductory chapter on what the eighth house encompasses). Even though you will be attempting to balance various responsibilities now, use this portal to create what you need and want. Meditation, visualization, conscious creation: find the technique that works best for you.

August 30 also features a second new moon, in Virgo, your seventh house. Saturn is within three degrees of this moon, indicating that all the opportunities that come to you and your partner now find their proper place, their proper structure, in your life. If you're not involved, this new moon indicates that you probably will be before the next new moon.

Dates to watch for: the eclipse dates, but also August 30, when three planets are transiting your seventh house. August 16 could be a bit problematic. Pluto in Sagittarius and Mars in Virgo are square to each other: power plays.

Best date: the new moon on August 30.

Pisces—September 2008

This month, compared to the last several, will seem like a piece of cake. It will be calmer, certainly, but with enough activity to keep you interested.

September 15, for instance, features a full moon in your sign, which illuminates a personal issue. Uranus forms a close angle to this moon, so whatever unfolds will happen suddenly, unexpectedly. Your imagination and intuition will be running at full tilt, so follow your hunches regardless of how outrageous they seem.

On September 23, Venus enters Scorpio and your ninth house. If you're traveling overseas, this transit could attract romance with someone you meet on the road. If you're not traveling, it could mean a relationship starts up with a foreign-born individual or someone connected to education or publishing. On another level, it could mean that your business or product now expands overseas or that your manuscript makes its way to the right agent or editor. You may be doing research or investigation, too, into a topic that intrigues you.

Mercury turns retrograde a day later, in Libra, your eighth house, and doesn't turn direct again until October 18. This movement should discourage you from applying for loans or mortgages or making changes in your will. All the other Mercury retrograde rules apply, too—about travel, backing up computer files, and so on—and remember to stick to the three Rs: revise, review, and reevaluate.

On September 29, the new moon in Libra opens opportunities to study esoteric topics. You may have a chance to attend a workshop on past lives, life after death, communication with the dead, or a similar subject. This new moon also indicates success in obtaining mortgages and loans. You may even get a tax or insurance break.

Date to watch for: the Mercury retrograde on September 24.

Best date: September 15, the full moon in your sign.

Pisces—October 2008

On October 3, Mars begins its transit of Scorpio, your ninth house. It stirs up all kinds of activities related to education, publishing, foreign countries and overseas travel. You may be doing research or investigating some facet of all these areas. If you're in search of a publisher for your novel, Mars helps you to find it. Mars is now forming a harmonious angle to your sun, so take advantage of this transit, which lasts through November 15.

Since Mars represents both our physical and sexual energy, you could get involved in a relationship that is based primarily on sex. This can be positive or negative, depending on what you're looking for in a relationship.

On October 14, the full moon in Aries lights up your second house and brings a culmination or completion to a financial issue or concern. Pluto forms a wide, harmonious angle with this moon, suggesting that the events unfolding make you aware of your own power.

Mercury turns direct again on October 15, in Libra, your eighth house. Now your mortgage and loan applications come through. Your partner or spouse may receive delayed checks. There's news about tax and insurance.

October 18 brings Venus into Sagittarius, your tenth house. This transit lasts until November 12 and really provides a window of opportunity professionally. Your ideas and projects will be well received now. You'll have a grasp on the much broader picture concerning your career and the people with whom you work. Venus here can also bring a romance or affair with a peer or a boss. Be careful, though, Pisces. You may not want to mix business with pleasure.

The new moon in Scorpio on October 28 falls in your ninth house. Opportunities arrive concerning overseas travel, education, publishing, and the law. Possibilities include a job offer that involves travel, travel related to research and investigation, courses you take related to publishing, travel, or the law. You get the idea here, Pisces. This new moon is compatible with your sun, so take advantage of it.

Date to watch for: October 26, when Mars and Jupiter form harmonious angles to each other and to your sun. Your physical and sexual energy are enhanced.

Best dates: October 19–31, when Jupiter and Saturn are trine to each other. You and your partner may get involved with groups or a group of friends who expand your vision of what is possible.

Pisces—November 2008

Two moons, four transits, and three planets changing direction: November is a powerhouse of activity.

Mercury enters Scorpio on November 4, joining Mars in your ninth house. This dynamic combo really gets things moving in terms of education, publishing, and overseas travel. Everything you do now in these areas brings about positive results.

Venus enters Capricorn, joining Jupiter in your eleventh house, on November 12. Anything you do now with friends or groups that support your interests should be very beneficial. When the two best planets are together like this, their energies mesh, so you may be involved in a romance with someone you meet through a group or through friends that expands your insights and talents. The very next day, the full moon in Taurus brings completion or a culmination to a communication project. Both Saturn and Uranus form harmonious angles to this moon, indicating that events unfold suddenly, but your emotions find a constructive outlet. One or both of your parents may figure into the situation that evolves.

On November 16, Mars transits into Sagittarius, your tenth house. This transit will coincide nicely with the transit of Mercury into Sagittarius on November 23, and a new moon in Sagittarius on November 27. Wow. The combinations are sure to bring an infusion of fresh energy and opportunities to your career. There will also be a lot of holiday socializing with peers and bosses. Network, Pisces, network like crazy!

Dates to watch for: November 19, when four planets line up and form harmonious angles to each other and to your sun. The planets are Mars, Jupiter, Saturn, and Uranus. There's no telling how this day will unfold for you—keep notes! Be attentive. November 26 is a landmark day: Pluto enters Capricorn again and begins its long, slow transit through your eleventh house.

Best dates: November 27, the new moon in Sagittarius. Keep an eye out for November 1, however, when Neptune turns direct in your twelfth house, and for November 27, when Uranus turns direct in your sign.

Pisces—December 2008

The last month of the year has every planet moving in direct motion, which means they're all functioning at maximum capacity. On December 7, Venus enters Aquarius and your twelfth house. One possible manifestation of this transit is a secret love affair or a romance that is extremely private, out of sight of family and friends. If that's the case, it won't remain secret for long. Once Venus enters your sign next year, you'll be shouting your news to everyone you know.

On December 12, there are two events to watch for. The first involves Mercury's transit into Capricorn and your eleventh house, and the second is a full moon in Gemini, your fourth house. Mercury's transit is great for discussions and social activities with friends. It's also good if you're a writer in search of a writing partner; you find the person you need.

The full moon in Gemini highlights your home and family life, just about perfect for this time of year. There could be some tension related to your professional responsibilities, but home and family win out for now. Plan something fun for your family on or around the date of this full moon.

On December 27, there are also two events: Mars's transit into Capricorn and your eleventh house, and the new moon in Capricorn. So let's pause a moment and take stock here. Right now, Mercury, Mars, Jupiter, and Pluto are all in your eleventh house. This is a lot of weight for one house and it indicates that friends, groups, and your own wishes and dreams are the focus for the rest of the year. The lesson here may be cooperation and team playing.

The new moon in Capricorn is close to both Pluto and Mars, with Mars at zero degrees Capricorn, a cardinal sign. Mars will stimulate the other cardinal points in your chart, so be prepared for more activity in your creativity, and with shared resources.

On New Year's Eve, Saturn turns retrograde in Virgo, your seventh house. The impact isn't immediate, but it may change the air between you and your partner.

Date to watch for: the new moon in Capricorn on December 27.

Best date: December 25, when Venus and Neptune are both in your twelfth house, bringing a deeper understanding of your past-life ties with the people around you.

Brainstorming

Envision yourself a year, two years, or four years from now. What is your life like? Where do you live? Is your work satisfying to you? Are you single, married, a parent? Are you happy? Do you have enough money? Is your health good? What are your spiritual beliefs? Are you a vehicle for change in your family or community? In the space below, describe the life you would like to be living a year or two or four up the line. Be as outrageous, creative, and wild as you want. After all, it's *your* life. If you can imagine it, then you can create it.

My Life in _____ (choose a year)

_____
_____
_____
_____
_____
_____
_____
_____
_____
_____
_____
_____
_____

HAPPY 2009!

PART TWO

What Other Astrologers
Are Saying

The Meaning of Numbers
by Rob MacGregor

What exactly is a number 9 day, and how did it get
to be that number? If you've been reading the dailies,
you've no doubt seen such numerological references.
Usually you'll find these numbers on the days when
the moon is transiting from one sign to another.

If you're familiar with numerology, you probably
know your life path number, which is derived from
your birth date. That number represents who you were
at birth and the traits that you'll carry throughout your
life. There are numerous books and Web sites that
will provide you with details on what the numbers
mean regarding your life path.

The numbers used in the dailies are found by adding
the numbers related to the astrological sign (1 for
Aries, 2 for Taurus, and so on), the year, the month,
and the day. For example, June 14, 2008, for a Libra
would be 7 for Libra, plus 1 (adding together the numbers in 2008: 2 + 8 = 10; 1+ 0 = 1), plus 6 for June,
plus 5 (1 + 4) for the day. That would be 7 + 1 + 6
+ 5 (sign + year + month + day) = 19 = 1 (1 + 9 =
10; 1 + 0 = 1).

So on that number 1 day, you might be advised that
you're getting a fresh start, a new beginning. You can
take the lead on something new. Stress originality, creativity. Explore and discover. You're inventive and
make connections that others overlook. Refuse to deal
with people who have closed minds.

Briefly, here are the meanings of the numbers; these

meanings are spelled out in more detail in the dailies themselves.

1. Taking the lead, getting a fresh start, making a new beginning
2. Cooperation, partnership, a new relationship, sensitivity
3. Harmony, beauty, pleasures of life, warmth, receptivity
4. Getting organized, working hard, being methodical, rebuilding, fulfilling your obligations
5. Freedom of thought and action, change, variety, thinking outside the box
6. A service day, being diplomatic, generous, tolerant, sympathetic
7. Mystery, secrets, investigations, research, detecting deception, exploration of the unknown, of the spiritual realms
8. Your power day, financial success, unexpected money, a windfall
9. Finishing a project, looking beyond the immediate, setting your goals, reflection, expansion.

Rob MacGregor is the author of seventeen novels and ten nonfiction books, including *Psychic Power* and *The Fog*. For more information, go to www.robmacgregor.net.

Men *and* Women Are from Mars *and* Venus
by Phyllis Vega

You already know your sun sign—the zodiacal sign occupied by the sun at the time you were born. The sun's position in your natal chart is important, because it defines your basic character and personality. Its sign denotes your public persona and shows how you act in social situations. For specific insight into the way you relate in more intimate situations, you need to look beyond the sun to the sign positions of the celestial lovers, Venus and Mars.

If you don't know the sign positions of Venus and Mars on the day of your birth, you can look them up on the World Wide Web at CafeAstrology.com: Venus Ephemeris Tables are at www.cafeastrology.com/venussignstables.html; Mars Ephemeris Tables are at www.cafeastrology.com/marssignstables.html.

Venus

Venus is love. Venus is romance. Venus is beauty. Its planetary energy is peaceable, harmonious, unifying, and creative. Venus's zodiacal sign defines your romantic persona. The planet's position in your birth chart exerts a strong influence on your sensuality, self-image, and attachments to others. Venus's natal placement is a clear indicator of the manner in which you approach relationships of the heart. Venus's sign determines what gives you pleasure, how you express that pleasure, and how you go about sharing it. The planet Venus also denotes sensuality. Venusian energy relates to the principles of love and attraction, and the drawing together of two separate individuals to create a unified whole.

Venus in Fire: Aries, Leo, Sagittarius

In the fire signs, Venus is romantic and idealistic. Your lovemaking is passionate, dramatic, and extravagant.

Venus in Earth: Taurus, Virgo, Capricorn

In the earth signs, Venus is sensuous and materialistic. You derive sensual pleasure from physical contact.

Venus in Air: Gemini, Libra, Aquarius

In the air signs, Venus is intellectual and communicative. You "feel" with your mind and connect to others on a mental level.

Venus in Water: Cancer, Scorpio, Pisces

In the water signs, Venus is sensitive and intuitive. You connect with your partner on a deep emotional level.

Venus Through the Signs of the Zodiac

VENUS IN ARIES

You want excitement and adventure in your love life. You're passionate and idealistic; sex and romance are equally important to you. You may experience some inner conflict between your desire for a committed relationship and your need for freedom and independence. Naturally daring and flirtatious, you become competitive when seeking the attentions and affections of others.

VENUS IN TAURUS

You appreciate the pleasures of the physical world and experience love in a straightforward, sensual manner. You enjoy good sex in much the same way you take pleasure in good food and luxurious surroundings. You want predictability and dependability in your romantic relationships. Resistance to change makes you rather possessive of the people you love.

VENUS IN GEMINI
Driven by a powerful intellectual curiosity, you want to sample everything life has to offer. Easily bored, you resist relationships that are too settled and comfortable. Variety, change, and excitement provide the spice you're looking for in your love life. You have a playful attitude toward romance and approach each new affair with optimism and high expectations.

VENUS IN CANCER
Easily hurt, you need a secure union with few surprises. You are extremely self-protective, but you hide your emotional vulnerability behind a dignified facade. Despite your total commitment to your beloved, there is a sense of caution as well. Rationality leaves you cold. You want a partner who is affectionate and not afraid to show it.

VENUS IN LEO
Venusian lions make passionate partners who love sincerely and wholeheartedly. Effusive, charming, and generous, you're lavish with your affections and attentions. Glamour and exuberance mark your courting style, and you relish the role of "star" in your own romantic drama. Although never one to discourage or ignore admirers, you pride yourself on remaining loyal to your lover.

VENUS IN VIRGO
You're seeking the perfect love on the one hand and a sensible partner on the other. The idealist in you yearns to place your beloved on a pedestal and worship from afar. Your practical side wants a solid, loving relationship that functions orderly and effi-

ciently. You'd rather be alone than with someone who doesn't meet your expectations.

VENUS IN LIBRA
Innately civilized and refined, you're easily upset by discord. An aesthete as well as a romantic, you surround yourself with art and beauty. Love makes your world go around, you fall in love effortlessly and often. In Libra, Venus is its most seductive, yet your sex appeal manifests in subtle ways that are neither vulgar nor overt.

VENUS IN SCORPIO
In Scorpio, Venus confers deep-rooted emotions and magnetic intensity. An extremist in life and love, you give yourself completely and demand total involvement in return. Your intimate relationships are based on loyalty, commitment, and unremitting focus on the beloved. With desires that are so powerful and overwhelming, you can become very jealous and possessive of your partner.

VENUS IN SAGITTARIUS
The idealistic wanderers with Venus in Sagittarius have a rather carefree attitude toward relationships. You're upbeat and easy to like, but not particularly dependable. Threats to your freedom make you extremely nervous. You fall in love easily, but like keeping things casual for as long as possible. The key to your heart is companionship and shared interests.

VENUS IN CAPRICORN
Venusian goats are dependable and self-controlled. A romantic at heart, you yearn for a loving partner. Your sexual needs and desires are strong, but reserve makes you cautious about expressing them. You want a caring, committed relationship, yet you are insecure and fearful of rejection. You actually prefer repressing your emotions to subjecting yourself to possible ridicule.

VENUS IN AQUARIUS

In Aquarius, Venus lives more in the mind than in the body. You set your own rules, with little regard for what others think. Your freewheeling attitude toward standards of behavior can be unusual to the point of eccentricity. With a head that's off somewhere in the stratosphere, romance is often the last thing on your mind.

VENUS IN PISCES

Venus in this sign is romantic and dreamy. You possess an ethereal charm and vulnerability that is both attractive and attracting. Naturally kind and unselfish, you willingly help others. Yet you're highly dependent yourself, and very much in need of a nurturing partner. You are seeking an otherworldly romance that's difficult to find on this Earth plane.

Mars

Mars is action. Mars is passion. Mars is desire. Mars is lust. Its planetary energy is impulsive, daring, and dynamic. Mars's zodiacal sign defines your sexual persona. The planet's position in your birth chart exerts a strong influence on your physical vitality, drive, determination, and spirit. Mars's natal placement is a clear indicator of the type of lovemaking you enjoy. Mars's sign defines what you desire, how you express that desire, and how you go about satisfying it. Martian energy also denotes basic modes of survival and the fight-or-flight instinct.

Mars in Fire: Aries, Leo, Sagittarius

In the fire signs Mars represents *physicality* and is dynamic and courageous.

Mars in Earth: Taurus, Virgo, Capricorn

In the earth signs, Mars represents *materiality* and is cautious and practical.

Mars in Air: Gemini, Libra, Aquarius

In the air signs, Mars represents *mentality* and is intellectual and communicative.

Mars in Water: Cancer, Scorpio, Pisces

In the water signs, Mars represents *emotionality* and is sensitive and feeling.

Mars Through the Signs of the Zodiac

MARS IN ARIES

In Aries, Mars represents high energy, courage, and initiative. Your sex drive is powerful and easily awakened. While living with you is never dull, it can be difficult. Impulsive and supremely confident, you're not inclined to look before you leap. Action is your middle name; when your passions are aroused you don't stop to consider possible consequences.

MARS IN TAURUS

Mars in Taurus is hedonistic, sensual, and deliberate. Your sex drive is strong but controlled. Your approach to lovemaking is straightforward and uncomplicated. Never rushed or anxious, you pursue your desires with dogged determination. Once you set your mind on someone, you're not easily discouraged. Patience and persistence allow you to wait for as long as it takes.

MARS IN GEMINI

Your sex drive is fueled by your mind as much as your body. Comfortable routine bores you; you seek out new experiences in order to maintain your interest. Since your intellect is your most active erogenous zone, your style of lovemaking is apt to be playful and inventive. Your preferred form of erotic communication is decidedly verbal.

MARS IN CANCER

The sensitive people born under Mars in Cancer are

subject to powerful mood swings. Your strong sex drive is tied to your emotions. You must feel safe and secure before you can let go. When you do, your responses are intense, magnetic, and seductive. With encouragement and reassurance, you're a romantic, thoughtful, and loving partner.

MARS IN LEO
An affectionate, physically demonstrative lover, you take pride in your sexual prowess. You're as easily aroused as any Mars in Aries, but your passions generally last longer. Mars in Leo natives enjoy sex more than most, especially when heavy doses of love and romance are part of the package. In love, you follow your leonine heart.

MARS IN VIRGO
An earthy, nervous sexuality characterizes those with Mars in this sign. Although your physical desires are strong, there is a shy, hesitant side to your nature that makes you fearful of letting go. Nevertheless, you are a perfectionist; in your lovemaking, as in everything else, you strive to be as skilled as possible at what you're doing.

MARS IN LIBRA
Aggressive Mars is decidedly uncomfortable in Libra, where its assertiveness is impeded by the desire for harmony, cooperation, and approval. More romantic than hot-blooded, you are seeking emotional and mental satisfaction rather than purely physical pleasures. Although you're generally amiable and agreeable, you are no pushover. There's a steely will lurking behind your smiling face.

MARS IN SCORPIO
Martian Scorpios display a magnetic sexual intensity with strong physical and emotional needs. Your sex drive is single-minded and passionate. You become deeply attached, sometimes obsessively so, to what-

ever or whomever you fancy. Outwardly cool and composed, your powerful feelings smolder just below the surface. An all-or-nothing extremist, you're not content with halfway measures.

MARS IN SAGITTARIUS

You approach sex as if it were a game to be enjoyed, but not taken seriously. Companionship and friendship are as important to you as love. In Sagittarius, Mars is not renowned for constancy in relationships. You value your independence too much. Afraid of being tied down, you may decide to run off if life gets boring.

MARS IN CAPRICORN

Your sex drive is powerful, with a full appreciation of sensual pleasures. Nevertheless, you believe that you must always be in control of yourself and your feelings. Despite your strong physical needs and desires, you generally choose self-discipline over self-indulgence. Yet beneath your restrained exterior, you're passionate, sensitive, and very much in need of love and affection.

MARS IN AQUARIUS

Your sex drive is fueled by intellect rather than physical or emotional responses. The sexual side of love is not all-important to you, yet you're intrigued by anything new and open to experimentation. Intense involvement scares you, but Aquarius is a fixed sign and you dislike change. When you commit to another, it's for the long haul.

MARS IN PISCES

The assertive energy of the planet Mars is tempered and diffused in Pisces. Innately romantic, idealistic, and sentimental, your greater need is emotional rather than physical. You go with the flow, letting life happen without attempting to control its direction. You look at relationships through rose-colored glasses, with high expectations that are rarely achieved in this world.

Phyllis Vega is an astrologer and tarot reader based in Miami, Florida. She is the author of five astrology books, including *Lovestrology* (2007), *What Your Birthday Reveals About You* (2005), and *Celtic Astrology* (2002). Ms. Vega may be contacted through her Web site at www.geocities.com/phyllisvega.

Signs to Make a Difference!
by Nancy McMoneagle

If you died tomorrow, what would you regret not having shared with the world? What would you like inscribed on your headstone or included in your obituary? If you would rather see "Made a positive difference in the world" than "Had the Most Toys" or "Watched the Most TV," read on!

Many of us feel at a loss to figure out how or if we can make a constructive impact in a world filled with terrorist acts, genocide, hunger, nuclear proliferation, poverty, crime, disease, and environmental disasters. Not being multimillionaires, celebrities, or politicians, we wonder how we can effect change at such a massive level.

The fact is, each of us is *already* making a difference in the world—for better or worse—every day. The question is, are you aware of what "gifts" you're leaving with each person you talk to or with each action you're taking? Do you bless the environment with each step you take, or do you unconsciously trample the earth?

The first step in making a positive difference is to become conscious of what kind of impact you have on others and your environment by what you say and do on a day-to-day basis. Are you expressing the more positive or negative qualities of your sun sign? Are you being a nurturing Cancer or a smothering one, an inventive Aquarius or a stubborn and rebellious one? Are others around you smiling, feeling comfortable and supported when in your presence, as they might from being around an optimistic, inspiring Sagittarius? Or do they feel judged, criticized, or powerless? As my wise Virgo mother used to point out, if everyone around you seems angry or out of sorts, look inside, because the problem isn't "out there"! The people around us are mirrors of ourselves, and as such are wonderful gifts for helping us become conscious of the kind of impact we're having in our world.

After becoming conscious of how we're affecting the world around us comes the important step of determining what our desires and intentions are.

Who do you truly want to be? An artist? President of the company? Loving partner? Nobel Prize winner? *How* do you want to be—wise, fun, serious, courageous, inspiring, powerful, spiritual, scientific, charismatic? What would you like to see happen in the world? What legacy would you like to leave the human race?

After gaining clarity about your intentions, keep your thoughts and actions in alignment with your intent. By being clear, intentional, and timely about the change you want to achieve in your world, you can't help but make a difference.

Unfortunately, many of us aren't clear about who we are, or what we really want, which is why we believe we'll never make much of a contribution to society. To make a positive difference in the world doesn't mean you have to be a Mother Teresa (who, by the way, initially wasn't well known, nor did she have any money) or J. K. Rowling (also not well known, nor did *she* have any money before her Harry Potter books and movies!); nor do you have to strive to be a Gandhi. But you do need to know your basic nature—your inclinations, innate talents and shortcomings, and decide how you want to impact your world.

What follows are some talents and challenges with which each zodiac sign has to work. Your raw material. Knowing your innately available abilities and strengths, as well as the less positive expression of each sign, will give you insights and ideas about how you can make the difference you'd like to see in our world. Make sure you also read the sign your moon and ascendant are in, as that will give you additional information. If you don't know what these are, a reputable astrologer can quickly determine these details for you.

Aries (March 21–April 19)

Your fiery, enthusiastic spirit and innovative leadership help carve the way for others, no matter where you're going or what you're doing—after all, look what Aries Thomas Jefferson accomplished! You're a pioneer—courageous, independent, and dynamic throughout. You have the gift of inspiration, so why not consider using such talent in your community? You could mentor young people, get the community enthused over supporting worthwhile endeavors, like adopting stray animals or starting a new enterprise that will benefit those in need. Aries, you are the consummate salesperson, so whatever you believe in, you can inspire others to join you in doing.

Just watch out for not following through, or being quick-tempered and intolerant, and possibly being a wee bit on the domineering side. Also make sure you are open and sensitive to the needs of others. Otherwise, Aries, *go for it!*

Taurus (April 20–May 20)

With your immense ability to be patient, determined, and cautious, you earthy Taureans offer stability, practicality, and follow-through to projects, events, relationships, and most everything else you put your hands to! Your love of and possible skill in the arts and music might also be something you could share with the world. Think of the delight Tauruses Barbra Streisand and Ella Fitzgerald have brought to so many with their amazing voices. Since many of you have a green thumb, you could be the Johnny Appleseed who helps renew our natural resources by planting trees where clear-cutting has taken place. Or you could make large sums of money and then use it constructively, like Taurus newspaper publisher William Randolph Hearst.

Since you enjoy the best in life, you need to watch out for being too self-indulgent, materialistic, or possessive. Also, dear Taurus, it's likely that you invented the word "stubborn," so take care not to be too slow-moving or obstinate. Even so, how fortunate to have such a firm foundation in life for success—and such good taste, too!

Gemini (May 21–June 21)

As the quick-witted, literary, and most expressive sign of the zodiac, you clever and curious holders of the "twins energy" have much to offer the world. Because you have the ability to communicate to all levels of society, you can educate, inspire, and stimulate people through what you write, say, or teach. What a gift! And since variety is your spice of life, you can fire people up on a number of topics, just as Gemini author Ralph Waldo Emerson did with his writings, and John F. Kennedy accomplished with "Ask not what your country can do for you. Ask what you can do for your country!"

Strive not to be too restless or scattered, which can make it difficult to follow through on your intentions. Also be careful about being too changeable as you jump from one subject, person, or activity to the next, as you may not allow for the depth of experience, feeling, or intimacy that comes with perseverance.

Otherwise, rejoice in your versatility, and grace the world with your wit and charm!

Cancer (June 22–July 22)

You moon-ruled Cancers have a maternal, caring, sympathetic, and thoughtful way of nurturing the rest of us. Cancerian actor Bill Cosby has done a good job of touching the public with his wonderful humor. Because you are the nurturers of the zodiac, you're often good cooks, so offering your services in feeding others could be a likely venue for making your mark on the world. Activities like operating a comfy B&B where you create a homey atmosphere and tasty meals for those away from home, or helping out the needy with Meals on Wheels or assisting the homeless, could suit your talents well. Of course, you could also be a banker, handling other people's resources, since you're typically careful with money and feel financial stability goes with emotional security.

In fact, emotional security is an area where you'll want to be especially conscious, as sometimes Cancers can be manipulative, whiney, or too dependent on others to get what they want. Since you are so sensitive, guard against being touchy, too easily hurt, or sorry for yourself. Instead, key into your ability to nurture and be nurtured as a way to make your mark on the world!

Leo (July 23–August 22)

Being the dramatic, creative, and self-assured soul you are, you can inspire enthusiasm and hope in people where others fail. You have the ability to express your fun side and love of life, spreading humor as Leos Mae West and Lucille Ball did through acting, or exercising your leadership through your powerful presence—Emperor

Napoleon Bonaparte certainly did! When you walk into a room, people notice; whether that's due to a regal bearing or your impressive attire and jewelry, you have more effect on people than you know, Leo. You're like the sun that people are attracted to for light and warmth, so your job is to be super-conscious of and responsible for how you use your magnetic energy! And, like the sun, you can put your life-giving energy to work anywhere you choose. Since you are particularly good with children, do something that positively affects their lives.

On the other side of this intensity and warmth, you Leos need to be careful not to be too "hot on yourself"—that is to say, being overbearing, vain, or pretentious. Giving others the chance to share their light, ideas, and opinions will go a long way in adding to your already extensive charisma. Use it or lose it, Leo—the world needs your warmth!

Virgo (August 23–September 22)

Serving others is of paramount importance to Virgos, which is why there are so many of you in the health and social service professions. You industrious souls have an in-built need to make a positive difference in the world—it's part of your raison d'être! Virgo Leonard Bernstein served us well with his soul-stirring music, Peter Sellers with his humorous roles on film, and Sophia Loren touched people worldwide with her exquisite beauty and acting talent. You Virgos are modest in how you go about making your mark on the world as you analyze the details and make order out of chaos. Whether you choose to help a friend get organized or write about the latest medical discovery, you are conscientious, practical, and painstaking about whatever you do.

As most of you Virgos already know, you have to watch out for being too critical or fault-finding. Don't overanalyze or you'll destroy the spontaneity and spirit of your own or others' feelings. If you mute a tendency to worry and don't get too fussy about the details, you Virgos can make a powerful and positive impact on the world by virtue of your practical abilities and strong desire to make the world a better place to live.

Libra (September 23–October 22)

You are the peacemakers and diplomats of the zodiac and have much to offer, given your sense of beauty and ability to help others achieve compromise. Libras have the uncanny gift to persuade even the most truculent, irascible people to relax and consider other, kinder options, showing both sides of a situation. Your talent could lead to more peaceful relations between people—at home or abroad. (One of the best-known Libras was Mahatma Gandhi.) With Libra's love of beauty, many of you will bring art and beauty to the world in some form, or teach others to see the beauty in and around themselves. Beatle John Lennon certainly touched the world through his love of music and peace.

Because you can see every side to a situation, Libras need to be careful about being indecisive, taking everyone's side, or looking for peace at any price. Libra, with your ability to be fair and put others at ease, you have a lot to give, making the world a more comfortable and beautiful place for us all!

Scorpio (October 23–November 21)

Intensity is your keyword, Scorpio, and as the probing, passionate, and penetrating person you are, you bring incredible insight to most matters. With your determination and need to be in control you're often a leader in authority over others, which you can use for constructive or destructive purposes, depending on your level of awareness and spiritual evolution. You have the power to facilitate change at fundamental levels, which can mean transformation on a major scale as you strive to help the world transform from tadpoles to frogs!

With all this passion and intensity, you need to be careful of being intolerant, suspicious, vengeful, or jealous. You have a great responsibility to use your power constructively. Murderer and cult leader Charles Manson is an example of a Scorpio who used his talents destructively, whereas Madame Curie used her Scorpio power to help discover properties of uranium, Johnny Carson used his Scorpionic talent to entertain millions, and Margaret Mead used hers to unearth secrets about the human race. Whether you use your Scorpio gifts for medicine, research, selling life insurance, or for intrigue, you have the possibility of transforming our world like no other. Good luck!

Sagittarius (November 22–December 21)

Philosophical and freedom-loving, you Sagittarians help the rest of us see a much broader scope of possibilities for living a more truthful and purposeful life. Like Libras, you love the idea of world peace, and help people expand beyond their limited thinking. You have a contagious enthusiasm and joyful approach to life that make you very popular, as does your marvelous sense of humor. In fact, as an extrovert and lover of travel, your influence can be felt worldwide, once you focus on what you most want to accomplish.

Having such a need for freedom and love of open possibilities might make it difficult for you to narrow your focus and complete what you set out to do.

You'd also want to be wary of exaggerating, procrastinating, or being too pushy or hot-headed, since you quite honestly believe you're right most of the time! Winston Churchill and Mark Twain are excellent examples of Sagittarians who made a positive impact on the world. Keep us informed and entertained, dear Sadge, and we'll be forever grateful!

Capricorn (December 22–January 19)

You scrupulously practical, cautious, and responsible Capricorns are typically the most dedicated, serious, and ambitious people around. Among many possibilities, you make excellent corporate CEOs and presidents, builders, teachers, mountain climbers (social climbers, too!), and are the ones we can depend on to make solid, reasonable decisions about the structures that affect our lives. There are many ways you might make a difference in our world given your high degree of responsibility. From being a leader, such as Capricorns Joan of Arc, Benjamin Franklin, and Martin Luther King, to forming a successful business, like Helena Rubinstein, you Capricorns have what it takes to build a viable structure around your dreams and make them work for the betterment of all.

Your more difficult traits include being egotistic, fatalistic, status-seeking, and feeling sorry for yourself. The good news is, you're always willing to work for whatever you get, and eventually you do get what you want!

Aquarius (January 20–February 18)

Imagining new possibilities beyond old, worn-out structures describes the way you inventive, progressive, and individualistic Aquarians approach the world. As the most unconventional members of the zodiac, you have the great ability to see around corners, gaining new perspectives and stretching beyond the norm to offer the world new approaches to most anything, such as cutting-edge inventions, and offering new philosophic approaches that challenge our old ways and broaden our understanding of the world. Naturalist Charles Darwin certainly did this, as did feminist Betty Friedan.

In your great desire to be knowledgeable and free, Aquarius, you'll need to be careful about being too rigid once you've made up your mind that you already know what's right! The world needs you to exercise your innate talents for being innovative, bringing people together for a common cause, and for helping us move forward in our evolution, wherever that may take us!

Pisces (February 19–March 20)

Enormously creative, compassionate, and sensitive, you Pisces help the rest of us escape from the harsher realities of the physical world and connect to a sense of the Divine. You do this through poetry, movies, music, art, and in the way you sympathize and care for others, as with men and women of the cloth, many of whom are Pisces. You bring a sense of the mystical and spiritual to our lives, helping us travel to other worlds. Piscean contributions that have helped us escape the everyday world include Handel's and Chopin's music, Elizabeth Browning's poetry, Renoir's art, and Elizabeth Taylor's magnificent film career—not to mention her Piscean charitableness in giving and raising great sums of money and awareness for conquering AIDS.

Because you like to escape the harsher realities, Pisces, you must be careful to avoid less productive avenues of evading reality: too much alcohol or drug use, or other kinds of addictive behavior. Instead, using your artistry in creating caring companies, beautiful music or art, serving those who are less fortunate or tucked away from society in such places as retirement homes, prisons, or who are otherwise banished from society would make a special difference in the world.

Remember—you are already making a difference in your world. It's up to you to decide what kind of difference you *intentionally* want to make! Just as it only takes one match to light a candle, which can ignite another candle, and so on down the line until a multitude of candles are lit, each of you has your own special light to share that can set the world ablaze!

Nancy McMoneagle is a professional astrologer and also works as a consultant with her husband, Joe, in their company, Intuitive Intelligence Applications (www.mceagle.com). In addition to her astrology practice, Nancy has served two terms as president of Virginia's Nelson County Chamber of Commerce and is a writer for Ivanhoe Broadcast News. She has received the title Dame and rank of Officer's Cross from one of the oldest organizations of European knighthood, The Order of Saint Stanislaus. She currently resides with her husband and their seven feline "fur children" in the mountains of central Virginia.

Sydney Omarr

Born on August 5, 1926, in Philadelphia, Pennsylvania, Sydney Omarr was the only person ever given full-time duty in the U.S. Army as an astrologer. He is regarded as the most erudite astrologer of our time and the best known, through his syndicated column and his radio and television programs (he was Merv Griffin's "resident astrologer"). Omarr has been called the most "knowledgeable astrologer since Evangeline Adams." His forecasts of Nixon's downfall, the end of World War II in mid-August of 1945, the assassination of John F. Kennedy, Roosevelt's election to a fourth term and his death in office . . . these and many others are on the record and quoted enough to be considered "legendary."

SYDNEY OMARR®'S
DAY-BY-DAY
ASTROLOGICAL GUIDES

Nationally syndicated astrologer
Sydney Omarr® guides fans into the new
year with his amazingly accurate
predictions—available for every sign.

Aquarius

Aries

Taurus

Pisces

Gemini

Cancer

Leo

Virgo

Libra

Scorpio

Sagittarius

Capricorn

Available wherever books are sold or at
penguin.com